A RECIPE FOR MAGIC AND MAYHEM

J.M. WALLACE

Books by J.M. Wallace

A Legacy of Darkness

A Legacy of Darkness

A Legacy of Nightmares

A Legacy of Destruction

Claiming Elfhame

Heir of Shadows and Ice

Heir of Embers and Ash

Heir of Starlight and Truth

Daughters of the Flame

A Crown Forged in Flame

Standalones

Bound by Blood and Sorrow

**Stay up to date on new releases by visiting
www.jmwallaceauthor.com**

A note before we begin...

My intention with *Ellamere Enchanted* was to create a comfortable space for my readers to escape to. This book is meant to give you the same feeling you get when you curl up with your favorite blanket with a warm cup of coffee or tea in that favorite mug of yours that you just can't seem to let go of no matter how many other mugs you buy.

Inside this story, you will find:
A charming town filled with unique characters,
A slow-burn, close proximity romance,
A woman struggling to move on from the grief of losing her family,
A sassy tabby cat,
And low stakes with a dash of magic and a pinch of danger.

Thank you so much for diving in with me,
J.M. Wallace

A RECIPE FOR MAGIC AND MAYHEM

For Pat (Trish) and Robert.
And for Mary and Tony.
(the Grandparents who showed me there is always a little
magic to be found in your partner)

Contents

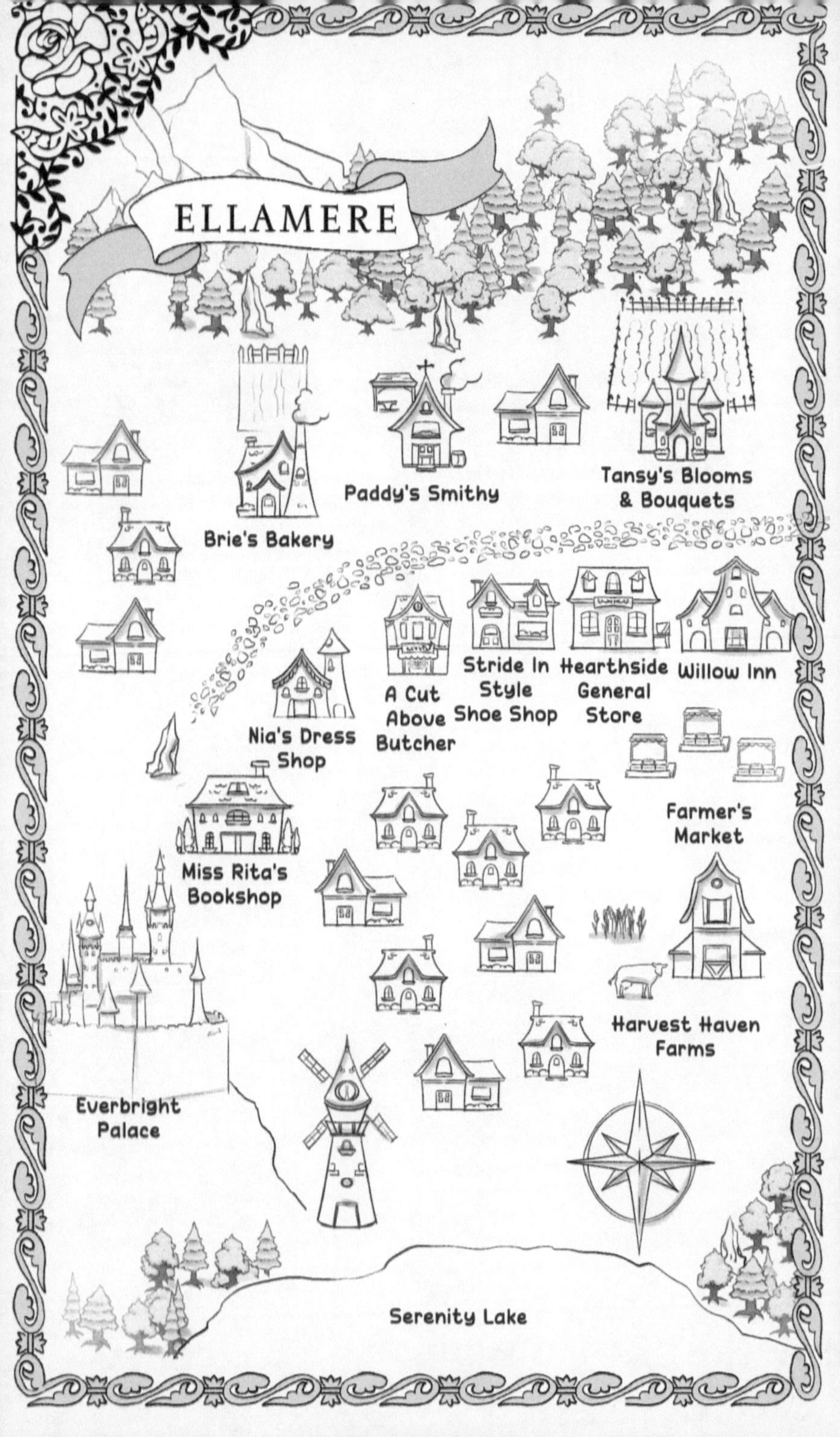

ELLAMERE
Paddy's Smithy
Tansy's Blooms & Bouquets
Brie's Bakery
Stride In Style Shoe Shop
Hearthside General Store
Willow Inn
A Cut Above Butcher
Nia's Dress Shop
Farmer's Market
Miss Rita's Bookshop
Harvest Haven Farms
Everbright Palace
Serenity Lake

Pronunciation Guide

Abrielle (ah-bree-el)
Armana (ar-mah-nah)
Deimos (day-mos)
Ellamere (ella-meer)
Erik (air-ick)
Greer (gr-eer)
Luna (loo-nah)
Nia (nee-ah)
Paddy (pad-ee)
Peakbottom (peak-bottom)
Raden (ray-din)
Robert (rob-ert)
Selanthia (sel-an-thia)
Tansy (tan-see)
Tinker (teen-ker)
Trish (tr-ish)
Vasiri (vas-eerie)

One

Chocolate batter, a dusting of flour, and something rather sticky coated Abrielle's freshly washed apron. This wasn't unusual considering her line of business, and after yet another long day, she didn't have the energy to mind it. No, what was bothering her now were the pages sitting on the table. They were taunting her. Again.

She had tried every recipe in her grandmother's cookbook; from warm melt-in-your-mouth chocolate morsel cookies to the most difficult meringue. She had spent her teenage years poring over those pages, learning every technique, every variant. But, at twenty-three years old, she still felt she hadn't mastered them yet. Nothing quite compared to when her grandmother made them.

She sighed, feeling the steady gaze from the painting of her grandparents. Placed in a simple wooden frame, it sat high on the shelf. Propped between a bag of flour and her grandmother's favorite clay bowls, it looked down on Abrielle like a faithful watchguard. It and the humble cottage and bakery were their legacy.

Her chest tightened with lingering grief, and she leaned over the cookbook resting on the tall table in the center of the kitchen. The pages were blurry, and she tried to blink away the tears threatening to fall. If only there was a recipe to perfect one's life. She blew a stray strand of dusty brown hair from her face and concentrated on the round ball of dough sitting in the center of the table. Its flour-dusted coating was a stark contrast to the silvery brown wood. Flour slipped into the grooves of the old table. It would be a pain to clean later. And although it was probably time to replace the antique, she couldn't bring herself to do it.

While the cookbooks and the treasures inside the kitchen were all she had left of her grandmother, the old oak table was a lovely reminder of her grandfather. It was one of the few things that remained of him. Well, that and the homey cottage that she called home. It was split into two sections—living quarters and a bakery, which included a kitchen as well as a space large enough to fit a few people at a time. He had built it all with his own nimble hands soon after he and her grandmother were wed. The cottage wasn't quite what it once was, but Abrielle loved it all the same. From the creaky floorboards to the large stone oven, it was home.

Tinker, the lazy old tabby cat, glanced up from her milk bowl and chirped. Abrielle patted her affectionately on the head and received a purr in return. She left the lovable feline alone to enjoy her breakfast and stepped up to the sink to give her hands another good wash. The first sliver of sunlight peeked through her yellow flowered curtains and her heart skipped a beat. Sunrise already? Abrielle quickly returned to the dough and rounded it gently, giving it one more dusting of flour, and hoping she would have enough time to get it in the oven before villagers showed up at her door.

Using her favorite serrated blade, she lightly sliced into the dough, making an arc over the top. Then, biting her lip in concentration, she carefully carved delicate details into it that resembled leaves. It was an unnecessary touch since the bread would taste the same either way, but lately, including designs in the loaves kept things a bit more interesting.

Her grandmother always said there was magic to be found in the mundane. But since losing her nearly ten months ago, Abrielle was finding that to be less and less true with each passing season. Winter had been a busy time with orders flooding in for Yule celebrations. And spring and summer had been prime picnic and travel seasons, giving her plenty to keep busy. But with the end of summer lull, Abrielle was becoming weary of the same commissions—fresh bread, pastries, and muffins with fresh fruit folded in, nearly every morning.

And, of course, there was the daily delivery to the palace, which consisted of the royal family's favorites. Peach scones, apricot tarts, and cinnamon swirl bread by order of the King of Ellamere himself. The commission had passed from her grandmother to her, and she knew she should be grateful. But surely the village, and even King Vasiri and his family, were as eager as she was to try something new.

Abrielle bit her lip and twisted her hands in the apron. Of course, there was the chance that they wouldn't like any new creations that she came up with as much as they liked the delights that came straight from the old cookbooks. Her grandmother's life's work was compiled in those pages. Trish Grainwick was renowned for her creations. To Abrielle, it was safer to stick to what she knew worked. Besides, it was a nice way to honor the memory of the woman who had taught it all to her.

Abrielle inhaled deeply through her nose and let the scent of fresh baked muffins overwhelm her senses. Then, straightening her apron, she decided her dilemma would have to wait. Knowing the day's work had to be done, she slipped the dough iron onto the hot embers and set about her other tasks while she waited.

When she finished, she took a moment to take a few steady breaths. She tried to ignore her disheveled reflection in the small mirror by the door, which showed her pale skin made paler by the flour which covered her nearly head to toe and had her chocolate brown eyes standing out like a spooked deer. Her favorite frilly white apron, embroidered with an A, hadn't helped much with the mess and she quickly tried to dust off the burnt orange dress she wore underneath. She washed her hands, which were turning pink from so much exposure to the hot water and lavender soap she had used several times that morning.

Cheerful, muffled voices grew louder outside as villagers began their day. Sensing that the first of her regular customers would soon be arriving, she folded the orders into parchment and set them aside. Then, she grabbed some specialty treats and placed them inside the glass display case her grandfather had installed on the little counter that stood between the kitchen and the bakery's sitting area. Customers—even her usuals—often enjoyed requesting jam filled breads or light pastries that caught their eye while they waited for their order.

Lastly, she made sure the shelves were well stocked with preservatives and dry mixtures that villagers could take home to bake themselves. Her favorites were the jars of ready-made mixes for cakes and cookies. But there were also pickled vegetables, and specialty spice mixes. It was another little touch she and her grandmother had thought up together. A way to lighten the load on themselves while still making sales.

The bells on the shop door chimed as one of the early risers entered. The sound was like music to her ears. A sign that the quaint, quiet home would soon fill with chatter and laughter again. Paddy Pepperwood, the blacksmith from next door, waddled in. He was a large man who had been quite spry and handsome in his youth. But years of bending over the anvil had been hard on his back, making him move much slower than he once had.

"Morning, Miss," he greeted her and approached the counter that separated the kitchen from the sitting area.

Abrielle, knowing he would be the first to come in, had his usual order already in hand. She smiled warmly at the familiar face and handed him a small bundle. With a wink, she said, "I included some extra blueberries and nuts."

Her grandmother had always said food could cure any ailment. Even though Abrielle had no idea if that was in fact true, she liked to try anyway.

Paddy's kind eyes brightened as he took the bundle in his calloused hands. "Much appreciated!"

Abrielle's gaze dropped to a dish sitting beside her. It wasn't one of her grandmother's recipes, so she hadn't set it out in the case. For years her grandmother had done an excellent job of making the bakery thrive. And truth be told, Abrielle worried if she didn't do things the same way, then it might fail under her care.

Still, the little dish taunted her from the corner of her eye. She grabbed it before she could lose her courage and too loudly asked, "Would you care to try this? On the house, of course."

She held up the dish, filled with a streusel topping from one of the pies. She had mixed the crumble with bits of raisins, cranberries, and nuts to make a more complex treat. But Paddy eyed it warily. She held up a finger for him to wait and rushed to grab some cream from the icebox.

Paddy was scratching his beard but waiting patiently when she returned. She spooned a bit of cream on top and frowned as it settled into the crumble in a sad sort of way. It took every bit of courage she had to hold the dish out to him. "It's something new I was trying."

He smiled politely, but she caught the doubt in his eyes as he said, "I'd love to give it a try."

Abrielle eagerly handed it to him and waited with bated breath. He took a bite and smiled when he finished. Heat rose to her face as she waited for him to say something.

"That's interesting!" he said cheerfully.

But Abrielle had been doing this long enough to know when a dish fell short of fantastic. And this was one of those times. He handed the creation back to her with an awkward smile. With a quiet sigh, she scooped the contents into the trash bin. She didn't blame him; it didn't look as appetizing as she had hoped. Although it tasted better than it looked, it *was* missing something. She just couldn't pinpoint what that something was.

Before Paddy finished counting out the coin he owed her, more customers trickled in.

The morning rush always went the same. Abrielle had the regulars' orders ready to go and was quick to fulfill the odd traveler's request. By the time she was done, sweat beaded on her temples. She plopped into one of the wooden chairs in the customer sitting area and wiped at her brow.

"Don't tell me I missed the rush." The familiar voice of her best friend, Tansy Fulbright, rang out over the sound of the bell as she slipped in. Her rich brown, curly hair was pulled away from her face with a bright yellow bandana. Her light brown skin had a brilliant glow from the heat of the morning and her amber flecked eyes sparkled with mischief.

Abrielle rolled her own eyes playfully at her dearest friend. "We both know you're not sorry that you weren't here to help out. You were only hoping to see Thomaz."

Tansy shrugged and walked around the counter to help herself to a warm cookie and a cup of tea. "The more I put myself in front of him, the more likely he is to get the hint."

Abrielle chuckled. "Why not just tell him you want to go to the Star Crossed festival together?"

It *was* a celebration of love, after all. Many of the eligible village women took the opportunity to ask the men they liked to go with them. And if a woman went without an escort, she would show up in her finest—adorned with beautifully bloomed flowers linked together to form a crown, and a special dress for the occasion—to catch the eye of the one they were pining after.

Tansy brought her breakfast to the table and sat across from Abrielle. "I could say the same to you."

Warmth flooded Abrielle's cheeks, and it wasn't because of the late summer heat. Although she didn't have anyone special in her life, she *had* mentioned Erik—the new guard who escorted her into the palace kitchens each morning—a few times. She wasn't one to pine, but he had caught her interest, nonetheless. How could he not? He looked like he had walked right out of a storybook with sunshine blonde hair and blue eyes that sparkled like the lake.

Abrielle sighed, sinking further into her seat. "I have my hands full with the bakery. Besides, Erik hardly knows that I exist, whereas Thomaz has shown his interest in you on many occasions."

He and Tansy had been sweethearts for as long as Abrielle could remember. They'd all grown up together in the village that sat at the edge of the palace gates. Anyone who knew the two of them would swear they were fated to marry one day. Even if neither of them was ready to admit it.

Tansy argued, "He would if you just put yourself out there. Plenty of men in the town would fall at your feet if you didn't always have your head buried in a cookbook."

Abrielle forced a laugh. Tansy sounded like her grandmother. Toward the end, she had joked often with Abrielle, asking when she was going to meet a nice young man.

When she didn't respond, Tansy's eyes widened and, with a mouthful of cookie crumbs, she exclaimed, "You *are* planning to come to the festival, aren't you? And not *just* with an armful of baked goods."

Abrielle bit her lip. Festivals were something she'd always looked forward to. She and her grandmother would spend weeks planning the menu and prepping the kitchen. Then, when the time came, they would stay up late telling stories to one another while they prepared parcel after parcel to be delivered to the event. It was something they'd always shared together. But things were different now.

Staying up late only reminded her of how empty the house was. The quiet always settled deep in her bones. It twisted her stomach into nervous knots just thinking about going to the festival without her grandmother.

Tansy insisted, "We'll have fun. I promise." She pursed her lips, glancing past Abrielle and into the kitchen where the painting rested on the shelf. "I have an idea! I can come over and help you bake for it. Then we can go together."

Abrielle's mood brightened a smidge. It wouldn't be quite the same as baking with her grandmother, but at least she wouldn't be alone. Tansy always knew how to lift her spirits. And it had become a tradition of sorts to rendezvous with her best friend after delivering goods to the festival tables. Maybe it would be fun to do all of it together this year.

Besides, she might even run into Erik there. For once he could see her when she wasn't covered in flour, with baked goods piled in her arms. Maybe she could even commission a new dress from Paddy's wife, Nia.

Feeling a bit more enthusiastic about it, she said, "I might take you up on that offer."

If her grandmother was still around, she would have told her to ditch the apron and go have a bit of fun. A smile tugged at Abrielle's lips as she imagined her grandmother's stern face and no-nonsense tone.

Tansy grinned and finished off her tea. Together, they went to the kitchen and gathered up the King's order. Abrielle pulled the bread from the oven, handing it to Tansy to wrap in the parchment, then she put out the fire. Next, they tied the rest of the bundles with neat little bows of twine to keep them safely covered during the walk. Then, with everything placed into handmade wicker baskets, Abrielle slipped her arms under the handles.

Tansy wrinkled her nose. "Do you want some help with those?"

Abrielle leaned back and lifted her arms. "I've got it."

"Are you sure?" Tansy asked skeptically as Abrielle stubbornly struggled to reach the door.

"Yup," she squeaked as she tried to figure out how to get it open with just her hip.

Tansy chuckled and slipped in front of her, turning the knob with ease.

Abrielle blushed. "Thanks, Tans."

It was much warmer outside than it was in the cottage. Her grandfather had smartly built their home so the breeze would waft through the kitchen just right, keeping it nice and cool even in the summer. But outside, with the rising sun beginning to beat down, Abrielle couldn't help but sweat. The wisps of hair that had escaped her braid stuck to her face. By the time she reached the palace, she would be a mess.

Tansy strolled by her side on the cobblestone street, making idle chit-chat. The two women waved at each neighbor they passed, giving them cheerful greetings and well wishes for the day. When they came to a fork in the road, Tansy gave her an encouraging wink.

Abrielle laughed, bidding her friend farewell, and continued on her way. On top of the hill, the palace glistened in the sun. The sandstone walls were adorned with elaborate arches and towers that loomed over the kingdom, giving a view of the land much farther than the little village below.

Abrielle had never been further than the kitchens, which were positioned on the ground floor. But even that was a marvel in and of itself, with massive ovens and rows of tables for the cooks to do their work without crowding one another.

Although they were more than capable of baking their own goods, King Vasiri graciously commissioned Abrielle's family long ago. Her grandmother had become the only commissioned baker in town, having the only kitchen—aside from the palace—capable of producing such large quantities. More than that, he believed in outsourcing work to his villagers. Ordering gowns from Nia for his wife and daughters, sending shoes for repair to Tansy's father, and regularly asking Abrielle for his favorites even after her grandmother passed.

Erik was waiting by the side gate, just as he had been all summer since he was first assigned to the palace. His midnight blue uniform was spotless without a crease in sight. The insignia on the front—a sun and moon intertwined with one another—almost seemed to glow with its silver thread.

The polite smile on his face made her chest tighten. Although she'd been seeing him every morning, they still hadn't made it past the acquaintance stage. A limbo that consisted of *how are you* and *have a nice day*.

Abrielle slipped past him as he swung the gate open for her. He followed quietly behind. She knew the way to the kitchens well and headed straight for the door at the side of the palace where the staff would be waiting to unload her burden. Erik held the door open for her and they both stepped inside. The kitchen was bustling with attendants preparing to take the royal family's breakfast upstairs. A symphony of voices filled the air along with the delicious aroma of bacon in the frying pan.

Erik waited patiently by the door while Abrielle took each item out of the baskets. The kitchen staff barely uttered a word to her as they placed the pastries and loaves of bread onto silver platters and shuffled to the stairs.

Abrielle, however, lingered a moment. If she could just work up the courage to ask Erik something personal, something that would give them a little push toward friendship... Sucking in a deep breath, she smoothed out her dress and turned to him.

"Miss Grainwick!" A shout from the stairs made her yelp.

The corner of Erik's mouth quirked upward. Was a laugh at her expense considered friendly? She didn't have time to consider it as one of the King's personal attendants called out for her again.

"Miss Grainwick! I'm so glad that I caught you. The chancellor would like to see you."

A lump formed in her throat. Why would the chancellor want to see her? He was the right-hand man to the King and rarely spoke to villagers himself.

"Oh?" was all she could bring herself to say.

The attendant clasped his hands together and raised his eyebrow. "To renew the contract."

Abrielle almost scoffed at herself. Of course. It was time for the yearly renewal of her services to the palace. She had been with her grandmother at the last one. By then, the illness had taken control, making it difficult for her to make the short trip to the palace on her own. It was hard to believe it had been nearly a year since she passed. Abrielle bit her cheek, trying to quell the pang in her heart.

The attendant nodded to Erik. "Please, see her upstairs to the library."

Erik gave him a curt nod in return and gestured to Abrielle to follow him. Eagerly, she did as he directed. Her grandmother had always taken care of the contract, but now it was Abrielle's job to oversee it. That meant venturing further into the palace. It also meant a chance to think of something clever and charming to say to Erik.

They took the long, narrow staircase up and Abrielle tried to count each breath she took in an effort to steady it. She was so winded from the climb that she couldn't even think of anything to say to the handsome guard in front of her, let alone actually *speak*.

When they reached the top, he wasn't so much as flushed. She on the other hand, had a cramp in her side. Erik studied her for a moment, and she smoothed her hair back, hoping she didn't look as disheveled as she felt.

Cautiously, he asked, "Are you alright? I know that's quite the climb..."

"Fine," she declared a little too loudly. Then, calmer, she added, "It's been a long morning."

"Tell me about it," Erik said as they walked down the hall side by side. He was much taller than her and she had trouble keeping her eyes off him as he spoke with ease. "The King has us practicing for the Star Crossed festival's opening ceremony."

Her heart doubled in speed. "Oh, so you're going to the festival?"

"Yes," he answered simply. "Isn't everyone?"

Abrielle tried to think of a smooth response, but all she came up with was, "Sure. They'd be crazy to miss it."

Ellamere's celebrations were always beautifully put on. Lively music, incredible food... and the bakery was always asked to make special cakes. This year, however, her focus might need to be shifted more to living up to her grandmother's legacy and providing the very best goods, rather than actually enjoying the festival itself.

The door up ahead was opened slightly and she could feel their opportunity to talk coming to an end. Erik stopped when they came to the library and gestured for her to go inside. Rather than say something charming to send him off with, she stumbled over the small lift in the doorway.

With more grace than she had, Erik caught her by the arm and helped her catch her footing. His touch sent butterflies fluttering wildly in the pit of her stomach. When he removed his hands from her, she realized she was staring at him, completely awestruck. He stared back and their eyes locked for a moment.

Say something... Anything. If only she were more like Tansy, who always knew just the right thing to say. Instead, Abrielle hiccupped, "Thanks."

Erik bowed his head to her. "I'll wait out here for you."

Abrielle remained there, smiling, even after he shut the door behind him. Once he was gone, she groaned. Now not only was she a bad flirt, but apparently, she was a klutz, too. Could things get any worse?

Two

Abrielle's cottage could have fit inside the library fifty times over. Books lined every wall as far as the eye could see. Based on the vastness, King Vasiri must have had every piece of published literature inside. Stuffing it to the brim like a fat, happy cat.

The chancellor sat at a large mahogany desk, mumbling as he looked over a stack of papers as high as his shoulders. Abrielle straightened her dress and tossed her braid behind her back. If she had known she would be attending a meeting like this then she would have worn something more professional. More silk and less flour...

She blushed when she noticed him peeking at her over his wire-framed spectacles. He cleared his throat and said, "Oh, Miss Grainwick, thank you so much for taking the time to see me."

"Of course." She joined him at the large desk and took the seat across from him.

"Now, we're here to discuss," he trailed off, shuffling through the mountain of papers stacked between them. "Ah, here it is," he mumbled, swiping a lone paper from the pile while he smiled. He set it in front of her with a flourish. "Your yearly commission renewal. You'll find it to be the same offer we gave your late grandmother."

Abrielle read over the document. It was simple, really. A generous payment each week in exchange for the royal family's favorites. As she scanned the parchment, she noted the offer for special commissions. The ones that included each celebration and ball they hosted. For larger events, King Vasiri would assign his kitchen staff to bake the bulk of what they would need, but Abrielle, like her grandmother before her, would receive double the coin in exchange for festive cakes and other specialties.

These commissions had belonged to her grandmother before Abrielle was even born. And it was an honor to know that the King trusted her to continue it. It also twisted the nerves in her stomach like braided bread. Could she continue to live up to the standard her grandmother had set? Was she even good enough to deserve such an honor?

The chancellor smiled pleasantly as he made small talk. "The contest should be interesting this year."

The contest. In all the business talk, Abrielle had forgotten about the annual dessert contest. Villagers from all over El-lamere were invited to compete for the coveted prize of coin from the King's treasury. It was a handsome sum. One that her grandmother had used year after year to fund the repairs to the cottage and bakery.

The chancellor, unaware of her thudding heart, continued, "Should be a piece of cake for you, eh?"

"We shall see." Abrielle wanted to sink low in her chair and disappear from plain sight.

Her grandmother won every year using a brand-new recipe she'd created from scratch. Although many lovely entries were presented for the contest, none had held a candle to her grandmother's creations. She was beloved in town and good at what she did. Yet, Abrielle hadn't even decided on what recipe she would use to enter this year.

Instinct told her to use one of her grandmother's, but if she did, there was no guarantee she would replicate it the same way. Even if others never seemed to notice—still coming in loyally each morning—she did. What if she wasn't up to the task? And what would losing mean for her bakery and reputation?

It wasn't that she didn't have enough business from the villagers, but losing the contest would be an embarrassment. Proof that she was in over her head. Heat crept across the bridge of her nose at the mere thought of the shame of losing. She tugged at the neck of her dress, hoping to relieve the tightness rising from her chest to her throat.

"Are you quite alright, Miss? I can have Erik fetch you some water."

"I'm fine," she said, horrified that she apparently looked as flustered as she felt.

The chancellor's eyes softened with sympathy. "Miss Grainwick, I recognize that this may be difficult for you." He gestured to the contract and continued, "Your family's longtime service does not go unnoticed. Trish Grainwick was an exceptional woman. She made a name for herself here when no one else had been up to the task. This could be your chance to do the same."

Despite his warm smile, Abrielle shrank with embarrassment. He could clearly sense her discomfort. Her grandmother had strived to build her business from the ground up. In truth, Abrielle had inherited it rather than earned it and the whole town probably knew it.

But she wasn't about to reveal her deepest doubts to the man in front of her, no matter how kind he was. Instead, she simply said, "Thank you. I appreciate your confidence in me."

The chancellor clasped his hands together and leaned forward eagerly. "Alright, then. You just need to sign here and here." He pointed to the blank spaces on the parchment.

Eager to continue with the relationship between her bakery and the palace, she took hold of the quill and dipped it into the ink.

As she began to sign her name, the chancellor spoke, "We, of course, would like to extend the offer as well for you to come and bake full time at the palace. We made the same offer to your grandmother every year, though she turned us down each time."

Abrielle chuckled. "That's not surprising. Having her own bakery was a dream she and my grandfather brought to life. Seeing as it's always been *my* dream to keep it running even long after they were gone, I'll have to respectfully decline."

The chancellor didn't look a bit surprised. "The King will understand. But the offer will continue to stand, should you change your mind."

Abrielle finished signing on the dotted line and slipped the baskets back over her arms as she stood. Offering her other hand, she said, "Thank you, Sir."

He embraced her with a warm grip. "See you at the festival."

Just this morning Abrielle had decided not to stress about the festival and instead enjoy it with her friend. But the contest was too important. The chancellor was right about it being her time to make a name for herself. But to do so, she would need an original recipe. Something no one had tasted before. A dish to really wow them. Her pulse picked up at the prospect. It wasn't just about the prize money. Her bakery would survive even if she lost. She would do the repairs herself if she had to. But her very reputation as a baker was on the line. She was going to impress the town with something new and exciting that would make her grandparents proud.

With a wide smile, she replied, "Of course."

A voice came from a door at the far end of the library. "Chancellor Rockwell, Princess Greer requires your services! She cannot find the new quills she purchased at the port!"

The chancellor chuckled. "Duty calls. You can see yourself out, right?"

"Of course." Abrielle dipped into a respectful curtsey.

Once the chancellor left, she wandered past the rows of bookshelves on her way to the door where Erik was waiting. It was her first time this deep in the palace, so she took her time peeking at the different titles on the shelves. There were books on the histories of Ellamere—*The Great Implementation of the Gemtowers*, *The Banishment of Magical Elements*, and *King Titus' Triumph*—to name a few. There were also fairytales about wicked creatures tricking unsuspecting humans, and even a few books on poetry.

She ran her fingers along the spines, wishing one of these books had the answers she was looking for. *How to Make a Man Who Barely Notices You're Alive Fall in Love With You* had a nice ring to it, didn't it? Or maybe *How to Move on When Your Family is Gone*. A lump formed in her throat. Instead of dwelling on things she couldn't change, she turned to irritation instead. Annoyance at her forgetfulness, mixed with another emotion she couldn't exactly pinpoint.

It was like a tug in her heart. Not grief or the loneliness that accompanied it in the quiet moments of her day. She'd felt plenty of that in the last year. And it wasn't the longing she'd become well acquainted with. Lately, she seemed to be in a constant state of that. Longing for something new. Whether it be romance or inspiration for new recipes. Anything to spice things up around their sweet little village.

This draw was something quite different altogether. Like a storybook siren summoning a sailor out to sea. She knew Erik would be waiting for her in the hall, but the tug turned into a pull as she followed the bookshelves. It was like someone had tied a string to her and was drawing it to them. She glanced around nervously, but there was no one there. Just her, the books, and a bit of dust. She came to a corner, shrouded in shadows. Cobwebs coated the shelves, and the books had a thicker layer of dust than the others she'd been looking at.

She reached up, running her finger over each title as she read. *Twelve Herbs to Cure a Broken Heart. Curses and Protection. Shielding One's Mind from The Otherworlds.* Each title alluded to spell work. It was a curious thing for King Vasiri to have in his private library, since he didn't have magic of his own. No one in Ellamere did as far as she knew. Not since the King's grandfather, the late King Titus, erected the gemtowers.

Old timers in town spoke of the magic that had been abundant years ago. Even her grandfather told stories of gifted individuals in hushed reverent tones. His favorite tale was the one about witches who would cast spells through shimmering potions. Or the winged creatures who enjoyed visiting human gardens. But that was before they put the eleven-foot-tall structures into place. The late King strategically placed them along the ley lines beneath the earth. Each one was said to hold great power.

Of course, not all the stories were quite as enchanting. Abrielle could remember many nights as a young girl when she had sat with Tansy listening to the King's youngest daughter, Princess Greer, telling horrifying tales of winged beasts that snorted fire and men with razor-sharp teeth who could devour little girls whole.

"Always keep salt on hand, just in case," Greer had said with a wicked wink. *"They won't be able to cross."*

Abrielle and Tansy had hung on to her every word, as if her advice might one day save their lives. Abrielle shook her head now at the naivety of her young self. There was no evidence that magic and the dangers that accompanied it still existed. The late King had intended to lock the magic out by using the gemtowers as a sort of gate, and as far as anyone in Ellamere knew, it had worked.

Still, there were a sprinkle of rumors throughout the years about outliers in the village having some power. A remnant of magic that had stayed behind like the scent of flowers carried on the wind. But Abrielle had never seen it for herself. And now that she was grown, she knew better than to put stock in gossip.

She continued to read the titles silently to herself until she came to a sloppily bound book. Compared to the others, this one was made by an amateur. It didn't have the same clean lines or smooth surface as its neighbors. Abrielle's hand grew heavy as she hovered over it, and the strange tug in her chest softened.

With a gentle touch, she pulled the book from the shelf and gasped at the title: *Mabel's Home Recipes*. She glanced around and saw no recipe section on the bookshelves nearby. How had it ended up here? Abrielle furrowed her brow, trying to recall anyone within the village that went by that name. She knew just about everyone but couldn't place a Mabel.

Regardless, with the contest still fresh in her mind, her heart fluttered. She blew the layer of dust off the top and flipped it open. Inside was a treasure trove of recipes she had never seen before. It was a mix of soups and meat pies, but when she came to the desserts section, she couldn't contain her rising excitement.

There were elegant rose-shaped pastries, delectable cookies, and towering cakes. All made with ingredients Abrielle hadn't thought to use before. And each was marked with little handwritten notes by who she guessed was Mabel.

The door at the other end of the library creaked open and Abrielle slammed the book shut with a squeak. With a glance over her shoulder, she spotted Erik peeking his head through the door.

It would have been a good time to slip the book back into its place. But whoever organized the library had clearly put it back in the wrong spot, and after all this time, it had gone unnoticed. Would anyone really miss it? It would be a shame to let the recipes go to waste. Especially when Abrielle had such a short time to come up with something to wow the judges at the contest.

Vibrating with nervous energy, she stuffed it into one of her baskets and folded the light cotton dishtowel over it. Surely no one would mind if she helped herself to the poor forgotten book. She could always return it later. Besides, recipes this intriguing deserved to be enjoyed, not kept hidden on a dusty shelf.

Erik's posture was nothing short of professional as she walked beside him to the stairwell. But something felt different. Maybe it was the weight of the stolen book in her basket or the prospect of getting home and trying out one of the new recipes. The thought emboldened her, giving her the courage to do other things she hadn't been brave enough to do before.

"I was thinking, we see quite a bit of each other now... Maybe we could share a drink at the festival." There. She'd said it. She had finally pushed past the veil of small talk. Now she held her breath.

He gave a halfhearted smirk as he said, "That would be great. I think some workers here at the palace will be joining up with one another as well." He allowed her to descend the stairs first with a gallant sweep of his arm.

Abrielle deflated. It wasn't exactly the response she was hoping for. But it was a step in the right direction. When they reached the bottom of the stairs, she turned to face him. "Right. That could be fun. I'm thinking of trying out some new recipes for it. Maybe I could bake you something?" Lamely, she added, "You know, as a thank you for escorting me every morning."

The moment she said it, heat bloomed across her cheeks, and she fought the urge to roll her eyes at herself. Escorting her was his job, why would she thank him? The recipe book weighed down the basket resting on her wrist and she had to tilt her arm back awkwardly to keep it from falling. She clutched her arms close to her stomach, hoping the stolen book would continue to give her courage.

"Do you have a favorite dessert?" Maybe her new treasure would contain the perfect thing to impress him, along with the rest of the town.

Erik's eyes flitted over her head, and he responded absent-mindedly, "I've never really had much of a sweet tooth."

Abrielle scrunched her nose. What sort of person didn't like dessert? And hadn't he been paying any attention at all? She was capable of more than sweets. Some of her best sellers were savory loaves of bread with dried meats or hot peppers folded in.

She opened her mouth to offer one of those instead, but Erik's face lit up. Confused at what had claimed his attention, she spun to find one of the Queen's lady's maids lingering in the doorway. The pretty girl waved merrily at Erik.

He placed a hand on Abrielle's arm and said, "Will you excuse me?"

Abrielle shuffled toward the door as she asked, "Don't you have to see me out?" As far as she knew, it was a rule. Though, who was she to judge when she'd just stolen from the King?

"That's okay! I trust you!" he called over his shoulder as he loped over to the girl waiting for him.

Abrielle deflated. But, determined not to let the additional minor hiccup ruin her day, she hurried out the door. Once she was far enough from the palace that it was no longer in sight, she reached into the basket. So today didn't go quite as planned. But she had done more this morning than she had all summer. She had said more than three words to Erik, and she had done something else she never had before.

Her stomach twisted into knots. She had *stolen* something. A laugh bubbled up from her throat. She had never done anything so reckless or bold in her life. It was exhilarating, but also made her feel a bit sick. What had begun as just another normal day was turning into the most exciting day of her life. Maybe her grandmother was right about finding a little magic in the mundane, if you just looked hard enough.

Three

Despite the excitement pulsing through Abrielle's veins, the stony old cottage looked the same as ever. It waited for her, like an old friend, and she hurried to the front door. But as she reached for the aged brass handle, a strong breeze blew one of the shutters, and it clanged against the house wildly, falling halfway off the hinge.

Abrielle grumbled under her breath and set the baskets down on the bakery's doorstep. She fumbled over the bushes which were overgrown and in serious need of trimming. Their branches scraped against her ankles and tugged at her dress, but she was determined. If she could rig the shutter until she was able to figure out how to properly fix it, then she wouldn't have to listen to it knocking all day and night.

A particularly large bush blocked her way and she stretched across, grasping for a hold on the faded sage green wood. Her fingers brushed against it just as she lost her balance and tumbled into a sea of greenery. She let out a yelp and attempted to untwist herself from the bush which seemed to be claiming her as its own.

Abrielle shut her eyes tight and stopped struggling, resigning herself to her embarrassing fate. She'd never been any good at this sort of thing. She was like Tinker; an indoor cat that didn't belong with the elements outside unless it was to collect things from her neatly kept garden.

A familiar feminine voice cut through her tumultuous thoughts. "Need a hand?"

Abrielle blushed, realizing Paddy's daughter, Luna, must have seen the whole thing. Luna's throat sounded tight, as if she was trying to hold in laughter. It made Abrielle cringe and want to sink deeper into the bush's overgrown branches. She attempted to wave her off.

"I'm quite alright, thank you, though."

Luna peeked over the bush and offered a hand, anyway. Reluctantly, Abrielle took it and was pulled out of the bush in the blink of an eye. Dusting herself off, she said, "Thank you. I think that bush may have it out for me."

"I'd say so. When's the last time you trimmed it?"

Abrielle was ashamed to admit that she couldn't remember. She'd been so busy lately with orders and the occasional experiment in the kitchen, that she might have let maintenance on the cottage fall behind a bit.

Instead, she said, "Thanks again."

Abrielle turned and began picking up the baskets, and Luna bent down to help. Her bright smile and rosy cheeks matched her father's, but she had gotten her mother's warm beige complexion and more petite frame. Even though she was a couple years older than Abrielle, she was much shorter. But there was a lot of power in that small package. Since she was big enough to lift a hammer, Luna had been helping her father at his blacksmithing workshop.

"You know, I could help you with that shutter. And maybe with the bushes, too." She held the basket with the cookbook out to Abrielle, who took it quickly and clutched it tight.

"I appreciate that, but I'm sure I can figure it out."

Luna was so capable. She'd been helping both of her parents with their businesses and never seemed to break a sweat. Abrielle admired that about her. She flashed a confident smile. Surely, she could get a handle on things and figure it out, one way or another.

Luna raised a skeptical eyebrow and shrugged. "The offer stands if you change your mind."

Abrielle nodded and said her goodbyes, thanking her neighbor once again. She shifted, trying to balance the baskets while she unlocked the bakery door. Before going inside, she shot a glare at the bush and the dangling shutter.

"I'll deal with you two later," she warned, then hopped inside.

Tinker trotted by her side into the kitchen, mewing loudly for treats. Abrielle put the baskets away and began preparations for the following day. She hummed to herself as she set dough out to rise. She could sense the recipe book sitting inside of the basket. The strange draw to it was still present, but she resisted. There was still work to be done and plenty of time to play later.

Abrielle didn't dare take the recipe book out of the wicker basket until nightfall. She wasn't sure why she was so nervous. No one would be looking for a forgotten, homemade book. And there would be no more customers today since they knew the bakery was always locked up in the evening. That time was reserved for prepping what she could for the next day.

Tinker walked between her legs, rubbing herself on Abrielle's stockings and leaving behind sharp pieces of black and gray fur. She patted the feline absentmindedly, eager to finally flip through the pages of her new treasure.

Even with the curtains drawn to hide from any stray passerby, she only lit a few small candles on the counter. A lantern might draw Tansy over for a late-night drink. It was warm with the windows closed, but Abrielle didn't mind. Not when her body was buzzing with anticipation.

If she could find the next great recipe to add to her menu, then sneaking the book out of the library would be worth it. It also might give her the inspiration she needed to come up with something on her own. And with the festival only a little over a week away, time was not on her side. She wanted something that would not only impress the villagers but would also win her the competition.

Although she preferred sweet desserts, she supposed she could try a savory one first. Maybe it would spark some creativity. Worst case scenario, she could always offer it to Erik. If Tansy insisted that she get out of her comfort zone, then it was worth a try.

Placing the book on the counter like it was a precious gemstone, she opened it to the dessert section. It might be a long shot, but she had nothing to lose. As she did, the candles sputtered, and Tinker's loud mew made her jump. Her heartbeat raced as she glanced at the windows, which were shut tight, keeping out any night breeze. Her nerves grew taut. Shaking off the strange feeling, she swatted at the pesty old tabby cat.

"Enough of that. I'm just going to try one little recipe and then we can go to bed."

The cat stuck an indignant nose in the air and padded over to the bundle of blankets Abrielle kept for her in the kitchen. Calmer now, Abrielle leaned over the pages to get a better look. She swiped through various desserts, taking mental notes of which ones she wanted to try next, then came to a soufflé. These were tedious to do, but maybe it was just the challenge she needed.

This particular one had a variation scribbled at the bottom. *Herb and cheese – Basil, Rosemary, or Wild Asparagus Root.* Abrielle jumped up and headed to the garden out back. She had used asparagus in things like tarts before, but never the root. It seemed just strange and different enough to try.

Ever since she was a young girl, she had delighted in watching her grandmother come up with new recipes. Sometimes she would sit there for hours as her grandmother set plate after plate in front of her to taste test. She never gave up until she got the recipe just right. That is precisely what Abrielle intended to do.

Creeping into the dark night, she came to the back edge of the garden. A glimmer in the shadows caught her eye and she took a moment to admire the gemtower sitting a few yards away. It was twice her height and was made of smooth stone that resembled quartz. The crystal-like surface mimicked a winter landscape with a cloudy blue color. It was tucked into the forest, but it cast a soft glow on the outer part of the garden.

The gemtower had been there long before her grandparents built the cottage—just one of five that lined the outskirts of the village. As a child she had tried to climb this one and in turn had received a scolding for playing with something that's sole purpose was to protect Ellamere's people—as was proclaimed when King Vasiri's grandfather had constructed them.

Thankful for the gentle light coming from it, she knelt and pushed aside sage and thyme until she found the wild asparagus that grew at the edge of the garden. The moonlight offered just enough clarity to find what she needed. With an expert hand, she plucked it out by the root.

Hurrying inside, she got to work. The lit stove cast a soft glow to the room, highlighting the drying herbs hanging from the ceiling and the little jars lining the shelves. Grabbing one of the smaller dishes, she coated it in a thin layer of butter, then sprinkled in breadcrumbs made with yesterday's stale bread.

While the flour and butter heated in a pan, she carefully chopped the asparagus and its roots. There was a calmness that these tasks brought her, and she reveled in it. There might have been moments outside of the cottage where she was awkward and clumsy, but in her grandmother's kitchen, she was confident and sure of herself. Knowing exactly what needed to be done and how to do it was rewarding.

Whisking in the last of the day's milk, she hummed to herself. It was a familiar, gentle tune. One she had grown up hearing in this very kitchen. As she added in the cheese and asparagus, she thought of what the new day would bring. Tomorrow she would carry the confidence she felt in the kitchen right up to the palace gates.

Glancing over the directions one last time, Abrielle noted that a line was crossed out beside the last step. The ink had been heavy, and it was impossible to read past it. She gnawed at her cheek, hoping she wasn't missing anything important. She didn't let it deter her, though. Many bakers jotted down extra notes, marking down little details from their experience with a particular recipe. Things they wouldn't do next time, or something they would do differently when they revisited it later.

Abrielle focused instead on what information she *did* have. A note with a star beside it stated that the mixing must be done in a clockwise motion. She narrowed her eyes at Mable's attention to detail. It was certainly a bit strange. She'd never made anything that required steps as specific as that. Still, she did as the recipe told her. If she had learned anything it was that recipes included details for a reason and not paying attention to those would only result in a failed attempt.

As she beat the egg whites into a stiff peak, she imagined how wonderful the festival would be if she had someone to share it with. And how grand it would be to have the villagers delight in her creations the way they had done for years with her grandmother. Folding in the cheese mixture, she thought of the reward in living up to her grandmother's legacy. To her true potential. It was in moments like this where she could truly reflect on what she wanted.

An icy chill crept up her spine as she poured the mixture into the dish. It was almost as if a ghostly touch had flitted along her skin, but she shrugged it off. She must have been exhausted. As soon as she was done with this, she would head straight to bed.

With a finishing touch, she smoothed the top using her favorite spoon—the one with little daisies engraved in it. Her grandfather had made it and gifted it to her on her tenth birthday. The first birthday she'd had after her mother passed. He had made her feel so special then, reminding her that they could still celebrate life even when the ones you loved had moved on.

Suddenly, even with Tinker's presence, she was struck by intense loneliness. It settled deep in her bones, filling her with a mixture of dread and heartache. What would her birthday be like this year, now that the last of her family had moved on? There would be no family to celebrate with. No laughter and joy filling the home. Only her and the soft creaks of the cottage.

A tear drifted down her cheek as she set the dish into the oven and lit the special candle that would track the time for her. The flame flickered in the warm light of the kitchen, allowing her to see the little tick marks Paddy had put on the silver piece for her. Then she waited. Once the candle burned down to the first tick, the soufflé would be ready. Just twenty minutes until she brought a little magic back into her home. A home that had been far too quiet and empty for too long.

Abrielle wasn't sure when she had dozed off on the hard wooden stool, but the faint scent of something burning woke her. With a quick glance at the candle that was keeping the time, she realized it had passed the twenty-minute mark. Scrambling for the oven, she nearly reached in with her bare hands.

"*Shoot.*" She hissed, drawing her hands away and grabbing the nearest paddle. She slipped it under the dish and pulled it out hastily. But as she lifted it over the counter, the dish slipped, banging onto the table. Her heart sank along with the soufflé's puffy top.

As it deflated—along with any hope that she'd perfect the recipe in time for the palace delivery in the morning—the candles circling the counter were snuffed out. The hairs on her arms stood on end as the room went nearly pitch dark, lit only by the glowing embers in the oven. Tinker let out a low, distressed growl, followed by a fearsome hiss.

Abrielle picked her up, holding her fluffy body close to her chest. The windows were still closed. No breeze drifted in, so there was no reason for the candles to have gone out like that. Running her hand along Tinker's back, she attempted to soothe both the frazzled cat and herself.

"It's alright. They must have been burning for too long." She nuzzled her face into Tinker's neck. "Let's go to bed. We can try again in the morning."

Tinker purred in response, and Abrielle held her while she spread the embers in the oven to make the fire die down faster. Together, they wandered into the living room. Too tired from the day, and feeling groggy from her cat nap, Abrielle didn't bother heading up the stairs. She'd have to be up in just a few hours anyway, so she curled up in her favorite armchair.

With the tabby cat on her lap, she pulled a soft woven blanket over them and tipped her head back. The sounds of crickets outside the window sang her to sleep in a soft symphony. And soon dreams came to her.

She was ten years old again and back in the forest with her grandmother, foraging for mushrooms. She chased after a delicate white butterfly, but it was always just out of reach. Her grandmother's warm laugh echoed through the trees, bringing a smile to Abrielle's face.

A soft breeze floated by ruffling Abrielle's hair. It caressed her like an old friend, and although her grandmother was off in the distance, she felt the faintest touch of someone pushing a stray strand from her face.

Her stomach dropped at the touch. The faint cloudiness that was often found in dreams told her she was still asleep. That this was just a figment of that. But then why did the touch feel all too real.

Four

Abrielle jolted awake to Tinker's rumbling growl. It grew louder than Abrielle's pounding heart and she glanced down to find the feline's blue eyes widened like saucers. She could still feel the ghost of a touch on her face and reached up swiftly. No hand or wind was found there. But it had felt so real. Not like the phantom touch of a dream.

The room was still dark with no sign of the rising sun. Drowsiness still disoriented her as she tried to peer out the window to judge the position of the moon. Just as she began to stand, something shifted in the corner near her bookshelf. The shadow wasn't shaped like anything she had in the living room. And besides, inanimate objects didn't have *moving* shadows.

Her heart leapt to her throat, and she moved slowly away from the armchair. The shadow froze and Abrielle's veins turned to ice. It most definitely wasn't one of the familiar objects in her family home. It was *someone* shaped like a man, and she wasn't sure if her eyes were playing tricks on her or if they really were as large as they appeared.

Fight or flight? Fight or flight? She couldn't decide. Whoever had broken into her house hadn't harmed her while she was asleep. But maybe now that they'd been caught, their tactics would change.

Beside her, Tinker's hair stood pin-straight on her arched back. With trembling limbs, Abrielle made a decision. *Run.* She grabbed the hefty cat and rushed to the kitchen, too afraid to try the front door in case the intruder got there first. Heavy footsteps followed behind her and her heart raced, spurring her on. If she could make it to the back door, then she could cut through the garden to Paddy and Nia's home.

Surely the intruder wouldn't follow her there. Maybe whoever it was would take what they wanted and leave without further assault. The kitchen was dark. Too dark. It was like the moonlight had been shut out of the room. Not even a sliver of it shined through the gap in the curtains.

With a screech, Tinker leapt from her arms. Abrielle scrambled to grab hold of her once more, but wasn't fast enough. The feline was gone. Hidden in whatever small space she was able to squeeze into, no doubt.

Which meant Abrielle was on her own. In her panic, she tripped over the stool she'd been sitting on earlier. She tumbled to the ground with a hard thud. Pain shot through her right arm, and she bit her lip to keep from crying out.

A man's rich, velvety voice called to her from the counter. "Ouch, that had to hurt."

She squinted, wishing her eyes would adjust to the dark. "Look. Whatever it is you want, just take it and leave." She grunted as she struggled to untangle her leg from the stool.

"What I want?" The stranger's voice was as smooth as honey. And it was close. Too close. "*You* summoned *me* here. How about you tell me what you want and then I can be on my merry way."

Abrielle scrunched her nose. "I most definitely did not invite you here to my home in the middle of the night."

What sort of arrogant ass blamed his breaking and entering on the victim?

He chuckled. "Foolish mortals. This is what happens when you trust a witch."

The floorboards creaked as he closed the gap between them. She could only make out his shape, which appeared broad and tall. She flinched as he knelt and pulled the stool off her and grabbed on to her left arm to help her up. Something she was grateful for since her right arm was throbbing.

She eyed him warily, but shadows shrouded his face making it impossible to get a good look at him. It didn't matter though. If he was there to rob or hurt her, he was doing a terrible job of it. What sort of criminal gave a helping hand to their victim? Adrenaline wracked her at the uncertainty of it all.

It was too late to run now that he had her literally in his clutches, so she took a long steadying breath and asked, "Witch? I don't know what you're talking about."

He was close to her. So close she could feel the warmth radiating from his body. Yet, shadows still danced around him, hiding his identity. The scent of juniper filled her nose. Like pine—both bitter and fresh. Had he come from the forest? She knew most of the villagers and couldn't place his voice.

Leaning in close enough that she could feel his breath on her cheek, he said, "You really have no idea, do you?" With a snap of his fingers, every candle in the kitchen blazed to life. Their flames sputtered for a moment before finding their strength.

It was like magic. She stammered, "H-how did you do that?"

Nausea rolled in her stomach. People didn't just spark candles to life like that. It wasn't possible. Not in Ellamere. All the scary stories Princess Greer had told her when they were children flooded in.

She took a step back, pressing herself against the table. Flight hadn't worked. So, it was time to fight. Without hesitation, using her uninjured arm, she grabbed the hefty rolling pin sitting on the table and swung. The intruder grunted as it slammed into the side of his head. The shadows around him fled like wisps of smoke. With one hand, he clutched his face and with the other, he snatched the rolling pin out of her grasp.

Based on the size of him, his strength shouldn't have surprised her, but she yelped just the same. The rolling pin clattered to the floor, and he reached out with surprising gentleness to grab on to her bicep. She pulled away from him but didn't run.

Curiosity overpowered her fear, and she raised her eyes to look at the intruder, who was still only inches away from her and cleared from the shadows. Expecting to find a vagrant with a mean mouth and a hateful, twisted face—things her imagination had prepared her for—she sucked in a breath. Instead, she locked eyes with an incredibly handsome man.

Dark, silky hair curled slightly at his ears. His eyes were dark pools, blotting out the whites that should have been there. They were so entrancing that she had trouble looking away from them. The shadows in the room seemed to gravitate toward him, keeping close to his skin as if eager to be a part of him.

When she recovered from the surprise, she remembered that handsome didn't mean *safe*. Her heart raced and tension built in her limbs making them feel incredibly heavy.

He narrowed his eyes as he said, "You're strong for such a little thing." Was that *admiration* in his voice?

There was a dangerous quality to him. Like a charming villain from a storybook. The one who locked the princess in the tower, claiming he did it to keep her away from the cold world. She shivered. Part of her screamed to run away. To call for the village guards. But another part of her didn't want to be separated from him. Not yet. Not until she uncovered the secrets surrounding his arrival.

His smile widened as if pleased with her reaction and he flashed dazzling white teeth. Abrielle leaned forward to get a closer look and nearly toppled over when she spotted the slight sharp points at the end of each tooth.

The man pulled back and watched her quizzically. "What are you doing?"

"Nothing," she replied quickly, straightening. In truth, she had gone cold all over thinking of Princess Greer's stories again. *Men with razor-sharp teeth who could devour little girls whole*, she had whispered over a campfire with a mischievous grin on her face.

With her hand on the counter to steady herself, Abrielle took a careful step back. Her gaze flitted to a glass shaker of salt sitting on the counter. The stranger made no move to follow, and the space between them allowed her to relax just a bit. Tinker, however, had no such plans and jumped onto the counter—something she was never under any circumstances allowed to do. Then the tabby placed herself between Abrielle and the man. If that's what she could call him.

There was something different about him. It was almost like when you took a walk in the forest and the hairs on the back of your neck rose, telling you there was danger nearby. Although the forest looked as it always had, you knew there must be a threat lurking out of sight.

The stranger didn't seem to be from her world. Instead, he was more like the ethereal creatures spoken about in stories passed down through the ages. From a time where magic still stirred in their land.

Abrielle swiftly grabbed the salt and gripped it in her hand, recalling the silly childhood superstitions Princess Greer had told along with her stories. At least, they had *seemed* silly at the time. That was before a stranger with pointed teeth entered her home.

Meanwhile, the man sneered at Tinker but did nothing to move the angry feline. Maybe he was frightened of cats? Though, Abrielle couldn't imagine a man of his size being afraid of anything or anyone. Her gaze drifted down to his clothes. The vest over his linen shirt seemed to be crafted out of some sort of bark and the leather belt around his pants was old and worn. His boots were even more curious than the rest, like thick leaves from a tree far larger than anything she'd ever seen in the forests around Ellamere.

She tilted the shaker, allowing salt to spill in front of her in a thin white line. She continued to spill it in a circle around her while the stranger watched with a tilted head. He made no move to stop her, instead observing her with a confused, yet entertained expression on his face. He raised his eyebrows and tendrils of shadows peered over his shoulder as if to watch her as well.

Feeling slightly safer with her little salty barricade, she asked with wonder, "Where did you come from?"

Tinker backed into her as the stranger leaned against the table. "I'll answer your question, once you answer mine. Why did you summon me here?"

"I told you; I did not invite you here. I was asleep when *you* broke into my living room."

A tinge of frustration creeped in. Why in the world would he think that she had asked him to come here? And in the middle of the night, no less?

Genuine confusion crossed his face. With a furrowed brow, he mused, "Impossible." Though he seemed to be talking more to himself than to her. He took a step forward, shuffling right through her should-be impenetrable barrier of salt.

Thanks a lot Greer, she thought with a scoff, suddenly feeling incredibly silly for thinking it would work. There was no doubt in her mind that this man wasn't from her world. But clearly, superstitions weren't going to help her get out of the mess she was in.

Heat blossomed on her face. The man, however, was thankfully too distracted to notice the burning blush forming across the bridge of her nose. He sifted through the ingredients left sitting out on the table. When he reached the old recipe book, he froze before continuing. Gingerly, he lifted it with two fingers as if he were afraid that it might give him the plague.

"Where did you get this?" he asked with a frown.

Abrielle didn't get the impression that he was an immediate threat to her. If he was, then he would have retaliated against her rolling pin assault. So, she crossed her arms, and demanded with more courage than she felt, "No. It's your turn to answer a question. Where did you come from?"

He arched an eyebrow in surprise. "Selanthia."

Abrielle had never heard of such a place. Not that she'd really paid much attention to geography during her schoolgirl years. She loved her village and her home and never imagined leaving it. She knew of all the villages within Ellamere's borders, but she had never traveled much. For all she knew, Selanthia rested across the sea.

The man pressed his lips into a hard line at her silence. As if inconvenienced by her ignorance, he huffed. "I believe you mortals refer to my lands as the Otherworlds."

Now *that* was a term she was familiar with. Despite her suspicions, Abrielle's jaw dropped at the confirmation that he truly wasn't from her realm. The land coined as the Otherworlds existed beyond her comprehension. It was a place of magic and mystery. When learning about the importance of the gemtowers, her teacher had briefly mentioned the Otherworlds; explaining that their realms were connected through the ley lines in which magical beings derived power. But there wasn't much knowledge on the land itself, so Abrielle didn't have many hard facts on the subject. Instead, she had to rely solely on word of mouth. Admittedly, the teachers had never mentioned Selanthia when speaking of the foreboding Otherworlds.

Regardless, she knew enough to expect trouble from anything that came from the forbidden realm. King Vasiri's grandfather must have had a good reason to close the doors to it. And the current king must have agreed since he had kept the gemtowers intact after all this time.

Yet, this stranger, despite his appearance, didn't seem like a monster. Unless it was all an act so he could prey on unsuspecting mortal women... Perhaps she was being foolish.

For all she knew, he *was* one of the men Greer had ominously spoke of. Maybe he was simply biding his time until he was ready to devour her.

She opened her mouth to ask more, but he held up a haughty finger. "My turn." Dangling the recipe book in front of her, he asked, "Where did you get this?"

Her chest tightened. She didn't know this man. She wasn't about to spill her thievery with a stranger. Especially one who had appeared from thin air. Everything in her screamed to see sense and call for the palace guards. But what would happen when they showed up and caught her red-handed with a cookbook from the King's private collection?

She opted for a vague truth. "I found it."

The side of his mouth tipped into a half frown. His voice dripped with disbelief. "You found it? And decided to flip to a random spell?"

Snatching the book from him, she pulled it into her chest and hugged it tightly. "It's a *cookbook*. There's nothing in here but ingredients and directions."

He rolled his eyes at her. It was the most human he'd looked to her since she first set eyes on him. "You literally just described a spell."

This time, she felt the blush creep along her face and down her neck. No doubt she was as red as the cherries sitting in the large bowl at the corner of the table. "I'm not a witch. I'm a baker. I don't know anything about spells or the Otherworlds. I was making a soufflé for goodness sake!" She gestured wildly to the sorry-looking dish sitting beside him.

Something nagged at the back of her mind as the words left her mouth. No one she knew had ever used magic before. But it had existed once upon a time, right? Maybe the book hadn't been placed in the spell section on accident. And maybe those strangely specific instructions had something to do with this mix-up. Go figure the one time she decided to try something new would backfire in such an alarming way. This was her punishment for not doing things the way her grandmother always had.

He picked up the dish and sniffed it. As he did, his eyes lit up like a hound who had caught a scent. "This reeks of intention and..." he sniffed again. "Wild asparagus root?" With a deepening frown, he suggested, "My guess is whoever wrote this recipe was trying to hide their spell work. Asparagus root coupled with strong intentions and," he shoved a finger roughly at the directions on stirring and scoffed, "stirring clockwise to *welcome* your wishes, must have weakened the veil between our realms."

She searched her memories for any deeper knowledge on the Otherworlds or veils but could think of none aside from the stale history of the King's grandfather and the rantings of a little girl who wanted to make her friends scream for the fun of it. It was becoming hard to decipher truth from fiction. Although in this moment with the strange man standing so close to her, it was easy to assume it was all real.

Despite that, Abrielle shook her head. No. She didn't have magic. She'd simply been trying to make something new and exciting. "That's not possible. The gemtowers keep magic out of Ellamere."

With a flourish, he gestured to himself with the dish still in one hand. "Yet, here I am."

The dish clinked on the table as he set it aside carelessly. She flinched at the recklessness in which he handled one of her grandmother's belongings. As she grabbed it quickly, checking for any chips, she kept quiet, waiting for him to speak again and hoping he wouldn't blame her for her mistake.

When he met her eyes, his demeanor softened. Even the shadows around him seemed to slide away slightly. "What did you wish for?"

Not wanting to share intimate details about her heart's desire with a total stranger, she replied, "It's my turn to ask—"

With an intense gentleness, he asked again, "What did you wish for?" Closing the gap between them, he placed his hands on her shoulders and gave her a gentle squeeze. "Please, answer."

Her mouth was as dry as bread that had been left out overnight. She licked her lips and answered, "I wished for excitement... and for someone to share it with."

He didn't laugh. Nor did he speak out in judgment. All he did was let out a low understanding hum. Abrielle wasn't sure what more there was to say. Why did he even care enough to ask? Her wish couldn't possibly make a difference, could it? Surely, he could just leave. Go back to where he came from and forget this ever happened.

Logically, she knew she should call on the guards. Except, how would she explain that she had pulled a book from the spell section and performed one? Either they would think she was daft, or that she had intentionally performed magic. Neither sounded appealing.

Nervously, she suggested, "It might be best for you to just go home now. Do that snappy thing you just did with the candles or something and whisk yourself back to your realm."

He righted the stool and sat, putting him at eye level with her now. "Well, seeing as you're the one who brought me here, only you can send me back."

Abrielle's heart sank. Of course, it couldn't be a simple fix. She tensed as Tinker inched closer to the man, feeling him out with her long whiskers. The stranger ignored the cat and stared at Abrielle expectantly.

She twisted the book in her hands and simply stated, "I don't know how."

"Then I suppose we will have to figure it out together." He peered around the kitchen. "Do you happen to have some tea? The spell dragged me out of my house rather roughly."

"Oh! Of course." She hurried to put the kettle on. She supposed even in the Otherworlds—or Selanthia as he called it—hostesses had manners.

From the corner of her eye, she caught him petting Tinker. To Abrielle's surprise, the old tabby laid down and allowed it to happen. That was something she *never* did with newcomers. And if Abrielle didn't know any better, she'd have thought the man looked quite proud of himself.

Taking two tiny teacups with little blue stars painted on them from the shelf, she introduced herself. "I'm Abrielle Grainwick, by the way..."

"Abrielle," he drawled pleasantly. It sounded as if he was savoring the way her name felt on his tongue, and her heart fluttered. Then he returned the courtesy. "You can call me Deimos."

Five

I t was as if Abrielle was caught in a bizarre dream. That was the only explanation for the broad, oddly attractive man sitting in her kitchen. Deimos—as he had just introduced himself—smirked at her with his hand extended. She stared down at it, uncertain.

"You do shake hands in this realm, do you not?" He tilted his head to the side curiously.

Abrielle froze as the much-anticipated sun peeked through the curtains, casting a pleasant glow on the kitchen. With Deimos' arrival, she was failing to go about her usual preparations for the morning rush. As much as she needed to deal with getting him out of her home and, well, frankly, out of Ellamere and back to where he belonged, she first needed to face her customers. Realizing the time, she pushed past his extended hand and scrambled to gather up any baked goods that hadn't gone stale from the day before.

Her right arm was sore, and she hissed as she shuffled through the cupboards. Using her left arm—the one she wasn't used to relying on—she clumsily grabbed what she could. A small voice inside her head told her to shove Deimos out the door. Let him find his own way home. But the other part of her worried what might happen if he was set free upon the village. Would he treat everyone as pleasantly as he'd treated her?

She peeked at her guest from the corner of her eye. He was larger than any of the men in the village. And he was a stranger. If he wanted to, he'd have no trouble hurting her with those strong arms that looked as if they were made for brute force.

Abruptly, she warned him, "I've offered to help you get home, but don't think for a moment I won't call for the guard if you try anything untoward."

"Noted," he chuckled warmly.

"I'm serious," she said with a raised eyebrow. "I won't hesitate."

Although she mustered the most serious tone she could, it was a slight fib. She knew calling for the guard would put her under scrutiny. But Deimos didn't. The last thing she wanted was for Erik and the other guards to come knocking on her door with questions she didn't have answers to. Even if Deimos wasn't a bad man, magic was banished for a reason and the King would surely want to act. There was no way he would allow someone from the Otherworlds to wander around their quiet town as if he was on holiday.

She wiped her sweaty palms on her apron and blew out a swift breath. It didn't help. Worries still swirled in her mind like cream being stirred into hot tea. If the guard came for him and tried to take him in, he might resist. Someone could get hurt.

She shook her head to clear the whirlwind of worries. It would be best for now if she attempted to handle her mistake herself. As she went back to work, she glanced at him from the corner of her eye again. He moved a stool to the corner, well out of her way. Then he lounged back and watched. It was thoughtful and she couldn't help but wonder if everyone in Selanthia had gracious manners. It was a far cry from the murmurs of danger and evil she had heard.

Dangerous or not, though, he seemed rather relaxed for a man who was just torn away from his home. It seemed she was doing enough panicking for the both of them. Curiosity gnawed at her as she asked, "Why don't you seem very worried about your predicament?"

His shadows slinked ominously, hugging close to him, but instead of answering, he drawled, "Do you always rush about like a ratawilly this early in the morning?"

"You didn't answer my question." Then, confused, she asked, "Wait, a *what*?"

With an exasperated sigh, he said, "It's like a..." he paused as if searching for the right word. "Like what you call a squirrel. Only larger. *Much* larger." He shivered but didn't elaborate further on what she suspected was a bad run in with one.

A million more questions about his world stormed her mind, but she didn't have time to dwell on them. Not right now, at least. She huffed. "Usually, I would have had everything freshly baked and ready to go by now. People will start trickling through that door any minute."

She froze and spun to look at the tall, dark stranger sitting in her kitchen. Even with rays of light falling on him, shadows seemed to creep from out of nowhere, edging as close to him as they could.

Anyone who set eyes on him would be able to tell he wasn't of this world. So not only had she allowed a man to stay all night, but she had allowed a... a... *whatever he was*, to come into their village. This wouldn't do at all.

After a moment of silence, Deimos spoke. "To answer your question, I'm not sure anyone really misses me back home. Maybe some time away was just what the fates ordered."

Loneliness settled over Abrielle. If he had someone back home waiting for him, then surely, they *were* missing him. It couldn't be all that bad. Not so bad that he would prefer being summoned by a clueless human, at least.

The bell at the door chimed cheerfully, and her heart leaped into her throat. Wide-eyed, she demanded, "You have to hide. Now!"

Paddy's voice carried across the room, "Morning, Miss Abrielle!"

She grabbed Deimos by the sleeve and tugged. He was much bigger than she was, and her efforts did little to move him. The smile plastered on his face was smug and he sat up straighter, as if trying to peer over the counter separating them from the old blacksmith.

"Morning, Paddy, I'll be just a moment," her voice was strained as she pulled harder on Deimos' arm. "I'm running just a bit behind today," she grunted.

Cheerfully, Paddy responded, "No worries. It's been quite a morning for us as well." A chair scraped across the floor and Abrielle sighed in relief, knowing he must be taking a seat. That meant he wouldn't be able to see over the counter.

As Paddy rattled on about his grass browning despite the recent rains, Abrielle turned on Deimos. His gaze dropped to where her hand lay on his arm and then flitted back to her eyes. With a desperate whisper, she pleaded with him, "Please, I won't know how to explain your presence here. Just hide."

With a shrug of his shoulders, he began to stand, but she leapt on him, dragging him low to the floor. "He'll see you," she reprimanded him and pointed to one of the larger cabinets where she kept the flour and grain.

Deimos whispered, "I won't fit in there."

"It's the best option we have. Now go." She pointed with as much authority as she could muster.

His eyes sparkled in the sunlight, and she noticed specks of purple in the large black irises. He was even more handsome in the daylight with a strong jawline and regal nose. But the ethereal quality to him was also more apparent now. The shadows that clung to him looked even more out of place and his presence seemed all wrong. It was like catching a bat lurking around in the daytime.

With wide, pleading eyes, she urged, "If anyone finds you here, they'll ask questions. You could be arrested by the King's guard and I along with you for bringing you here in the first place."

She thought of the witches who were said to have caused the King's grandfather to take action against magic. If she recalled correctly, they had become powerful enough to ignore the laws in Ellamere and in turn, had put those without magic at risk. What if King Vasiri accused *her* of being a rogue witch? One who was trying to undermine his authority and break down the symbolic walls that kept magic out?

She wasn't sure what the ramifications would be for summoning a man from another realm, but it was something she didn't want to find out firsthand. If the King thought she was trying to stir up trouble, he might withdraw her commission. And if the villagers found out, it might deter them from coming to her shop. How would she explain Deimos without admitting she'd stolen a book from the King's personal library and accidentally cast a summoning spell? Her stomach turned at the prospect of what might happen to the bakery in that scenario. King Vasiri could shut her down. Or her neighbors might be too frightened to buy from her if they thought for a moment that she was enchanting the recipes.

Finally, Deimos conceded with a lopsided frown, shoving the large sacks out of the way so he could cram his massive frame into the cupboard. He had to draw his knees up to his chest and duck low to fit. If Abrielle hadn't been so on edge, she would have laughed at the sight.

There was concern in Paddy's voice as he asked, "Are you sure everything is alright back there? I could lend a hand if you need it."

"No, no," she insisted, shutting the cupboard door quickly. "Everything is fine. I just..." she paused, trying to think of an excuse, "slept in a bit longer than usual."

A few muffins that were stored properly in an air-tight container caught her eye and she tossed them into a basket, along with a few tarts that had held up well since the day before. Paddy didn't seem to mind as she handed him the day-old baked goods. But still, feeling sorry for the poor assortment, she offered, "It's on the house."

"No, I couldn't accept that." Paddy shook his head fervently.

Desperate just to get him out of there, she offered instead, "Half price then. I insist."

It truly wasn't a problem since she typically put together day old packages to sell for half price, anyway. She hated for things to go to waste.

Seemingly appeased by that, Paddy pulled the coin from his pocket and put it in her hand. "Are you sure you're alright? You look flushed."

Abrielle forced a smile. "I might be coming down with something, but I'll be fine, I promise."

Paddy tipped his head to her and on his way out, said, "If you need anything at all, let Nia or Luna know. Best to lean on your friends when you're feeling under the weather."

Abrielle's heart warmed at the offer, and now she gave him a *genuine* smile. "Thank you, Paddy."

A few villagers slipped by him as he left, and Abrielle's stomach twisted into knots. How long would Deimos stay put? She had to get this over with quickly, so she scurried, dodging Tinker who followed her every move, and gathered up everything she had ready in the kitchen. She gave them all the same excuse and half-priced offer she'd given Paddy, and no one seemed bothered by the goods she handed them.

When the last customer exited, she finally took a full, solid breath. The day was far from over, though, and there was the matter of the demon-like man hiding in her cupboard. He called out gingerly, "Can I come out now?"

"Yes." She gasped as she caught sight of Tansy just outside the door. "I mean, no! Stay there!"

He groaned loudly, but the sound was drowned out by the bell as Tansy came inside. Her cheeks were rosy, and she began speaking before Abrielle could greet her. "It is madness out there. Did you know Thomaz's entire flock of sheep fainted last night? Simultaneously. And this morning they're walking around in a complete daze. He can't get any of them to stay with the herd. They keep wandering in all sorts of directions and even the pups can't get them to heel."

Tansy headed for the kitchen and Abrielle clumsily intercepted. She hit her side on the counter, trying to get around it, and groaned. Surprise flashed across Tansy's face as Abrielle took her hand and pulled her back into the dining area.

Trying to distract her friend, she said, "I suppose that's strange."

Though, nothing seemed as strange as having a shadow man appear in the dead of night. She bit down on the inside of her cheek. Did Deimos' arrival had something to do with the odd occurrences? She shook her head as if she could dust off the absurdity and suppressed a groan, hoping nothing else would go wrong.

Tansy plopped into her seat and continued, "It's not just that. I woke to find every one of my prize-winning roses withered. But there was no sign of a frost. It's still too early for that." Her face fell into a pout. Tansy's garden was her pride and joy, and Abrielle felt sorry for her.

"That's terrible. Is there any way to salvage them?"

"I'm not sure. I suppose if I—"

A loud clanging came from the kitchen and panic rushed through Abrielle, making the hairs on her arms stand on end. She froze, praying there would be no more noise. It didn't work. The cupboard banged shut, and she held her breath, scrambling for a way to explain Deimos to her best friend.

Footsteps padded on the floorboards, but rather than an alarmingly handsome man, a grotesque dog-like creature walked around the counter. His fur was black and mangey, long and tangled like it hadn't had a good washing in quite some time. The creature's fangs poked out from between its lips as if too big to fit in its mouth. And it was enormous. Larger than even the wolves she'd seen in the forest. But its eyes... They were dark pools with purple specks. Deimos' eyes.

The shock left her speechless. She desperately wished she'd had more time to figure Deimos out before now. Too much mystery surrounded him and, much like her recipes, Abrielle preferred all the information laid out before her. The uncertainty left her with a metallic tang in her mouth. Perhaps she was further in over her head than she thought.

Her brow furrowed as she watched him glance at his reflection in one of the glass cases that housed jars of jam and preserves. When he did, a strangled gurgling sound escaped him and he shook his head, taking a few alarmed steps back.

Abrielle thought she might faint. What other abilities did he have that she didn't know about? She hoped she wouldn't find out. At least, not until Tansy left. Deimos stalked away from his reflection and padded over to the table with a strangely human-like huff. One that didn't match his feral appearance.

Tansy drew her legs onto the chair and wrapped her arms around her knees. "What *is* that thing?"

Abrielle hesitated, not quite sure herself. "It's uh, I found it. Last night."

Silently, she added shapeshifting to the many questions she still needed to ask him. What other tricks did he have up his sleeve? She tensed as the beast strolled up to her side and sat like an obedient pup with its head held high.

Tansy cringed as she said, "That's not any sort of dog I've ever seen before."

Tinker hissed in agreement from the counter with her hackles raised. The dog... or Deimos, responded with a snort in Tinker's direction. The tabby turned away indignantly and leapt from the counter back into the kitchen.

Abrielle awkwardly patted Deimos' head and gave a strained smile, trying to look as if she wasn't repulsed by him.

"I think he's a long way from home. He needed a place to stay." With a pointed look in his direction, she added, "Just for the night."

"Right." Tansy, who typically fawned over any animal she came across, stared at him warily. "Well, you should definitely keep him hidden from the customers. He'll frighten them right back out of that door."

Deimos snorted again, as if insulted. Abrielle pulled at his ear in warning. As she did, her arm throbbed. Maybe the fall had hurt her worse than she thought. Her chest tightened at the thought of having to prepare for the Star Crossed festival with an injury.

Swallowing the growing lump in her throat, she turned her attention back to Tansy and said, "Um... Do you think maybe you could make the delivery for me this morning?"

Leaving a stranger in her home made her uneasy but leaving someone or *something* like Deimos alone in the little cottage brought on a wave of panic. And what was to stop him from wandering into town on his own? Still unsure of what exactly he was capable of, it was too big a risk.

Tansy's brows were knitted together. "To the palace? Are you sure?"

Abrielle stood quickly and grabbed the bundle of baskets she had set aside for the royal family. It wasn't the best she had to offer, but it was better than not showing up with anything at all. "Yes. Just tell them I'm not feeling well, but I will deliver their usual order tomorrow."

"Okay..." Tansy's voice dripped with suspicion. "Are you sure everything's alright?"

"Of course," she squeaked.

Tansy tilted her head. "It's just... you very rarely ask for help. Did something happen between you and Erik? Is that why you're avoiding the palace?"

Deimos whipped his head toward Abrielle, and she shifted uncomfortably under his scrutinizing gaze. "No," she answered truthfully. To be honest, she hadn't thought of Erik at all. There had been more pressing matters to attend to. "I'm just not feeling the best. I think I need to take the day to rest."

Tansy seemed to relax at that. "You do work hard. I keep telling you, you need to take some time for yourself." She took the baskets from Abrielle. "I'm happy to help out. And I can come back to check on you later."

"No!" Abrielle answered too loudly and a bit too fast. "I'll be alright. I'm just going to curl up with a good book and," she paused, glancing down at the rabid-looking mutt, "deal with Deimos." The name slipped out without her realizing it.

"You *named* it?" Tansy scrunched her nose.

With a forced nonchalant shrug, she replied, "I had to call him something. *Fluffy* didn't have quite the right ring to it." Abrielle hid a smile behind her hand as Deimos stomped an offended foot against the floor.

"Alright then." Tansy shot one last suspicious look at him, then headed for the door. "I'll see you later!"

"Bye!" Abrielle practically shoved her through the door, then shut it tight and flipped the lock.

Once her friend was down the road and out of sight, Abrielle grabbed a piece of parchment and a quill and scribbled: *Closed today. Open again in the morning.* She poked a hole in the top of it with the tip of the quill and strung frayed twine through it. Hanging it on the window of the door, she raised her chin, ready to get down to business.

To herself, she said, "That should do it."

The padding of footsteps behind her sent a tingling rush of adrenaline through her limbs. It had been a long time since she'd had anyone linger after the morning rush in the bakery. It was saddening how quickly she was becoming accustomed to the absence of her family.

When she turned, she drew in a sharp breath. Deimos was back in his human-like form again. His shirt was missing, and his pants hung low on his hips. He was like a bronze statue, and he was standing so close, she wasn't sure how she hadn't noticed him there sooner. Suddenly, she was immensely aware of his presence. The heat of his body emanated to hers. Even his shadows seemed to envelope her, slinking around to her peripheral.

Frozen in place and trying to resist the urge to reach out and run her fingers over his broad chest, she asked, "Where is your shirt?"

He pointed behind him to a crumpled heap on the kitchen floor.

Abrielle raised an eyebrow. "So, you were... naked? In my kitchen," her voice reached a higher pitch.

Defensively, he said, "Only for a moment."

She considered chastising him about bakery etiquette. Instead, she had to bite back a snicker as he scratched his ear—a gesture very similar to something a dog might do. But the worried frown on his face made her hold back.

It was the first time she had seen him show any sign of uncertainty, and she had to admit it was a bit satisfying. After all, why should she be the only one twisted with worry? She raised an eyebrow and asked, "Are you alright?" For all she knew, shifting into the beast was painful.

"What sort of question is that?" he practically shouted. "Did you *see* how disgusting I looked?"

"Yes," she quipped. "Did you not mean for that to happen?"

With his jaw clenched, he said, "I meant to shift. But not into whatever *that* was. Something's wrong."

"Yeah, you need a good grooming because now Tansy thinks I've lost my mind and adopted a horrifying stray."

All sense of his carefree attitude from earlier dissipated. Deimos bared his teeth slightly, showing razor sharp fangs, reminding her that he wasn't of their world. And that she, in fact, had no idea who this stranger was that she'd brought into her home.

He shook out his arms, clenching and unclenching his fists and added, "I've never had trouble with... performing."

Abrielle bit her lip at the implication. She honestly wasn't sure how to respond to that. "Maybe you just need some rest. I'm sure it happens to a lot of guys with your," she coughed, "abilities."

He took a step closer to her, and heat flooded her chest. She had to crane her neck to look up at him as he spoke. "You don't understand. My abilities are weak here. That is a *problem*."

Worry welled in his eyes, making him look much more human than she knew he was. It was hard to imagine anyone who looked as intimidating as him being afraid.

If he insisted it was a problem, then she wasn't about to question it. Between the two of them, he knew much better than she did when it came to magic. That much had already been made clear in her mistaken spell work.

Abrielle gulped. "Then we need to focus on getting you back home."

She took an unsteady step away from him, feeling the sudden need to put distance between her and his strong, solid body.

His footsteps pounded on the floor as he followed her to the kitchen. It was a jarring sound since she was used to total quiet after the morning rush. Once she reached the counter, she flipped the cookbook—or spell book, she supposed—open to the recipe she'd used the night before.

Hoping Deimos would have some insight, she asked, "Do you know anything about this sort of magic?"

He grumbled, "Kitchen witchery isn't really my area of expertise."

Abrielle bit her lip. "What exactly *is* your area of expertise?" To be honest, she was afraid of the answer.

"My family deals more in... nature."

She bit back a frustrated sigh. He was being coy for a reason. It made her wonder how bad it had to be for him to only give partial explanations. But judging by his silence, he wouldn't be sharing any more information with her. So, she turned back to the matter at hand. If she sent him home successfully, then she wouldn't need any answers from him at all. He could go back to the Otherworlds, and she could go back to focusing on the bakery and the upcoming festival.

She worried at her bottom lip as she ran her finger along the page of the cookbook. It looked so harmless. Like the most mundane thing in the world. She skimmed the recipe again, looking for any hidden meaning in the words, but found none. Her eyes settled on the scribbled-out sections, and she sighed. If only there was some way to restore it to its original state.

She brushed her hair to one side of her shoulder and felt Deimos' breath on the base of her neck. He was hovering over her, bending to peer at the recipe book.

She turned slightly and chided him, "Do you mind?"

"Not at all." He smirked at her and remained where he was.

She pushed the book away and turned to face him. Pressed between him and the counter, her breath hitched in her throat. *Fates be damned, he was attractive.*

She huffed, "I need a little space if I am to figure out a way to send you back home."

He chuckled. "Be honest. You have no idea what you're doing." Although his tone was mocking, his shadows whirled around him quickly, as if in anticipation.

"Well…" she paused, irritated by his condescending tone, "I haven't heard you come up with any ideas. You're the one with powers. Shouldn't you be able to just snap your way back?"

He shook his head. "This is beyond the extent of my knowledge. All I know is that *you* summoned me here and only *you* can send me back."

Her heart dropped and she pinched the bridge of her nose, willing an answer to come. "I could try the recipe again. Maybe it will open a doorway."

He scoffed and gestured to himself. "It was clearly a *summoning* spell. Unless you want to invite all of my neighbors, I suggest you never try that spell again."

Her pulse quickened at the prospect. "How many of you are there?"

The shadows that clung to him passed over his face. "More than you would be prepared to deal with."

Goosebumps prickled along her arms. "Okay, so that idea is out the window. But maybe there is another recipe in here that will work."

With a shrug, he said, "It's worth a try."

Abrielle stared down at the book with uncertainty. She didn't need to *try*; she needed to succeed. The sooner she sent him home, the sooner things could get back to normal. When she had hoped to spice things up, Deimos certainly wasn't what she had in mind.

Six

A brielle leaned over, pressing her forehead to the counter. She and Deimos had been flipping through recipes in Mable's cookbook for hours, with nothing to show for it. Each recipe had notes redacted with angry little scribbles. Short of picking a random one to try, it seemed they wouldn't find any answers there.

Deimos sat across from her, tapping on the table with his long fingers and wearing a slackened look on his face. The pressure was already on, and his impatience added to her own made her rattled. She glared up at him. "Could you stop that?"

A sly smile spread across his face, lighting it up despite the shadows dancing at the corners of his eyes. He chuckled as he pointed to his forehead and said, "You have a little flour... right there."

Abrielle rubbed at her skin and fought the urge to roll her eyes. If he was so worried about his abilities misbehaving in her world, he needed to take this more seriously. She lowered her hand and asked, "Is it gone?"

With a curt shake of his head, he stood and leaned over the table. "Here."

He grabbed a blue striped kitchen towel and wiped it along her brow. His fingers brushed against her skin, and despite the warmth of his touch, she shivered. It had been so long since she'd been touched like this.

There was no denying the physical reaction her body had any time he was especially close. Even now, absentmindedly, she leaned into his touch. Pleasant nerves twisted in her stomach. The sort that one got when they rode too fast on a horse. Nerves that indicated both excitement and terror. His hand lingered there near her face, the towel dangling between his pinched fingers, and she blinked rapidly, snapping out of it.

Maybe it was because she'd been on her own for too long. Or maybe it was that a man like him—one who didn't have the boyish charm like others she'd met—had never touched her so informally before. Deimos was far from reserved when it came to his interactions with her, and it was disarming. As was the dimple in his cheek when he smiled...

But she wasn't a foolish schoolgirl. She was a woman. One with responsibilities. She cleared her throat and shook out her skirts as if doing so might also shake away the way her body was reacting to his every touch. It was nearly evening, and she still had to prep for the morning. Between that and finding a solution for sending him home, there was no room for distractions.

She leaned away and gestured angrily at the cookbook. "This is getting us nowhere. We need to try something else."

Deimos' expression turned solemn. "You're right." He perked up and suggested, "Maybe we should go back to where you got it."

It was like a candle flickered to life in her mind. The library! Why hadn't she thought of that earlier? There were rows of spell books on King Vasiri's shelves. If she could sneak back in, then she could search for something to undo a summoning spell.

But it was nearly nightfall. She couldn't very well walk up to the palace and demand to visit the private library. Her eyes flitted to the cold, dark oven. If she didn't start prepping now, then she would have nothing to give her customers in the morning.

Deflated, she said, "I can try to sneak into the library where I found it tomorrow morning. I'll find a way to do it when I take the delivery to the palace."

That seemed to please Deimos. "Perfect. Now that we have a plan, can we eat?"

Abrielle's stomach growled in response. She'd been so consumed with finding answers, she had missed lunch. Even Tinker mewed at her, as if scolding her for forgetting to feed them all. She ruffled the tabby's fur and stood.

Deimos remained where he was, resting his elbows on the table. Both he and the cat were watching her with starving, pitiful eyes. She stifled a smile and set to work, opening a jar of smoked salmon. She spooned it into Tinker's dish and set it on the floor for her. Eagerly, the greedy feline jumped down and began to gobble it up.

Now for Deimos. She opened the pantry, which was stocked full of staple foods. Dinner had always been a grand affair with her grandparents. Since they were often too busy in the morning for a big breakfast, dinner was the time they made up for it. Every night had been spent around the table exchanging town gossip or sharing their dreams. Her grandfather would tell stories of faraway places he had seen when he was in the King's army and her grandmother would chime in with little tidbits that he forgot to include.

Since their passing, dinners were small, quiet, and uneventful. Except for tonight, she supposed. It almost brought a smile to her face. That is until she remembered her dinner guest was a magical being from a land she knew next to nothing about. With a worried gasp, she turned to him.

"What sort of food do you eat?" She hadn't even considered that he might have a particular diet. Did he eat meat? If so, she prayed it was game from the forest and not something more sinister. The sharp points at the ends of his teeth made her hold her breath in anticipation of his answer.

Deimos simply shrugged. "Boar, serpent, stag…" he paused, "Why are you smiling?"

Abrielle hadn't realized she was. But she supposed she couldn't hide the relief she was filled with as he listed basic wildlife. "No reason." She spun to face the pantry. "Well, I can't say that I have boar or," she paused and cringed, "serpent. But

I do have some dried venison here. And I could sauté some vegetables to go with it."

"Sounds grand."

She eyed him studiously for a moment. Stories of the Otherworlds spoke of dangerous magic and creatures not fit for the mortal realm. But Deimos seemed more than at home in her little cottage and were it not for his strange appearance and the fact that he'd shifted into a monstrous hound earlier, she would have felt as if he were any other traveler passing through town on his way to the festival. As confusing as his presence was, it was also a little exhilarating.

I really need to get out more, Abrielle thought to herself as she reached for the sack of potatoes on the top shelf. All thoughts of Deimos fled her mind as intense pain shot up her right arm. She cried out and recoiled from the pantry, hugging her arm close to her chest. Deimos was instantly by her side. He took her hand gently and pulled her arm toward him.

As he pushed her sleeve up to her elbow, his shadows inched close to her skin as if inspecting it, too. Abrielle's stomach dropped when she saw the large, blackened bruise on her forearm. It was smudged with purple, reminding her a bit of Deimos' eyes.

More formally than the way he was touching her, he said, "You are hurt."

She bit the inside of her cheek. "I was hoping it would just go away. I didn't realize it was this bad."

Deimos grazed his thumb along the inside of her wrist sending pleasant goosebumps along her arms. "Did this happen last night when you fell?"

"Yes." Instead of meeting his eyes, she watched his thumb as it began to run little circles around the softest part of her skin. Clearing her throat as if it could erase the delightful chills running through her body, she said, "I'll be alright. I'm sure it just needs some ice."

"I'll get it," he offered instantly.

"No. It's fine." The last thing she needed was for someone to spot him lurking outside in her garden. "The icehouse is just out back. I'll run and grab it."

His face twisted with what she suspected was guilt. "It's my fault that you're hurt."

Without thinking, she placed her other hand on his upper arm and gave it a squeeze. "It was an accident."

His shadows inched toward her hand, and she withdrew it quickly. It was difficult to tell if they were a part of him or just drawn to him. They seemed to mirror his feelings, but at the same time, they moved curiously, as if they had a mind of their own.

In all the books she had read in her life, she couldn't recall any beings that commanded the shadows. Not in any history books nor any fairytales she had read. Eyeing them warily, she asked, "Deimos, would you please tell me what you are?"

His nostrils flared slightly as he answered, "It's hard to explain."

Was it truly hard, or did he just not want to? His gaze dropped to the floor and Abrielle sensed something like shame in the quiet way he spoke.

"Just trust me when I say it's easier if you don't worry about it. What I do back home is of no consequence here so long as I return soon."

The implication that if he didn't return soon, then there *would* be consequences, sent an unpleasant shiver up the back of her neck. Abrielle wasn't sure if it was stubbornness or embarrassment that was holding him back, but either way, she decided to drop the subject. Instead, she said, "How about you cut the potatoes while I get the ice?"

Reluctantly, he agreed. "I can do that."

Before he could change his mind and try to come outside with her, she stepped away and ran out back with a small pail in hand. It was a crisp night, and the moon was already out, challenging the sun in a race to see who would get to light the late evening.

To her right, a few yards away, she spotted Paddy in his workshop. His daughter, Luna, was beside him singing as they worked. Abrielle waved at them and enjoyed a moment of knowing she had been right in keeping Deimos hidden inside.

She treaded carefully around the planted fruits and vegetables until she came to the little old icehouse her grandfather had built. It was dug into a large mound of earth. The moss on top was thick and soft to the touch. She opened the creaky door that had been hinged into the earth and stepped into the underground chamber.

Her grandfather, ever the craftsman, had found a way to create a series of drains and vents that allowed the harvested ice to stay cool until winter came around again. It worked well and Abrielle was grateful for it.

She found an ice block and clumsily used a pick with her left hand to chip away at it. It took much longer than it should have, and she couldn't ignore the hint of regret at not having Deimos do it for her.

There was an echo through the chamber as bits of ice clinked into the pail. Already she could imagine the relief that it would bring her tender arm. If she didn't get it back to working condition, it was going to slow her down severely. That was something she couldn't afford. Especially not with the festival on the horizon.

With a sufficient amount of ice resting in the bottom of the pail, she stepped outside. Paddy and Luna were no longer in sight—likely calling it a day to have dinner together as a family. So, Abrielle started for the house, wondering how her own meal was faring under Deimos' care.

Carefully, she followed the thin trails that ran between each patch of fruits and vegetables that littered the small plot of land behind her house. But when a faint glimmer of light twinkled out of the corner of her eye, she stopped short. Squinting into the shadow filled forest, she spotted the gemtower. At first glance, it was as it always had been. Standing firm and tucked into the thicket of the woods.

But the shine that always emanated from it flickered slightly now. It gave Abrielle a twisted feeling in the pit of her stomach. It had never wavered before. At least, not that she had noticed. It had been there her entire life, and not once had it ever shown even the slightest change. If anything, it was the *one* constant in her life. The only thing she felt sure would be left whole, even after everything else she cared about was gone.

With the pail draped over her uninjured arm, she jogged to the far side of the garden. Peering through the tree line, she could make out only the slightest hairline fracture on the smooth gem-like stone. It snaked along the front, running from the base to the top in a jagged line. Again, the soft glow flickered, making Abrielle's heart skip a beat.

A stranger in her home. Strange occurrences in town. And now this. She gripped the pail tightly and forced herself to turn away from the gemtower with a decisive step. If these things were all related, then it was her fault. And it would be up to her to fix them. Starting with Deimos.

Seven

"Is something wrong with the food?" Deimos inquired with a thoughtful gaze.

Abrielle promptly stopped shuffling the vegetables around on her plate and smiled at him. "No, it's great." She hoped her smile concealed the grimace she felt coming on.

"Liar," he laughed and shoved a forkful into his mouth. His teeth flashed—sharp and made for slicing into more than vegetables softened over the hearth—reminding her once again that this was no mortal man in her company.

It was puzzling how she could sit across the dinner table from him without fear. If he was hesitant to tell her what he was, then it must be very bad. A dark warlock perhaps? Or a lycanthrope? Maybe he was wanted and on the run for a nefarious reason. Or he might be a demon who made deals with poor souls at the crossroads. Even as these possibilities circulated in her mind, her impulse wasn't to run from him.

Instead, it filled her with more curiosity. All she knew for sure was that he didn't belong in her home... in her world. And yet, here he was. Here *she* was. Eating and lying to him. Because the meal he had made them, in all actuality, was horrific. The vegetables were sticky clumps of mush and she blamed herself for letting him cook the meal on his own.

A lump formed in her throat as she forced down a sticky cluster of carrots. But it wasn't from the food. The hairline fracture on the gemtower lingered in the back of her mind in a nagging sensation. Deimos had no idea, of course. She still wasn't sure how much she could trust him. Oblivious to her paranoia, he grabbed a piece of smoked venison, then snuck his hand under the table. A pleased purr rumbled from below in response.

Abrielle chided, "I see you've bought Tinker's love with scraps of your dinner."

Quickly, he withdrew his hands and folded them on the table. "Similar to what you do, no?"

She furrowed her brow, trying to gauge whether he was insulting her or not. "No."

"Do you not make this food so that people will be drawn to your doorstep?" He leaned back nonchalantly, but there was an inquisitive glimmer in his dark eyes. As if he was trying to figure her out. Like *she* was the Otherworlder in the room and not him.

"I bake so that people will come and buy from me. So I can make money to survive. That's how businesses work here. It's how people make a living."

"Goods in exchange for money." He frowned. "Yes, I am aware of how that works. But that's not the only reason you do it, is it? I see the care you put into it."

He gestured to the loaves rising on the counter. Then to the cookies baking in the oven. She frowned back at him now. Of course, she put great care into her work. Otherwise, it would never be good enough. It would never measure up to the craftsmanship her grandmother had mastered. But it wasn't so people would love her.

As determined as she was in her stance, tears of embarrassment threatened to well in her eyes. She blinked rapidly, wishing for them to go away before they could fall. Then, hoping to shift the subject off her, she asked, "What about you? I know you do not wish to tell me what you are exactly, but what is it that you do at home? We've spent the entire day together, yet I still know next to nothing about you."

He sighed. "I'm in what you would call the *family business.*"

"Really? What sort of business?" She leaned forward, intrigued. She supposed she was in the family business as well, taking over for her grandmother. It was interesting to find out that she and Deimos had that in common. That they could have *anything* in common.

But as his shadows shifted over his face, masking his emotion, she realized he might not feel the same way about it as she did. She recalled the comment about needing space from his home. Maybe she had overstepped her bounds.

A beat later, she relaxed with relief as he answered more cheerfully than he appeared. "We are keepers of our land. Tasked with maintaining balance."

She crinkled her nose at the vague answer. There were so many things she wanted to ask him, but as she opened her mouth, the shadows around him hovered in close as if to shield him and the secrets they held. So, she decided to drop it. For now.

As she stood to clear the table, Deimos joined her, grabbing the plates up before she had a chance. She followed him to the sink with Tinker mewing behind them. Ignoring the greedy cat who no doubt wanted the leftovers, Abrielle grabbed a bucket to fill with water for washing.

"I'll take that," Deimos offered. "It's the least I can do."

She clutched it tighter, worried that he was bad at more than just cooking. What if he accidentally broke a dish, or made a bigger mess while she still had so many other things to attend to? Trying to deter him, she offered, "But you cooked, so really, cleaning up is the least I can do."

"I insist," he said. When he took the bucket, his hand brushed against her own, sending goose-prickles along her arms.

She gulped. "Okay." She watched with uncertainty as he slipped from the door. It was dark outside now and the water-spout was just beyond the threshold. Hopefully, no one would see him. How would she explain it?

He was back before she had much time to dwell on the dangers that came with having him found out. There was a carefree smile on his face, as if he never considered the consequences. Was he truly not afraid, or was he just clueless?

She decided to warn him. "I don't know how much you know about Ellamere, but magic isn't exactly welcomed in our community."

He hummed in response.

Biting her lip, she continued, "If they find out about you, they might try to arrest you. It's best that you keep a low profile. Avoid drawing attention for both our sakes."

"You're afraid you'll get in trouble?" He inched closer to her and gazed down with an intensity that made her shift.

"I just don't need anything else to go wrong. I need to prepare for the festival." She pointed at the kitchen window, which was in a poor state with the hinge loosening. "There's this contest, you see. If I win, I not only show that I've earned my position in this bakery, but I can afford to buy supplies to fix things up around here."

"I see." Deimos studied the window for a moment before going to work washing the dishes.

Abrielle walked over to the other end of the counter. To fill the silence between them, she admitted, "My grandfather used to do all the repairs. He took beautiful care of this place. But when he passed, my grandmother figured out how to do a lot of those things herself. She taught me the best she could. And what we couldn't do ourselves, we saved to hire someone." She didn't care to admit that she hadn't quite mastered handiwork as well as she'd mastered braiding her favorite ham and cheese bread.

Deimos didn't look up at her as he spoke, and his dish scrubbing slowed. "It must have been nice to have a family to rely on like that."

Pity for him struck her but was followed by the familiar twinge of grief. She knew she had been very lucky. That's what made losing her grandparents so hard.

She was glad when he didn't say any more on the subject, and the two of them fell into a comfortable silence. It gave Abrielle the opportunity to finish prepping for the morning. It was always easiest to prepare the dough and fillings the night before. That way, when she woke before sunrise, she could simply place everything together and have time for it to bake.

The flour was unbelievably soft as she sprinkled it onto the counter. When she was a toddler, coating the surface was one of the things her grandmother would task her with doing. Still, after all this time, it gave her a sense of comfort and joy to feel it sift between her fingers.

Deimos hummed a merry tune as he scrubbed the dishes. And for a moment, Abrielle lost herself in his peaceful presence. It had been so long since she had shared a moment like this with anyone that it didn't matter to her if it was with a mysterious stranger. She nodded along to his song and grabbed the nearest rising loaf. Placing it on top of the flour, she readied it for one last kneading.

Rising to her tippy toes, she grabbed the furthest end and drew it toward her. Her arm still ached from earlier, but the ice had helped with the swelling. Except, as she pressed into the dough, smashing it into itself, pain shot up to her elbow. She hissed and drew away from the counter, clutching her bruised arm.

Deimos was at her side in an instant. His face was drawn down in concern, but he didn't move to touch her. Instead, he and his shadows hovered over her as if trying to decide how to help.

Abrielle assured them, "It's alright. I'm fine."

"You're still hurt. Don't exert yourself. I can do it." He nodded to the dough.

"I don't know…" Again, she worried he might make a mess of things. Not only that, but she had rarely had anyone else in the kitchen. It had always been her and her grandmother. Or Tansy, in the very few instances that Abrielle had allowed it.

There was something almost invasive about it. Like letting Deimos help meant sharing something more intimate with him. And as handsome as he was, she had no intention of doing anything more than working with him to send him back home. It was a simple arrangement. They were not friends.

"Don't be stubborn." He dragged the stool over and gestured for her to sit. "You can tell me exactly what to do and I'll do it."

There was that disarming smile spreading across his face once again. Her arm ached in a painful reminder that she might not have a choice but to accept his help. Reluctantly, she sat, still cradling her arm against her chest. Deimos listened closely and followed each direction she gave him. His hands were a sticky mess, dotted with light brown dough and stark white flour. Try as he might to pull it off of him, it only continued to stick to the fingers he was using. Soon he gave up on trying to stay clean and before they knew it, each loaf was kneaded properly and ready to rise for the night.

He moved to the sink and attempted to shed the mess. It only turned slimy and impossible to get off. When Abrielle joined him, he held his messy hands up in defeat.

"Let me." She grabbed the lavender rosemary soap and began rubbing it gently on him. She concentrated on removing the dough from around his nail beds and could feel his gaze settled on her.

As she rinsed the soap from his hands, she snuck a peek at him. His dark eyes bore into hers and there was a soft, content smile on his face. She swallowed heavily and took a step back. "That should do it." She handed him a towel and put more space between them.

Now that she didn't have anything left to focus on, the pit in her stomach grew with each passing second. Even if she had brought him to her world unknowingly, she had still dragged him away from his home, nonetheless. And now, here she was relying on him to help *her*.

Between that guilt and the knowledge of what the next day would bring, she felt as if she was spiraling. Silently, she made a list inside her head, like writing down ingredients to a recipe:

Deliver the morning order to the palace.

Sneak into the library to find the answers we need.

Send this attractive man home before I do something to make a fool of myself.

Focus on the festival and the baking competition.

It all seemed simple and to the point. But in reality, things had not been going her way. Glancing at the portrait hanging above her, she said a silent plea in her head. *Grandmother, I wish you were here to tell me what to do. To tell me how to fix this.* As always, there was no response. Just her grandmother's sure smile beaming down on her.

Beside her, Deimos asked, "That is your family?"

"Yes," her voice cracked as she spoke.

"And they've both passed on?"

"Yes. It's just me now." Abrielle squeezed her eyes shut.

"They were kind?" There was a note of longing in his voice.

Abrielle nodded and held back a sob. "The kindest. They taught me everything I know. And loved me."

Deimos' hand rested on her shoulder, and he gave it a light squeeze. "I admit, I do not know what it is like to miss family. To have had that sort of love. But I do know that it is okay to grieve a loss and to let yourself move on without them."

In this moment, she couldn't remember why she had ever been frightened of him. Would an evil or dangerous man be going out of his way to comfort her?

Abrielle gazed up at him and met his eyes. The pain in her heart lightened slightly, and she found the strength to speak. "We should put all this away."

He nodded and followed her lead, putting everything in its place so she would have an easy time preparing for the rush first thing in the morning. Tinker no longer followed them around. It seemed she had tired of them once realizing she would get no more food.

After everything was safely tucked away, Abrielle and Deimos stood awkwardly in the doorway that led to the rest of her home. She hadn't considered what having him there overnight would mean. It hadn't occurred to her that waiting until the morning to find answers in the King's library would mean having a man spend the night alone with her.

"I uh…" she paused, unsure of what to do with him. There were only two rooms in the house and she wasn't sure which one to put him in. The thought of having a stranger sleep in her grandparents' room made her uneasy. But so did the idea of sleeping in there herself. In truth, she'd only been inside twice since her grandmother passed away. It was too painful to look at so many intimate reminders of them.

She twisted her hands together and offered, "Take my room. I can sleep down here."

Deimos stepped closer to her, resting his arm on the door-frame above her head. The warmth of his body made her realize just how cold the rest of the room was without the fire lit. She pressed her back against the wall and stared up at him.

He leaned over her and smirked. "What sort of gentleman would I be if I threw a lady out of her own room?" He gave a curt nod in the direction of the stairway. "You sleep in your own bed. I'll take the armchair."

"Are you sure?" It didn't seem very polite for her to agree too easily.

"I'm sure."

His gaze was intense, contrasting with the easy smirk on his face. Heat welled in her chest and warm shivers ran down her spine, but before she could dwell on what those sensations meant, she ducked under his arm and sidestepped over to the chair. Beside it, in a wicker basket, were a colorful array of hand knitted blankets. She grabbed as many as she could and tossed them onto the chair.

Deimos swaggered over to it and plopped down on the cushions. It creaked under his weight and his limbs stuck out over the arm, making for a ridiculous sight. He was far too large for the chair. A laugh bubbled up from her throat and she covered her mouth with one of her hands.

Then she gestured to the sofa sitting across from them. "Maybe that will be more comfortable."

Deimos chuckled. "You're probably right."

He crossed the space in just two steps and lowered himself onto the large cushy couch. Even then, he was far too tall, and his legs still hung over the arm. Abrielle pinched her lips together to keep from laughing at him. "Are you sure my bed wouldn't be more comfortable?"

He shifted awkwardly, trying to get the blanket to reach over his toes. "I'm plenty comfortable."

Abrielle shook her head, allowing the laughter out. Then she grabbed another blanket and draped it over his feet. Proudly, she stated, "Two blankets seem to do the trick." Next, she handed him one of the throw pillows and he took it gratefully.

As she walked to the stairs, Deimos called out, "Goodnight, Abrielle." Her name seemed to roll off his tongue like the tune he'd been humming earlier.

From the first step of the staircase, she called back, "Goodnight, Deimos."

Then, with Tinker rubbing against her legs, she ascended the stairs. The day had brought many surprises, and there was no telling what new ones would arise tomorrow. But for now, with Deimos drifting off to sleep on her couch, she felt content. In some small way, the house felt a little bit warmer than it had in a while.

Eight

Something silky soft trailed along the side of Abrielle's face and shifted to tickle her nose. She crinkled the bridge of it and shook her head, too deep in her dreams to actually open her eyes to see what it was. All night she had been visited with smiling images of her grandparents. Just now, they were gesturing for her to go. To walk ahead toward the sparkling lake where the festival would be held. The sun was beating down brightly, as it always did on the very best days.

But again, something tickled her cheek, and she knew it was a call back to the world of the living. She peeked one eye open and groaned groggily. When she saw what was trying to wake her up, both eyes popped open in surprise. Although the sun had not fully risen yet, a gentle glow from the window gave her a clear view of the shadows.

The ones belonging to Deimos.

Her curiosity rose, clotting out any fear she knew she should be feeling at the sight of his shadows in her room. She lit the candle beside her bed and found that there was no sign of him. The shadows shifted, backing away like a frightened animal caught rooting around in the garden. It was almost as if they had a mind of their own. When they were close to Deimos, they seemed to mirror his own thoughts and emotions, but here in her room, they behaved of their own accord. It only furthered her suspicions that they weren't necessarily a part of him but were rather drawn to him. Like a moth to a flame. But in this case, darkness was being drawn to… whatever sort of creature he truly was.

The shadows drifted around her bed, but there was still no sign of their master. Instead, the inky black tendrils looped around in an early morning dance. They reached down to touch the handmade quilt lined with little embroidered white daisies. But when they noticed Abrielle watching them, they froze.

She offered a polite smile, hoping they might go away and leave her to her morning routine. Instead, it gave them courage. With a slight jittery movement, like a dog shaking his butt just before he pounces, they leaped for her.

She gave a small gasp as they reached for her face, fluttering under her hair and around her neck. They seemed eager and delighted; like they were saying good morning to her. She was surprised at how buttery soft they felt. Like the velvet of a moth's wing.

Abrielle knew she should be screaming with fright. After all, who in their right mind enjoyed being woken up by disembodied shadows with a mind of their own? In truth, she was simply startled. It had been so long since anyone besides Tinker had woken her up and she was left with an anticipatory feeling at breaking fast with someone other than the cranky old cat.

The shadows shimmied away from her and inched toward the door. They paused before crossing the threshold as Abrielle tossed the blankets off and tiptoed on the ice-cold floor to her wardrobe. She swung the doors open to find a suitable dress for the day.

Quickly, she landed on one of her favorites. A white lace top with a dark sage green linen skirt. She untied the back of her nightgown and began to draw it down but froze when she sensed that she still had an audience. It didn't matter whether the mysterious inky black tendrils were a part of Deimos or simply gravitated toward him. She had no desire to give them a show either way.

She whipped around to catch the shadows in the act of spying on her but raised an eyebrow when she found them twisting themselves in the direction of the hall. She wasn't sure if or how they had the ability to see, but they always seemed to know where they were going and what they were doing. And the way they craned themselves toward the doorway now reminded her of someone turning their head awkwardly to give someone privacy.

Not willing to take any chances, she padded across the room and shut the door swiftly before getting changed into the new day's clothes. Her hair was another matter entirely. She brushed out the massive bedhead she had going on and tied it neatly back with a strip of white lace. A few shorter strands fell into her eyes, and she brushed them back with her hand before grabbing the candlestick and opening the door.

The shadows were gone. Seemingly, they had gotten the hint that women in this realm required privacy. The rest of the cottage was quiet. Maybe her unwanted guest was still sleeping. She did, after all, rise much earlier than most. So many things needed to be done. The stove needed heating, bread needed baking, delicacies needed detailing... And demon-like men needed *unsummoning*.

After a few steps down the hall, Abrielle found herself frozen in place. The door to her grandparents' room was ajar, just like always. In the last year, she had rarely gone inside, but also couldn't bring herself to shut the door entirely. Having it propped open slightly gave her a moment each morning to pretend that they were still inside. That if she peeked in, her grandmother would be sitting at the dusty rose-pink vanity brushing her hair while her grandfather tied his boots at the foot of the bed.

Abrielle bit the inside of her cheek. Deimos would need a change of clothes, and she certainly didn't have anything suitable for him in her room. With an uncomfortable sigh, she pushed open the door. It creaked from lack of use and inside a sliver of bronze sunlight and candlelight gave sight to a thin layer of dust coating the furniture. Guilt gnawed at her as she dusted a cobweb off her grandmother's mirror.

She should have been taking better care of the space. Dusting and sweeping at the very least. But as the deep ache of loss began to weigh on her, making her chest feel heavy, yet hollow at the same time, she remembered why she hadn't.

She needed to get what she came for and get out of there before the loneliness paralyzed her. Swiftly, she moved to the closet and shuffled through her grandfather's old shirts. They no longer smelled of freshly sawed pine—no longer smelled like him—but they were hung neatly as if he might come back at any moment to put one on.

Deimos was much larger than the older man had been before he passed, but it was better to offer her guest something rather than nothing. Blindly, she grabbed the first one her hand met and withdrew it from the wooden hanger her grandfather had carved. Next, she reached into the trunk at the end of the bed and plucked out a pair of brown pants. They were made of light linen, perfect for the late summer heat.

With the clothing clutched too tightly in her hands, she moved for the door, but stopped short. Underwear... He would need those, too. She cringed at the thought of going through her grandfather's drawers, let alone giving them to Deimos to wear. But what was worse? Having a strange and unnervingly attractive man wear her late grandfather's braies or having him go without anything at all beneath his pants?

Deciding the former was better—and less distracting—than the latter, she opened the drawer to the large pine dresser and reached in. Her breathing was becoming short and erratic as it usually did when she dwelled too long on her loss, so she hurriedly grabbed what she needed and ran from the room without looking back.

Once she descended the stairs, the space between her and the bedroom was enough to let her relax. She took a steady breath, clutching both the candle and the clothes in separate hands and walked into the dark living room. The sun still hadn't fully risen, and she estimated that she would have just enough time to bake the bread before customers began strolling in. But only if she hurried.

Deimos called out to her from the sofa. "Good morning, Brie."

She turned toward him, and her gaze landed on his flexing muscles as he stretched out and groaned groggily. A thin stream of dusty light shined on his dark hair, which was tousled from a good night's sleep. Tinker rubbed along the side of the sofa, and he reached down to scratch her on the back.

Abrielle raised an eyebrow. "*Brie*?"

Tinker laid down and rolled onto her back in invitation for Deimos to give her a good rub. He did so as he responded, "Short for *Abrielle*." He peeked up at her quizzically, as if she should have been witty enough to understand.

Which she was. She bit her lip and said, "No, I know that. It's just..." she paused, trying to hold in a laugh. "Brie is a stinky cheese."

Still scratching Tinker's belly, Deimos chuckled and said, "Oh." He opened his mouth as if to say more, but Tinker—who apparently had a change of heart about the belly rubs—nipped him on the hand.

As he cursed in a hushed tone, the candle Abrielle was holding snuffed out, leaving them with nothing but dim morning light. Tinker's nails made click, click, click sounds as she scurried off to find solace, leaving a hurt looking Deimos behind.

Abrielle's hand shook slightly at the surprise of her candle flame extinguishing at the exact moment that Deimos was bitten. Just as they had sputtered when she had completed the recipe. *Spell*, she corrected.

She grabbed a matchstick and relit the candle, stepping closer to Deimos to shine it on his hand in order to see just how badly the old tabby had gotten him. He sat up and she knelt on the floor in front of him. There were no marks on his skin, but the tendrils of shadows wisped around his hand as if trying to soothe him and tell him everything was alright.

"Are you okay?" she asked as she noted the look of hurt still in his eyes. "Did she hurt you?"

"Just my pride," he said solemnly. "I really thought we were becoming friends."

Abrielle reassured him. "Cats can be finicky. Don't take it personally."

The corner of his mouth quirked up at that, and he locked eyes with her. Even his shadows seemed to brighten as they loosened their hold on his hand and leaned in closer to her.

She watched them in fascination and asked, "Are the shadows a part of you? Do you control them?" She blushed thinking of their presence as she dressed for the day, and continued, "Or see through them?"

Deimos shook his head. "I am not connected to them directly. *They* found *me*, actually. When I was a little boy."

Abrielle tilted her head, eager to hear more.

He continued, "There was a forest near my childhood home. It was dark. Forbidden. Which made it the perfect hiding place."

"Who were you hiding from?" The words escaped her before she thought better of it. It wasn't truly her business. But she was itching to know something—anything—about him. To make him feel less like a stranger if she was going to be spending yet another day with him.

His Adam's apple bobbed before he answered. "My brothers. My father. My responsibilities." He huffed a bitter laugh. "You name it, I was probably trying to hide from it."

Abrielle's heart hurt as she imagined a young Deimos hiding in a forbidden forest all alone. Even from a young age, she had never liked being alone. She had always sought out the company of her family. When that failed, she had turned to Tansy. It wasn't until recently that she had begun shutting herself away in the bakery. Too consumed with her duties and, to be honest, a little afraid that she would lose yet another person closest to her. The possibility of that terrified her.

Her voice came out soft as she asked, "And the shadows? They were in the forest?"

Deimos smiled at them as they perked up, lifting until they were near his head. "Yes," he said, "the shadows were there, keeping me company, until one day they simply followed me home. We've been together ever since."

Abrielle smiled at that. What a blessing to have found something comforting at such a dark time. Even if the thing doing the comforting was frightening at first sight. Deimos' lips parted as they gazed at one another and suddenly, Abrielle realized how close she was to him, kneeling before him like a lover might do.

She sniffed and stood quickly. "I uh, I need to get started on the morning orders. You're welcome to help yourself to anything you'd like for breakfast." She glanced down at the clothes she had set beside her when she went to check on him and added, "I got you a change of clothes. You're welcome to them if you'd like."

With a flourish, she turned away and hoped he didn't have time to notice the frown that was pulling at her lips. The sofa creaked and Deimos' heavy footsteps followed her through the bakery and into the kitchen. They didn't speak a word as she lit enough candles to grant her the light she would need to move around unhindered until the sun made its full appearance.

A stool scraped across the floor behind her, and Deimos cleared his throat loudly before speaking. "When will we go to the library?"

Abrielle took frosting from the small icebox beneath the floorboards and pulled out a few piping bags. She answered as she scooped the vanilla-flavored cream into them. "I deliver to the palace every morning after the rush. Once I'm there, I'll have to find a way upstairs. They'll be expecting me in the kitchens, but I've never wandered any further inside by myself."

Doubt about their plan working crept in. What if she was caught wandering where she shouldn't be? King Vasiri was a kind man, but no one liked to have visitors meandering through their homes and popping their heads into places they hadn't been invited to. She shot a pointed look at Deimos' peeping shadows, which were huddled at his shoulders.

He shrugged. "That part should be easy enough. Assuming my magic isn't still acting all topsy-turvy, I should be able to shroud us long enough to get in and out without being seen."

Abrielle dropped one of the piping bags on the floor as she shot up to her feet. "Us?" She laughed haughtily. "No way. You're not coming with me."

Deimos furrowed his brow. "Why not?"

She gestured wildly at him. "Look at you. You'll stand out for sure. Everyone will know you don't belong here."

A deep look of pain spread from his eyes to his mouth, which settled into a hard line. Abrielle swallowed a large lump in her throat. She hadn't meant to hurt his feelings. Deimos didn't respond, as if her words left him speechless, which made her feel twice as bad.

She tried to rectify things as she explained, "I'm trying to keep us both safe and out of trouble. Please, Deimos, just trust me."

He had no reason to. She knew that. But she had shown a great deal of trust by allowing him to remain in her home. If he had been summoned into another villager's house, they might not have shown him the same courtesy. He likely would have been in the palace dungeons at this point. But she didn't want to see him harmed. Not when he hadn't done anything to indicate he deserved it. Not when he hadn't asked for any of this. She only wanted to fix her mistake.

Wordlessly, he stalked away. His footsteps echoed on the creaky floorboards as he left the bakery side of the home and disappeared into the private living quarters. Abrielle grabbed a maroon pinstriped apron from the hook and twisted her hands in it. She would apologize again later. For now, she needed to focus on getting things ready for her customers. If she let things slip with the bakery because of the mess she'd gotten herself into, then she'd never forgive herself. Her grandmother's bakery came first. Always.

Nine

"No," Abrielle whispered in shock. The dough that Deimos had kneaded the night before was sunken and gray when it should have been puffy and beautifully tan. All six loaves looked the same, and each emanated a putrid smell that reminded her of gas from the swamp deep inside the forest.

She glanced back at the doorway where Deimos had stalked away. He hadn't made so much as a peep since she told him he couldn't come with her to the palace library. That was a solid twenty minutes ago. Since then, she had piped frosting onto the pastries and filled the tarts with cherry filling.

But the bread... Making a new batch of dough and waiting for it to rise was out of the question. Customers would be gracing her doorstep within the hour. Already, a soft glow was drifting through the kitchen windows and giving light to the wildflowers on the sill.

Abrielle still needed to water them and change out their vases, but the bread was the key issue at the moment. She had plenty of other goods to offer—fat-topped mulberry muffins, flaky cherry tarts, and foldovers lined with vanilla-bean frosting. But this would be the second day that she didn't have steaming fresh bread to offer her patrons. Her grandmother *never* would have allowed such a thing to happen twice in a row.

Even when Abrielle's grandfather had fallen off the roof and twisted his ankle, her grandmother had both tended to him and baked seven loaves for a traveling troupe of troubadours. When Abrielle had come down with a fever that put her in bed for a week, her grandmother had made soup for her each and every morning while opening the bakery without fail.

Abrielle frowned at the rotten dough. She'd never had anything like this happen before. Nor had she ever seen anything like it happen to her grandmother. Dough didn't go bad overnight. It just simply didn't happen.

Knots twisted in the pit of her stomach like snakes doing a dance as she thought of Deimos kneading the dough. He had done everything precisely as she said. Nothing different than she would have done. Yet, at his hands, the dough had gone sour...

The door chimed and Abrielle whipped around to find Tansy with a hand on her hip and baskets slung over her other arm. Her dark curls were pulled back in a purple bandana that highlighted the blush on her light brown cheeks.

She strolled into the kitchen uninvited and set the baskets from the previous day's orders on the counter. Then in a stern voice, asked, "How are you feeling?" Before Abrielle could answer, she added, "Don't even bother lying to me, because I'll be able to tell by that little nose twitch you do."

Abrielle glanced worriedly at the doorway to the rest of the house. *Please let him have the good sense to stay hidden,* she thought nervously. Then to Tansy, she said, "I had a good night's rest. Don't worry. And I'm ready to make today's deliveries," she drifted off as Tansy peeked under the dish towels covering the horrendous sight that was once considered dough.

Tansy grimaced and covered her nose. "What *happened?*"

Abrielle sighed. "I don't know. Humidity maybe? Bad grain?" She knew neither of those were the cause. She had been getting her grain from the same family that her grandmother had gone to for the last decade. And the weather had been exceptionally chilled at night for summertime. But she had no other explanation to offer her friend unless she wanted to explain the rather large man in her living room whose best friends were shadows.

Tansy shook her head. "You seem tense. I think you're working too hard."

Tansy always thought Abrielle was working too hard. She thought *everyone* was working too hard. From the little old lady down the street who sold her garden seed to the man who played guitar on the road to Ellamere's port.

"I'm fine," Abrielle promised.

The bell chimed again as Paddy and Luna walked in.

"Morning girls!" she exclaimed as she and her father stepped up to the counter.

Abrielle made sure the dough was covered and hoped they wouldn't notice the stench from where they were. Then she grabbed the other baked goods she had ready to go and carried them with her to the counter. She put them inside the glass case merrily but could feel Tansy's watchful gaze on her back.

Just so long as that gaze didn't wander further than the bakery... Abrielle shook her head and made polite conversation with Paddy and Luna. She handed Paddy his selection, but as he passed her his coin, he asked, "Everything alright over here, Miss Abrielle?"

Fatherly concern clouded his eyes and Abrielle shrugged as she replied, "Of course, why do you ask?"

His eyes narrowed for the slightest second—so quick she almost didn't catch it—before he said, "Thought I saw a man rootin' through your yard last night by the back door. Had half a mind to come check it out myself, but in the blink of an eye he was gone. Nia and Luna said my eyes just aren't what they used to be."

Abrielle mustered a smile. "It was just me here," the lie came out tight in her throat, "could have been the shadows playing tricks." Her eyes darted to the doorway. If only Paddy knew the truth—that some shadows did in fact like to play tricks for their own amusement.

"Alright, then." Paddy seemed satisfied with her answer, and he handed the bundle of baked goods to Luna. "Just remember, if you need anythin'. Anythin' at all, you just call on us."

"Of course," Abrielle squeaked. It was a nice offer. One he and his family gave often. But her grandmother hadn't needed anyone. And Abrielle knew if she just tried hard enough, then she wouldn't need anyone either.

As they left, she caught the faintest whisper as Paddy leaned in close to Luna. "Proud like her grandpa was. Needs to learn to lean on someone once in a while."

Luna hushed him and shoved him through the door with an apologetic smile cast quickly at Abrielle. Tansy placed a hand on her shoulder and steered her back into the kitchen just in time for several more townsfolk to scurry into the bakery.

The rest of the early morning was a haze. It was finally starting to feel like things were normal again, despite the strange sensation that shadows were watching her from the corners of the room. A reminder of her guest and the weight that rested on her shoulders to send him home. Still, putting on a practiced smile, Abrielle tied twine on package after package and made small pleasantries with each person who walked in. Meanwhile, Tansy sat on the counter with Tinker resting snugly on her lap.

Only every once in a while, did Abrielle sneak a glance in the direction of the rest of the cottage. She couldn't begin to guess what Deimos was doing in there, but she was grateful that he seemed to be listening to her pleas for him to keep a low profile.

Once the last customer left, leaving through the door with a soft clink of the bell, Abrielle dusted off her hands and removed the apron. Tansy had graciously packed up the palace order and it was all set to be delivered.

The two women said their goodbyes to one another, but as Tansy headed for the door, she stopped dead in her tracks and turned to Abrielle. She was only a few feet away from the doorway to the private quarters of the cottage and Abrielle held her breath. If Tansy looked to the right of her, she would see directly into the living room, where Deimos might very well be.

Tansy crinkled her brow. "I forgot to ask, whatever happened to that... dog?"

Abrielle licked her lips. Her mouth had gone as dry as the summer sands on the Ellamere coast. "Oh, he's somewhere around here." She waved a dismissive hand, hoping that would be the end of it.

Tansy raised an eyebrow. "You're not hiding something from me, are you?"

Abrielle didn't want to lie to her best friend, but she also didn't want to drag her into her mess. The last thing she wanted was to get Tansy into any sort of trouble. And she wasn't sure how Deimos would feel about it. After all, it wasn't just her secret. It was *theirs*. This affected him as much as it did her.

As she answered, she remembered Tansy's comment about wrinkling her nose when she lied. She reached up and scratched the bridge of it, attempting to cover it casually as she said, "Of course not." Then hurrying her out the door, she said, "I'll see you tomorrow, Tans."

She watched closely out the small windowpane in the door until Tansy was out of sight. She only glanced back twice, which gave Abrielle some small semblance of relief. Maybe she had convinced her friend enough that she would drop it until Deimos was sent back. Then she could come clean and tell her everything.

Abrielle had just finished putting the *closed* sign on the bakery door when Deimos stalked into the small sitting area. Rather than the mopey expression she expected to see on his face, he had a look of determination in his eyes. They were focused and his jaw was hard set.

A muscle twitched in his neck as he greeted her. "Ready to go?"

Abrielle shook her head and pushed past him to the kitchen. "I told you. It's not safe. It's too dangerous for you to be out there."

He followed close behind. His voice was clipped as he said, "What do you know of danger?"

Abrielle reached the far counter where the dough was still sitting and spun to face him. With her hands braced on the wooden tabletop, she gripped it hard and snapped back. "I know that having a strange man in my house is dangerous. I know that you have abilities beyond my understanding. And *that* alone—not knowing—is dangerous. But you don't seem to care."

Deimos scrunched his nose, then raised his chin to sniff in the air. "What is that smell?"

Abrielle groaned and stepped aside. She snatched the dishtowel off one of the loaves to reveal the monstrosity underneath. "That would be the bread. Or what was supposed to be bread."

Deimos' jaw dropped. Through clenched teeth, he said, "Shit."

"What is it? What's wrong?" Abrielle clenched the towel in her hand.

Ignoring her question, he insisted, "You need to let me come. You said it yourself that you don't know anything about magic. It comes from my world. Runs in my veins. I might be more help than you think." He blew out a heavy sigh. "You might need me whether you care to admit it or not."

Abrielle bit her lip. He had a point. She had no clue what she was looking for beyond knowing that she needed to go back to that one section in the library. Tinker mewed loudly and rubbed along Deimos' legs as if taking his side in the disagreement.

"Fine," Abrielle relented. "But please do try to shift into something less intimidating."

Deimos took a step back and shook his hands out in front of him. He looked like one of the jesters in the King's court that liked to play sleight of hand. Except rather than pulling a card from his sleeve, Deimos pulled darkness. It was nothing like the shadows that gravitated toward him. This was like the darkest of the night sky. Like the void when you closed your eyes in the pitch dark with no light to offer a bit of color behind them.

It was nothingness. And it engulfed him entirely.

Abrielle's instinct was to stumble back, but she bumped into the counter. Tinker catapulted in her direction, forcing her plump feline body between Abrielle's legs and the cabinets. Meanwhile, any darkness in the room seemed to be pulled into Deimos' direction. Sucked from the corners of the ceiling, away from the shelves, and even her own shadow that was cast on the floor from the morning sun, tore away from her to join Deimos and his ensemble of darkness.

Abrielle's heart pounded in her chest. Just when she thought it might burst right out of her, Deimos returned to view. But now, instead of the incredibly handsome man, all that was left standing was the massive wolf-sized mutt with wild fur and tattered claws.

"Fates help me," she gasped. How was she supposed to walk around town with *that* and go unnoticed?

Deimos dropped to his hindquarters and scratched his ear with his back leg. Tinker, wanting nothing to do with him in this form, scurried into the other room and out of sight. This was going to make for an interesting trip. Would the palace even let him into the kitchen looking like that? They might have to find another way in.

What was done was done, though. Abrielle glanced at the pants and shirt that had fallen off of him during the shift.

Quickly, she grabbed the change of clothes she'd laid out for him in the living room, then returned to scoop up the baskets for the palace. Deimos padded behind her to the door. She opened it to let him pass, but his massive frame knocked into her, nearly sending her tumbling down the steps. Swiftly, he was there to stop her, using his side to catch her like a guardrail and setting her upright.

"Thank you," she said. Although it was his fault she fell in the first place.

He gave a snort, which she interpreted as *you're welcome.* And they were off. They curved down the winding cobblestone street, passing familiar homes made either of stone or timber. Birds perched themselves on several of the slated roofs, with heads cocked in Deimos' direction. One of the alley cats scurried away from them with a hiss. Even the flowers in the front yard gardens seemed to sway and tilt away from him as they passed.

Ellamere's little capital was quaint and charming, but the people were vibrant, making the streets a lively place to be. There were a few villagers on the road, headed to their respective places of work, and each jumped and hopscotched out of Abrielle and the beast's path. A few even graced them with a curse under their breath or a horrified gasp, but none tried to stop them.

The village was a small one and almost everyone knew Abrielle from the bakery. But this morning, most friendly neighbors failed to wave at her. She blamed the homely dog beside her, but supposed it was preferable to them gawking at his Otherworldly appearance in his natural form.

Abrielle was glad when the gemtower nearest to the palace came into view, signaling their upcoming arrival. Her nerves grew taut as she realized this was the easy part of their little journey. She still had no idea how she would get him inside.

When they reached the gemtower, Abrielle took a moment to peer at it. She didn't see any jagged lines or hairline fractures. Not like the one behind her garden. She supposed she should be relieved, but part of her grew more anxious at the thought. If the barricade nearest to her home was the only one affected, then that as good as proved that Deimos was the cause. That it was her fault for breaking one of the decades old towers that were supposed to keep their kingdom safe.

If a doorway of sorts had been opened to let Deimos through, then would it let other creatures in? Ones much worse than him? She supposed she should be thanking the fates for sending an inherently decent Selanthian man into her home instead of something like the ratawilly he had mentioned before.

Deimos trotted alongside her, his head whipping left and right, as if taking in every sight and detail along the way. Talk of the Otherworlds always made her imagine it was a stark contrast to her own world. But Deimos wasn't exactly what she had imagined, so maybe the same was true for Selanthia. She couldn't help but wonder if he preferred Ellamere or if he was finally getting homesick. Something told her by the way his tongue was hanging out of his mouth that it was the former. A warm smile spread across her face and her fingers itched to reach out and pat him on the head.

That is, until they reached the palace gate. Erik was already there waiting with a polite smile. But when he looked down at Deimos, he drew away and sneered. "By the fates. That thing is hideous."

Deimos raised his hackles in response and let out a low, guttural growl. Abrielle placed a steady hand on him and willed him to remember why they were there. Reluctantly, he took a step back, allowing her to place herself between him and Erik.

"It's my uh... I'm just caring for him for a little while." She gave a tight-lipped smile.

Erik watched Deimos warily as he opened the gate to let them pass. The King's guardsman gave Deimos a wide berth as he walked with them to the kitchen doors. Before opening the door for Abrielle as he usually did, he paused and said, "That thing can't go in there."

Abrielle's eyes darted between Erik and Deimos. There was no chance that Erik was going to budge no matter what excuse she came up with. She had no choice but to go in alone and figure out another way to get him in.

She crouched in front of Deimos and whispered low so Erik wouldn't overhear. "Stay here and keep out of trouble." He shot a glare in Erik's direction, so she added, "Please, I am begging you."

With a subtle, curt nod, Deimos sat down. His tail, which she only just now noticed was tangled with the thin tendrils of shadows that were always accompanying him, swished in annoyance.

Erik stepped forward to open the door for her and she thanked him.

Despite his distaste for Deimos, he looked particularly handsome today with a slight sunburn freckling the bridge of his nose. A warm blush crept up her neck and to her cheeks as he gazed down at her and smiled.

"Have you had a nice morning?" she asked lamely, hoping to sway the subject away from the canine watching them intently.

"It's been hectic, actually. Complaints are coming in from the north side of town."

Abrielle sucked in a breath. That was her side of town. Hesitantly, she asked, "What sort of complaints?"

Erik continued, "Apparently the crops have a strange, white cobweb-like substance coating them and it just appeared out of nowhere this morning. And Thomaz's sheep fainted again last night. I think he must not be giving them enough iron or something." Erik prattled on as he held open the door to the kitchen.

His body brushed against hers as he did and all worries about Deimos and the town were replaced with a tightness in her chest. His body was hard and lean, and she had the strangest urge to reach out and touch it. Instead, she tripped over her own two feet and nearly spilled the entire palace order on the ground between them.

Erik caught the baskets with ease and handed them back to her. Her face burned with embarrassment, and she wanted nothing more than to crawl into the void-like darkness that Deimos had called on earlier.

Deimos let out a snort from a few feet away that sounded an awful lot like a human laugh and Abrielle shot him a warning glare. He needed to behave. She wagged a finger in his direction and followed Erik into the kitchen quickly.

Without making polite morning pleasantries with the kitchen staff, Abrielle dropped the order on the table, apologized for the missing bread, and scurried back out the door. Erik's eyebrows rose in surprise, likely at how eager she was to get out of there, but he said nothing as she waved to him and jogged back to the gate without him escorting her.

Deimos followed and she heard him grunt as Erik called after them. "Maybe consider sending that thing back where it came from."

She glanced over her shoulder to find him pointing at Deimos. With a forced laugh, she replied loudly, "Oh, if only I could."

Deimos loped behind with a groan as she picked up her pace. They exited the gate and rounded the corner until they were far enough away to not be seen by anyone coming and going from the palace. The curve of the old stone wall gave them the privacy they needed.

Abrielle wiped at her sweat-soaked brow and leaned down to Deimos. Unsure if he could talk in this form, she asked hesitantly, "What now?"

Deimos wagged his tail, and the shadows clung to it as if holding on for dear life.

"That's not an answer," she huffed. Twirling a stray strand of her hair, she considered all the entrances into the palace. Aside from the main doors, there were several servants' entrances in the back. But each might be patrolled by a guard at random. It was too risky.

Deimos nudged her with his nose. Staring into his eyes was incredibly confusing. They were the one thing to give away the disguise. To tell her that he was in there, hidden beneath the shapeshifted form. And right now, they were serious and silencing. She quieted to allow him a moment.

The nothingness from before crept out from his chest. More of the darkness followed, flowing from his paws, back, and head. The friendly shadows that were riding along on his tail shrunk away into the wall as if trying to escape Deimos' void while still shying away from the sun.

The nothingness spread and Abrielle whimpered in shock as it enveloped her, plunging her into the painfully cold dark. Surprisingly warm shadows soon wrapped around her shoulders and pulled her in. Deimos' voice, which came out as a half bark, echoed in the dark as he said, "Just trust me."

Abrielle wanted to argue and tell him this was absolutely insane. To demand that he release her from whatever magic this was. But the strength of the taut muscles in his fur covered side that was pressed against her made her hold her tongue. She had asked him to trust her. Now it was time to repay the favor.

Ten

The magic shrouding them was strange to say the least. Abrielle could see through the shimmering veil easily, and Deimos walked on in his hound-like form with confidence. They huddled together as they walked, which forced them to move slowly through the palace garden and into one of the entrances reserved for the household staff.

Between the heat of Deimos' side pressed against hers snuggly, and the anticipation of being caught, Abrielle was becoming lightheaded. She clutched her baskets close to her. They were empty since she unloaded the delivery earlier, except for the clothing she'd brought for Deimos to change into when they reached the library.

The magic he used to get them through the palace unnoticed seemed to drown out any sound their footsteps made. It was as if the void was sucking the noise into itself and trapping it. As they rounded the corner upstairs, a group of lady's maids swished by them in a sea of petticoats and giggles. Not once did one of them glance in Abrielle and Deimos' direction.

Still, she did not take a full breath until they reached the library door. Worry swelled in her chest as she wondered if the chancellor—or worse, the King—might be inside. She cracked the door open carefully and peeked through. The chancellor's desk was empty, and she couldn't hear anyone else. Perhaps everyone was in the dining hall enjoying their breakfast. Hopefully, they weren't too disappointed about the absent bread...

Abrielle was so busy glancing at each corner of the room for any sign that they weren't alone, that she didn't notice the magic veil had dropped. She blinked rapidly, realizing there was no shimmer clouding her vision, and spun to face Deimos.

She lowered her gaze, expecting to find the scruffy canine, but instead, she was met with bare, muscular thighs. Her eyes traced up and widened when she found a fully nude Deimos standing before her. He was... remarkably blessed, and it made her pulse quicken.

He cleared his throat, and her eyes roved up over his broad chest to his grinning face. She was becoming accustomed to the slight points on his teeth and actually admired the easy way he smiled. Except for right now. Right now, she wanted to slap him. This was wildly inappropriate. As was the way her lower stomach clenched in anticipation at the thought of taking a step closer to run her hands along his... She squirmed, suddenly feeling very antsy.

Keeping her eyes pinned on his face and not allowing them to drift below his neck like they were inclined to do, she dropped all the baskets except for the one holding her late grandfather's clothes and threw it at him with a snap, "Put these on!"

He begrudgingly pulled the clothes out of the basket and began dressing as he asked, "Are all mortals from your realm this squeamish around nudity?"

"Are people from your realm *not*?"

Deimos chuckled. "We don't run around butt-naked if that's what you're asking. But we also don't blush at the sight of it."

"I'm not blushing." She reached up, hoping to cool her cheeks with her hands.

Once he was finished buttoning the shirt, he held his hands out wide and said, "There. All covered."

Abrielle bit her lip as she took in the ridiculous appearance of him. The pants were too short for him with the hem stopping well above his ankles. The shirt sleeves were short as well and the shoulders strained at the seams when he moved. Her grandfather had been a tall and broad-built man, but Deimos was like one of the marble statues of storybook heroes in the palace courtyard.

It was his turn to blush. "I think I'm a bit too large."

"It'll do for now. With any luck, we'll have you home before nightfall." She gestured to him to follow her to the far corner where she had found the cookbook. *Spell book*, she corrected herself again with an internal groan.

Deimos' shadow friends were back now that he had dropped the void. They snaked around him and peered over his shoulder at the bookshelves. Abrielle led the way to the far corner where the strange tug in her chest had drawn her before. Had the book itself been calling out to her? Had it been using its power to lull an unsuspecting mortal into releasing its magic on Ellamere? Surely, it wasn't capable of malicious intent. It was nothing but paper bound together.

She side-eyed Deimos. Paper with scribbles of words that could summon someone as large and strong as him. That could rip open the gates between worlds. Suddenly her hands and face felt cold and clammy. The only comfort she found as they neared the magic section was that nothing was tugging at her now. It was by her own will that she was marching toward the dusty, cobweb-filled shelves.

The moment they reached the books, Deimos dove in. He drew out book after book. Many were titled with some sort of spell work. *Spells for the Full Moon, Enchanting Your Heart's Desire,* and *Spell Bound.* He plopped onto the floor with his shadows and began flipping through the pages.

Abrielle had no such direction. She meandered aimlessly along the shelf running her fingers over the spines. Although she should be eager to find answers as quickly as possible—considering they were technically trespassing at the moment—she couldn't shake the feeling that something was wrong outside of the palace walls.

"Deimos, did you hear Erik talking about the crops and livestock? Rumors seem to be coming in from everyone. Him, Tansy, even Paddy mentioned something." She bit her lip before adding, "And then there's the dough this morning..."

Deimos didn't look up from the book in his hands. Instead, he stared intently at a page with a flower the size of a full-grown man and pressed his lips in a thin, hard line. After a few minutes, he failed to respond to her. Was he going to pretend it was no big deal? Had it not been for his abrupt appearance and the hairline crack in the gemstone near her house, she might have brushed these things off as strange coincidences, too. But the timeline connection was hard to ignore.

She gulped, unsure if she really wanted an answer to her next question. Grabbing a random book from the shelf, she held it close to her chest and turned to him. "Are all of these things happening because of you?"

He said nothing. Did that mean he was guilty? Abrielle studied him. His mouth was down turned, and his knuckles were white from clutching the book on his lap too tightly. A wave of nausea turned her stomach. If these things were happening because of him, then ultimately, they were her fault.

She joined him on the floor, sitting cross-legged across from him. Waiting until he was ready to speak—to give her answers—she opened the book she had grabbed.

Instead of answering her, he changed the subject. "What's with you and the boy?"

Abrielle was taken aback. Surely, he wasn't referring to Paddy. She tilted her head to the side. "You mean Erik? Nothing." She attempted to scoff, but it came out clumsily. "He's just someone who works at the palace. I see him nearly every day, so of course we're friendly."

"You mean, *you're* friendly. *He's* excruciatingly dull and clueless to boot."

"What do you mean, clueless?"

"Anyone within half a mile of you two can see that you're pining after him."

That set her teeth on edge. Not only had he evaded her questions, but now he was making her out to be some silly schoolgirl. She was not pining. Just because she thought Erik was pleasant to look at and wanted to get to know him better, didn't mean she was head over heels. She thought Deimos was attractive, too. And she was kind to him. It didn't mean she wanted him.

Her stomach dipped in protest as she recalled the sight of him naked.

She shook the memory away. Either way, it was none of his business. Indignantly she sniped, "So what if I am?"

"Well, I can tell you, you're never going to get his attention like that." He dusted his fingers along her cheekbone, sending warm shivers down her neck. "Blushing will do nothing to woo him. If you want, I could help."

Abrielle leaned into the touch before drawing away from him and positioning the book in her hands between the two of them. She didn't need his help. She didn't need anyone's help. If she wanted to win Erik's heart, then she would find a way to do it herself.

She ignored Deimos, turning her attention back to the book on her lap. The title read: *Otherworlds Deities and Lords.*

Her eyes flitted to Deimos who had gone back to intently reading through the pile he had grabbed. She should be looking for books on spells as well. But curiosity gnawed at her. Especially after he had so successfully evaded her question with talk of her love life. Perhaps she would feel better if she could understand a bit more about his world. Maybe an answer to sending him back lay within his own world's history.

Or she was just kidding herself. Fooling herself into thinking that solving Deimos would solve the problem of sending him away. Either way, she opened the book. It was filled with pictures of strange creatures. Massive monstrous men who wore giant spiked turtle shells and lithe women with bat wings and long talons for nails, amongst others.

Each time Abrielle flipped a page, her stomach sank further. Occasionally, she came across depictions of ethereally beautiful men and women who wore seashells or leaves, but it didn't lessen her horror at the more frightening beings she saw in those pages.

When she turned to a chapter on lords of the realm, it was as if the wind had been knocked out of her. There on the page stood several tall, broad men. Each was handsome in his own right with dark hair and pitch-black eyes. A few smiled, revealing slightly pointed teeth. The ground around them was withered. The grass nearest to them, brown and dead. A few of the men held wilted flowers.

Beneath the portrait read:

Lords of Pestilence. Bringers of blight. Masters of Mayhem.

Abrielle shivered as her gaze landed on the man in the middle. "Deimos," his name came out as a whisper.

"Yes?" he asked, finally looking up from the newest book he had begun flipping through. It was one titled, *Spelling Someone into Spilling the Truth.*

Abrielle wanted to laugh at the irony. Instead, she held her book out in front of him. "You're a *God*?" They had spent days together now and he never alluded to just how much power he had.

"What?" His face flushed as he attempted to snatch the book from her hands.

"Is this you?" She jabbed her finger on what she assumed was a family portrait.

Deimos' paled. The shadows almost seemed to quake behind him and lowered themselves out of sight behind his back. Abrielle raised her chin, determined not to let the matter go this time. Pestilence, blight, and mayhem. He should have been honest with her from the start. Should have warned her about the sort of damage he could do to their world. Unless he *meant* to do these things. Purposefully ate away at Ellamere's land. For what? To what end?

The next page had a brief description and she read out loud, panic rising with each word, "*Whose sole purpose it is to maintain balance and harmony within the realm. Where there is light and life, there must be darkness and death. Without the Masters of Mayhem, Selanthia would fall out of its natural cycle. Should they fail in their endeavors, there will be no rebirth.*"

She pushed the book under his nose. "That *is* you. You're a God. Or a Deity. Whatever they call it."

"A lord," he mumbled.

"Why did you keep this from me? Is this the family business you spoke of? Are you trying to destroy my town?" The questions poured out of her like a dam had been broken.

Deimos grabbed the book from her and with one quick grimace in the direction of the family painting, he slammed it shut. Then, standing quickly, he shoved it back onto the dusty shelf and said, "Yes." His words came out tight as he continued, "That is me and those are my brothers. No, I am not *trying* to destroy your town. I told you; something is wrong with my powers. I am trying with all my might to keep a handle on things. To keep my magic from doing any real damage like you see in that book." He blew out a frustrated breath.

Abrielle could sense the turmoil inside him as he picked up one of the spell books and clenched it tightly in his hands. She could practically feel the tension rolling off him in the way he spoke as if straining to make her understand. The muscle in his jawline ticked, and he shook his head.

She stood, too, now, and quietly asked, "If you mean no harm, then why didn't you tell me all of this sooner?"

Deimos looked her in the eyes now. For a moment, she thought she saw a flicker of fear as he said, "I hoped I could get control of it before you found out. I was born into this power and position. I did not choose it. My family isn't bad, Brie. We uphold the balance of nature. Every beginning must have an end. But ending things can be tiresome. When I woke up in your bakery, I thought maybe, just maybe, this was my chance. That I could be something else for a little while. If I could just suppress my nature, then I could enjoy a holiday away from Selanthia and my familial responsibilities."

Abrielle furrowed her brow. "But you can't suppress it."

"Something is interfering with my control."

"The gemtowers," she guessed. "They keep magic out of Ellamere, but the one behind my garden is fractured. Maybe that's why you still have access to your power."

"It's possible. And the fact that it's only fractured but not completely broken would explain why I don't have the strength to fully control it." He scratched at the back of his ear. "It's hard to be certain. I don't know of anyone who has crossed through the ley lines since they erected the towers."

Deimos' eyes clouded with worry and his shadow companions closed in around him. He chuckled, but it sounded more bitter than sincere. "Father would certainly be proud of me right now."

"How so?"

"The prospect of his own son being the one to bring magic back to the mortal realm after all this time..." Deimos clucked his teeth. "Some in Selanthia are still bitter about being forced out of Ellamere. But my father? Well, he just loves a little mayhem."

Abrielle wasn't sure how to respond to that. Her grandfather had been the closest thing she had to a father, and he had loved order and peace. Robert Grainwick had been the one who others came to when things became too chaotic for them.

She sighed. "There aren't any answers in these books, are there?" Abrielle hadn't had high hopes of finding their solution in the library, but Deimos' dismay only confirmed it.

He shook his head. "Your King seems to have only kept minor spell work. Love potions and such. As well as protections from my kind. But nothing on summoning one of us. I suppose that was why the spell was so well hidden within the recipe."

Abrielle nodded solemnly. All that sneaking for nothing. She picked up the rest of the books and carefully placed them back on the shelves in their designated spots. They couldn't afford to leave behind any trace that they'd been there.

She peeked out an open window. Clouds had swept in, making it appear much later than it was. And a musty, earthy scent drifted on a small breeze into the room. A storm was brewing. They'd best get home quickly, unless they wanted to be caught in a downpour.

Her gaze drifted to Deimos who was squinting out the window at the clouds. If they were going to get out of the palace unnoticed, she would have to go back under the blanket of darkness with him again. She hesitated. Did knowing what he was change things? She had spent two days with him. Had slept under the same roof as him. And he had not hurt her.

True, strange things were happening around town, but if he had truly wanted to harm Ellamere, wouldn't he be powerful enough to do real damage?

"Deimos... the town—"

"I will do everything I can to make sure nothing truly bad happens to it."

"How can you be sure?"

He offered his arm to her as he said, "I can't. But I can promise to try."

In answer, she picked up her baskets and looped her arm through his. As the shadowy void enveloped the two of them, she couldn't ignore the twisted feeling in the pit of her stomach. A nagging voice in the back of her mind was telling her it was a mistake to put so much faith in someone else and their word. It could very well backfire on her.

Each step they took through the palace and down to the gate weighed heavily on her. She spotted a goat who seemed to see right through the void. When it looked at them—or more accurately, Deimos—it stood on its hind legs and began to spin in circles.

Further on down the road, closer to home, a bunny hopped alongside them and began chirping like a bird. A cow which was pulling Thomaz's cart full of fainted sheep, barked in Deimos' direction. Each time, a deep blush formed on his cheeks which were illuminated by faint sunlight that had wiggled its way through his void.

Abrielle watched each strange occurrence with an air of amusement. The book that had depicted Deimos' family was foreboding and ominous. But the things she was witnessing now were a bit on the silly side. Strange, yes. But dangerous? Not quite.

If barking cows and chirping bunnies were the worst that happened while he tried to suppress his magic, then maybe the town would be safe for a day or two more while they figured out a plan b. In the meantime, she would just have to keep him well hidden. Maybe being confined to the house would keep the magical occurrences to a minimum.

The moment they reached the threshold of the bakery, raindrops started to fall. They *tinked* on the roof in a rhythmic *tap, tap, tap*. It wasn't likely that any patrons would be dropping in the rest of the day, which meant Abrielle would have enough time to prepare for the next morning. If she could put out a new batch of dough, and bake a few things the rest of the afternoon, then there might be plenty of time for a drink... or four. After the week she was having, she would need something stronger than even Deimos' magic.

Eleven

Rain tapped relentlessly on the roof of the cottage. Despite the chill the storm had carried in, the bakery's kitchen was toasty. Warmth radiated from the stone oven which was filled with several pastries. A familiar sweet sugary scent filled the air, expanding into every crevice of the room.

Abrielle pressed her fists into the dough, thankful that the pain in her right arm had subsided. Icing it and resting it had helped; even if doing so had resulted in an entire day's worth of dough going to waste. Now she worked vigorously on a whole new batch, prepping it for the next morning.

Since coming back from the library, Deimos had been nose-deep in Mable's recipe book. He sat across from Abrielle, content with working in silence. The steady hum of the wind sang them a stormy night song. Nights like these were her favorites. It calmed her very soul to listen to the constant rainfall and occasional thunder and lightning off in the distance.

It also made the annoyance she was holding onto lessen just a tad. Deimos should have told her who he was from the very start. She might not have been so quick to trust him, but she deserved to have all the facts.

She snuck a glance in his direction. It was hard to imagine him coursing through his land with a destructive hand. Were his brothers different than him? He made it sound as if he didn't quite fit in with his family. It only helped to soften her disposition towards him. Internally, she sighed. She had never been very good at holding a grudge.

Deimos' shadow companions danced around in front of her. They seemed delighted by the storm, swirling between them and hovering well above the counter. The end of each tendril leaned over to watch her knead the dough but took a break each time Deimos made any sort of noise. Each cough, throat clearing, or hum, grabbed their attention along with Abrielle's. But each time they were all disappointed to find that he was simply making the sounds of someone who had been sitting in one spot for too long without anything to drink, rather than the sounds of someone who had found the answer to all their magical questions.

Abrielle abandoned the dough for the whistling teapot. She paused before pouring and asked, "How do you like to take your tea?"

Without looking up from the spell book, he replied, "With a dash of fungus root and a bit of nightshade."

Alarmed, Abrielle stared at him with her mouth gaping open. "Um... I can't say I have any fungus root. But you do know the second of those is poisonous, right?"

A blush bloomed across the bridge of his regal nose, and he finally looked up, giving her a sheepish grin. "Right. How about you just make it the way you normally drink yours."

Unconvinced she would ever get used to the little reminders that he wasn't mortal, she plopped two spoons of sugar and a splash of cream into it. Just the way she liked it. When she pushed the cup in front of him, he smiled broadly.

"Thanks." He took a long sip, and she watched the veins on the backs of his large hands stand out. The dainty teacup looked out of place held between them, but she couldn't take her eyes away, wondering what it would feel like to be in the teacup's place.

She blinked rapidly, snapping out of it as he set it down carefully and gestured to the book. "I'm getting nowhere with this."

Abrielle nodded. She hadn't had high hopes for another look into Mable's book. If there had been anything to find, they would have come across it by now. With a sigh, she grabbed each kneaded dough and placed it into its bowl. Then, covering each with a dishtowel, she set them aside.

There were still two left out on the counter and Deimos stood, reaching out as if to grab it.

Abrielle shouted, "No!"

She leaped across the floor and grabbed the dough before he had the chance to touch it. She tensed as she placed the dough in its bowl. She hadn't meant to shout at him. But there was no way she could risk letting him touch anything edible again. His eyes popped open in surprise.

Apologetically, she said, "Better safe than sorry."

He sat back down looking like a sorry pup with his head hung low. Tinker leapt onto his lap and mewed wildly in an effort to get his attention. With a smirk, he brushed his hand along the tabby cat's back and she settled in happily.

He looked so content with a soft smile, but Abrielle still felt sorry for making him feel bad about the dough. Biting her lip, she eyed the cupboard, high to the right of the sink. The one she always needed to climb on the counter in order to reach. There was one thing in there that was sure to cure rainy night blues. She pulled one of the drawers out and clumsily tried to get the right footing to climb.

Deimos' voice dripped with uncertainty as he asked, "Do you need a hand?"

She grunted in response, "No, I've got it."

"It looks like you might need a hand." The stool scooted across the floor, and she could hear his approaching footsteps behind her.

She argued stubbornly, "Really, I think I'm capable of grabbing something off the shelf."

Despite her assurances, arching her back and stretching her arm as high as it would go didn't seem to do the trick. Her fingers brushed against the glass bottles, but she couldn't get a grasp on the one she wanted. In a most ungraceful manner, her foot slipped, pulling the drawer out and leaving her with nothing to stand on.

She yelped as Deimos caught her in both his arms. He smelled like a summer night—like evergreens in the evening air. Once her feet were back on steady ground, she gazed up at him breathlessly.

With a wicked grin, he purred, "Capable, huh?"

Stubborn pride swelled in her chest. With her chin tilted high, she countered, "You distracted me." But she couldn't help the smile pulling at her lips. She might be capable of a great many things, but maybe reaching things on the high shelf wasn't one of them.

"So, are you going to let me help now?"

Rolling her eyes playfully, she relented. "Yes."

"Yes what?" He licked his lips and suddenly she became aware of his hands still around her waist.

I suppose this is one way to find out what being the teacup would feel like. She liked it as much as she imagined she would.

She gulped. "Yes, Deimos, I would very much like your help."

He flashed her a smile so dazzling that she couldn't remember why his sharpened teeth had frightened her when they first met. His smile lit up his whole face, despite the shadowy air that constantly surrounded him.

He reached around her, pressing his body into hers. He barely had to lift his arm above his head to reach the cupboard. Abrielle's pulse quickened at the close proximity, but she couldn't bring herself to move. Instead, she watched as he raised an eyebrow at the large, clear bottles filled with liquids that varied in amber, red, and even some purple.

Abrielle pointed to one nearly the color of molasses. "That one, please!" she squeaked.

Deimos drew it from the cupboard and held it between the two of them, creating a bit of space. She despised that bottle for a moment. Then, with a shake of her head, she took it and stepped away from him. What was she thinking? She had absolutely no business lusting after him. Didn't she have more pressing matters to attend to? Like sending him home in time for the festival.

She set the bottle on the table in the middle of the kitchen and tried to shake the lingering sensation of his body pressed against hers. Her hands trembled slightly as she finished setting the bread dough aside and placing the cookie dough beneath the floorboards in the mini-icebox. Then she joined him at the table with two glasses in hand.

The glass was a deep green and had been hand blown in town by one of the talented glassmakers. They were her favorite ones to use after a long, exceptionally hard day when she and Tansy would drink near the fire; reading to one another from their favorite books or sharing the latest town gossip.

Tonight, it seemed, her company would be found in a *lord* of the Otherworlds. She measured him with her gaze. Did that mean he was like royalty in his realm? Did women throw themselves at his feet? Or were they frightened of how much power he held. Surely, the women she had seen in the book who had leathery wings, or glittering shells covering their breasts wouldn't be afraid of someone like him. A jolt of jealousy ran through her. It was an unfamiliar and discomforting feeling, and she imagined it was similar to being struck by lightning.

She forced a smile as he filled her glass first. It occurred to her suddenly that maybe *she* was as brave as those Selanthian women. That she hadn't been frightened of him enough to call for the guard or throw him out. Or was she just foolish and naïve for thinking she was safe in his presence?

Wow. She really needed this drink, or she'd find herself wasting the night away with all these thoughts.

She held up a finger before Deimos could take a drink. He waited patiently while she jogged to the spice shelf and grabbed the jar that held cinnamon sticks. She plucked out two of the twisted sticks of bark and placed them in each of the glasses.

Deimos eyed them warily, but she assured him, "Cinnamon goes just right with the spice in the mead. Trust me."

The corner of his mouth twitched upward, and he held his glass up to her. "Here's to trusting each other."

Abrielle raised her glass in response, but chimed in with, "I might be trusting you for now, but I haven't forgiven you yet for keeping the truth from me."

She gazed at him hotly over her glass as she took a drink. The mead burned going down, but the sweetness of it gave her delightful shivers. She wasn't going to let him think he'd gotten off that easily.

Deimos took a swig from his glass and grimaced. "This is... *potent*."

Proudly, Abrielle stated, "It's my grandfather's recipe."

"The man certainly knew how to make a drink." Deimos seemed impressed as he raised it to his lips again.

Abrielle smiled at the compliment, then commanded, "Grab the bottle."

After taking a quick moment to pull everything from the oven, she put out the fire and gestured for Deimos and the shadows to follow her into the living room. With everything set out to cool, her work was done for the night.

Deimos eyed the recipe book as he picked up the bottle. Abrielle shook her head and said, "There's nothing more that thing is going to give us. Unless we're willing to try recipes at random and see what happens."

He visibly shivered. "No way. Witches are unpredictable." He abandoned the book and followed Abrielle through the doorway.

She removed a few pillows from the armchair and tossed them to the floor. Then she grabbed her favorite, purple-knitted blanket and wrapped it around her shoulders with one hand, careful not to spill her drink in the other.

Deimos took a seat on the sofa he'd slept on the night before and Abrielle sat across from him on the pillows she'd thrown on the floor. She crossed her legs comfortably and reached for the bottle he had set on the short table between them.

Filling her drink, she said, "We should play that game."

Deimos raised an eyebrow. "What game?"

"The one we played the night I summoned you. An answer for an answer."

She drank her mead, enjoying the way it warmed her chest as if a fire was being lit inside it. Drinking with him could be a very bad idea. She would get far too bold. And with the ghostly touch of his hands lingering on her waist, there was no telling what foolish things she might say... or do. But then again, she'd been full of terrible ideas lately. What was one more?

Tinker made her way onto Abrielle's lap and snuggled in like a fat little potato. She purred loudly as Abrielle ran a hand along her back. Meanwhile, the shadowy tendrils settled in as well, resting on the back of the couch behind Deimos' head. Abrielle had to admit, she was getting used to them. She nearly laughed at the ridiculousness of it. Was she really so desperate for company that she was willing to accept a lord of destruction and his shadow friends?

Deimos started with the first question of the game. "What do you see in that boy?"

Abrielle frowned.

He corrected with an exasperated sigh, "Erik. What do you see in him?" He leaned back and crossed his leg, resting his ankle on his knee. "As far as mortals go, he doesn't seem all that special."

Abrielle's chest tightened. She really didn't want to discuss a silly crush with someone like Deimos. Who, judging by the ease with which he'd displayed his naked body earlier, was likely well versed and confident when it came to the opposite sex.

But it *had* been her idea to play the game, so she answered, "He's handsome." She tried to think of more to recommend him as a desirable suitor, but to be honest, she didn't know him that well. She bit her lip, trying to think of what other girls in town would want in a man. She took a drink and said over her glass, "And he's motivated. He's risen in the ranks quite fast. It's impressive."

"Ah, so you're looking for someone who is career driven."

Abrielle shrugged. "I'm not looking for anyone, really. I have my hands full with the bakery. Asking Erik to the Star Crossed festival was Tansy's idea. It's common to go with someone you like."

"I see..." His face twisted into a skeptical look.

"My turn," she hiccupped. Uh oh. The mead *was* really strong. "Why do you care so much about what I see in Erik?"

Deimos furrowed his brow. "Who says I do?"

She clucked her teeth and wagged a finger at him. "You can't answer a question with a question."

He chuckled. "Fine, I just think you can do better." Before she could respond, he took his turn. "Do you enjoy *my* company?"

"Yes," she answered confidently, before thinking. "I mean, I think you are quite..."

"Go on."

"Charming. In your own way." She took a bigger gulp of her drink.

Deimos laughed and her cheeks burned. She needed to steer the conversation in another direction before she mentioned wanting to feel his hands on her once more. Or to put her own hands on that chiseled chest of his. So, she asked, "What do you have against witches?" It wasn't the most creative question, but his statement about witches being unpredictable was still fairly fresh in her mind.

The shadows quivered behind him as he answered, "They were once mortal, just as you are. But they found a way to harness the magic in my land. At first, it was for the betterment of them and the people in their villages. They would use it to heal both the mind and body. But as always, there were a few who reached too far." He turned the glass in his hand, watching the cinnamon stick swirl around in the mead.

Abrielle sat forward with interest and was rewarded with a scolding meow from Tinker. She ignored the old tabby as Deimos continued, "The ones who weren't content to borrow magic, began to grasp more of it for themselves. They found ways to harness it for their own gain. Some to make themselves more beautiful, or to extend their lifespan. Others made worse choices. Like trying to make a play for political power here in your realm. Thinking they could become more powerful than even a king."

She thought of King Vasiri's grandfather. He'd been so frightened of those witches that he'd exiled magic altogether. For the first time, she wondered what it had been like to experience the good sides of magic firsthand.

Deimos' voice was grave as he said, "I say they are unpredictable, because they are clever. They create spells that work only for the author. Or they hide incantations within books like a sort of spy's code." He nodded to Abrielle. "You could have been hurt. If things had gone wrong, who knows what could have happened." There was a hint of anger behind his words as if the thought of her being in harm's way bothered him.

She shivered at the thought of something worse happening than summoning a dark lord from the Otherworlds. Goosebumps prickled along her back and neck and suddenly there was a pounding at the door. She nearly jumped out of her skin, spilling her drink in the process.

Deimos froze, his brow furrowed in concern. "Are you expecting anyone?"

"No—" she cut off abruptly and planted her face in the palm of her hand. "Shoot! It's Tansy. She must have seen the lanternlight."

There was more pounding accompanied by Tansy's shivering voice. "It's freezing out here! I'm coming in!"

Deimos hissed, "Did you lock the door?"

Abrielle rolled her eyes. "It won't matter, Tansy will just pick it. You need to hide!" She stood quickly to intercept her friend before she walked in on the strange little party, but swayed on her feet. The effects of the mead had definitely already kicked in.

Deimos argued with a whine, "I don't want to hide." His jet-black eyes were glossed over making the purple specks shimmer in the warm glow of the lantern. Apparently Selanthians weren't immune to her grandfather's concoctions.

She swatted at him. "Well do *something*. She's coming!"

The door handle jiggled in the bakery, and she rushed to the wide doorway between it and the living quarters to block Tansy's view as she stepped inside. Her hair was matted to her face, and she shoved it away from her eyes with a murmur. "It's really coming down out there."

Abrielle leaned awkwardly against the doorframe with her arm raised. She slipped as she tried to rest her head on her hand and opted for just leaning her back against the old wood. "Yeah, seems we were overdue for some rain."

Tansy wrinkled her nose. "It rained like four days ago. Listen, I know you're busy with festival preparations, but I *really* need a girls' night. Thomaz and I had one of our long talks and now we're going to the festival as *friends*. And I'm swamped with flower orders for the floral crowns and..." Her gaze drifted passed Abrielle to the bottle sitting on the living room table. With a laugh, she said, "Already broke into the good stuff I see."

Abrielle practically tripped over her own two feet as she rushed past Tansy and into the other room. She tried to think of a way to explain Deimos, but her mind was a chaotic swirl of drunken thoughts. Claiming to have met him on the street wouldn't do. A distant cousin, perhaps? Tansy was no fool. She'd never buy it.

All her scrambling was apparently for nothing, though, because sitting in Deimos' place on the couch was the now all too familiar hound. Its scruffy ears perked up as Tansy walked into the room. When she joined him on the couch, Abrielle held her breath.

Tansy sat beside him and reached out gingerly to touch his snout. "You still haven't sent this guy packing, huh?"

Abrielle sat back down on the floor and drained her cup. She was going to need a lot more mead to get through this strange interaction. She breathed heavily as she said, "Nope. Seems he's here to stay a while longer."

Tansy studied him for a split second, then scratched him on the side. He leaned back, embracing the attention and soon he was laying down with his stomach exposed. Abrielle held in a snort as Tansy rubbed his belly like he was a run of the mill stray dog.

Deimos shamelessly reveled in the affection. Soon his hind leg was kicking rapidly as if she had found precisely the right spot to scratch. It was all too much. Abrielle completely lost it and cackled with laughter. Tansy gaped at her in surprise, and Abrielle knew this would be impossible to explain away. But it was too late. Once she started laughing, she couldn't stop. A cramp ran up her side and she took several deep breaths before being able to sit up straight.

Once she had the laughter under control, guilt crept in. She had never kept anything from Tansy. She was the best friend Abrielle had ever had. And now that her grandparents were gone, she was the closest thing she had to family. Her eyes stung at the thought of lying to her anymore and she sucked in a nervous breath. Maybe it was the mead clouding her judgment, or the disappointment of not coming any closer to a solution to her Deimos problem, but she couldn't hold the secret back any longer.

The truth burst from her like a hiccup. "Deimos is a demon from another realm. I summoned him the other night with a soufflé."

Tansy laughed uncomfortably and stared at Abrielle as if waiting for a punchline to the joke. When none came, she gingerly lifted her hand from Deimos. As she did, the bleak darkness wound around him.

Knowing what was coming, Abrielle threw a pillow at him and scolded, "You'd better cover up before those shadows disappear! Don't be indecent!"

The void shifted for a moment, reaching down beside the arm of the couch where Deimos' clothes had been strewn about. After a moment, the darkness dissipated, and standing before them in all his *clothed* glory, was Deimos.

Twelve

Tansy took the big reveal better than Abrielle could have hoped. True, she looked as if she might pass out with her eyes as round as saucers. But at least she hadn't run screaming for the palace guards. Not that she expected her to. Tansy was the most understanding, brave person she knew. And already, the relief of sharing the secret released a weight Abrielle hadn't realized she'd been carrying.

Deimos had the good grace to sit in the armchair beside Abrielle instead of taking his previous place next to Tansy. He cast her a haughty smile that made Abrielle want to pinch him. But she supposed she should be relieved that he wasn't offended she had spilled their secret without running it by him first.

He practically purred as he said, "You have quite a way with your hands."

This time Abrielle did pinch him. He yelped and rubbed the side of his calf.

Tansy's eyes darted back and forth as she stuttered, "H-how did he..." She pointed to the sofa where he'd been sitting then to him.

Abrielle shoved the bottle of mead in her direction. She was going to have to catch up if she was going to hear the whole story. Tansy took it with trembling hands and drank straight from the neck.

Deimos remained silent as Abrielle explained everything. She started with the shapeshifting then backtracked to finding the book in the King's library. All the while, the three of them continued to drink. By the time she finished her tale, the bottle was empty, and Tansy was in awe.

She shook her head wildly, sending her curls flying. "You. Miss *work first, play later*, have been out gallivanting with..." she paused and looked Deimos up and down admiringly then finished, "him."

He raised his chin and grinned proudly.

Tansy tipped the empty bottle upside down and slurred, "Seems we're out." She leaped up and grabbed Abrielle by the arm. "We'll be right back."

Abrielle giggled as Tansy whisked her out of the room and into the bakery. The kitchen was spinning, and she gladly let Tansy make the climb up to the cupboard to grab another bottle. When she jumped down, she took Abrielle's shoulders firmly.

With a laugh of disbelief, Tansy said, "This is not at all what I meant when I told you to put yourself out there and try something new."

Abrielle bit her lip. "Trust me, I know."

"So, what are you going to do?"

"I was hoping maybe you'd have some ideas." Abrielle grabbed the jar of cinnamon and tucked it under her arm so she could carry the bottle and a glass for Tansy.

Her friend stared at her incredulously. "Honestly, I have no idea. It... it's amazing really. You've stumbled into uncharted territory." She leaned in, growing serious. "And he's been kind? He hasn't done anything untoward?"

"Unless you count showing me his..." Abrielle pointed her gaze downward and said, "his *you know what*."

"Excuse me?" Tansy shrieked.

Abrielle swatted her with her free hand. "We were in the King's library, so it really wasn't a big deal."

Tansy burst into laughter. "That actually sounds much worse."

Abrielle shook her head. "No, really, he's been fine. I just don't want anyone to get hurt."

There was a moment of silence and then a dramatic shout from the living room. "Brie! I'm parched!"

"Okay, maybe he's a bit needy," Abrielle joked as she and Tansy strolled back to Deimos.

Abrielle filled all three glasses and found her seat on the floor again. With the alcohol settling in and the warmth of the fire Deimos had started, a steady calm washed over her. She leaned back against the armchair and didn't flinch when Deimos' leg brushed against her shoulder.

It wasn't long before they were all sharing stories like old friends. Tansy told Deimos about the many adventures she and Abrielle had as children. And Abrielle confessed that the reason she had sprinkled salt on the floor the night he appeared was because of the Princess' superstitions.

Deimos revealed a bit about his childhood, leaving out any bits about his family which only made Abrielle more intrigued. Instead, he shared stories about fairies fluttering about in the gardens and the time a ratawilly chased him up to the roof of his childhood home.

Once the bottle was nearly gone, they all seemed to give a collective sigh. After a moment, Deimos broke the silence. "I like it here."

Tansy responded sarcastically, "Sure, what's not to like?" She scoffed. "It's the same predictable stuff every day."

Abrielle crinkled her nose. "What's wrong with that? There are still plenty of ways to spice things up."

Tansy snorted. "Like summoning a... what are you called again?"

Deimos grabbed a strand of Abrielle's hair and twirled it around his finger. She gave a delighted sigh and tilted her head back slightly. He was slouched in the chair and his eyes were heavy with drunkenness. "I'm just Deimos."

Tansy ignored the evasiveness. "Anyway, you summoned him and now things are finally getting exciting."

Abrielle felt her own eyelids growing heavy. Between that and Deimos playing with her hair, she was sure to drift off any minute now. Groggily, she said, "You're right, it is pretty exciting. But what's *not* exciting is staring at the recipes—or spells, I should say—in Mable's book."

Tansy bolted upright and hit her forehead with the palm of her hand. "That's it!"

"What's *it*?" Abrielle and Deimos said in unison.

"The answer has been in front of the two of you this entire time. You need to go to the source. Find this Mayline—"

"Mable." They said again at the same time.

Tansy snapped her fingers. "Yes. Mable. Find the one who wrote the damned spell and there you have it! She can tell you how to reverse it. Or write a new spell to accomplish the same goal."

It was painfully obvious, and Abrielle was embarrassed to admit she hadn't thought of it first. The book appeared to be incredibly old judging by the yellowing, crinkled pages. It never crossed her mind that the author might still be around. Especially with magic exiled from the land. Could they truly have been scrambling for an answer when it was there all along? She had never heard of a woman by that name before. Surely in a town as small as theirs, she would have.

As if reading her mind, Tansy offered, "I can ask around town tomorrow. That way no suspicion falls on you. I'll simply say that my mother would like to get a recipe from her."

"It is a good idea." Abrielle glanced at Deimos who looked unsure. "What do we have to lose?"

A quiet calm befell the group again until out of nowhere, Deimos sighed. "I'm not sure I really want to go back."

Abrielle shifted to look up at him. "Really?"

He shrugged and released her hair. "Ellamere is just so different from my lands. It's more homey here. I don't know..." he drifted off with a sad look in his eyes.

Abrielle bit the inside of her cheek and shifted to face him. She leaned on the cushion and rested her chin on her arms. "You said you ran from your responsibilities back home. If you could do anything else in the world, what would it be?"

He was thoughtful for a moment before answering, "I would do the opposite of what I do now."

A smile tugged at her lips. "How so?"

He leaned forward, resting his elbows on his legs. "I would build things. Once my eldest brother decided he wanted a treehouse. One so high that none of our other brothers could reach it." His eyes lit up, the purple specks sparkling in the lanternlight. "He of course didn't want to actually do any of the work. Which is probably why he let me in on that little secret of his."

Abrielle laughed lightly. "So, he delegated while you did the work."

With a shrug, he said, "I didn't mind. It felt good to create rather than destroy."

Sadness washed over her for young Deimos. Without thinking, she brushed her fingers against the back of his hand. They stared at one another intently until Tansy's snores broke the somber moment.

Sheepishly, Abrielle said, "I should get her to bed."

"Do you need help getting her upstairs?" Deimos was already standing and smoothing out his wrinkled shirt.

She shook her head. "No, I've got it."

"Really?" he drawled. "This I've got to see."

Abrielle stuck her nose in the air and strutted up to Tansy who was sprawled out on the sofa. She tilted her head, trying to gauge how best to grasp onto her friend's arms. Then, bending over, she slipped her arms under Tansy's armpits and sat her up. Tansy let out a loud snort, but still didn't wake from her drunken slumber.

Abrielle grunted with an *oof* and hugged Tansy tight as she tried to lift her. Her body was limp and impossible to move. With a huff Abrielle turned to Deimos and put a hand on her jutted hip. "Fine. Maybe I need a little help."

In the blink of an eye Deimos gallantly swooped Tansy up and followed Abrielle to the stairs. Abrielle went first, tripping on the first step and making Deimos tumble into her. Tansy didn't even stir. Laughter bubbled up from Abrielle as she grabbed the rail.

Deimos laughed, too, as he said, "Perhaps I should have carried you up first."

Feigning offense, she quipped, "I'll have you know; I am no damsel in distress."

"Of course not. But those stairs seem to be putting up quite the fight."

She was inclined to agree as she stumbled up to her room.

Moonlight lit her bed, and she moved the quilt before gesturing for Deimos to set Tansy down. This time it was his turn to lose his balance as he plopped Tansy onto the bed. Abrielle leaped forward, landing on her knees, and reached across to help right him before he could fall onto her sleeping friend.

Abrielle gripped his arms and although he had regained his balance, she didn't let go. Instead, kneeling on the bed, she and Deimos stared intently into each other's eyes. If she'd been any taller, they would have been nose to nose.

She cleared her throat as her gaze dropped to the beautiful curve of his mouth. He leaned forward slightly, and Abrielle's lips parted invitingly. The butterflies which had been puttering around in her stomach lately, took full flight. Leaning in, she began to close her eyes. That is what women did, right? It had been so long since she'd kissed anyone.

Time slowed. The warmth of his breath reached her lips, and it was like the nerves in her body were firing all at once.

Suddenly, Tansy let out a snore that rivaled even the wild boar in the forest. Deimos looked down in alarm as he whispered, "I thought only beasts in Selanthia made noises like that."

Abrielle released her hold on him and clapped her hands over her mouth to keep from crying out with laughter.

With the moment broken, she stood quickly and headed for the door with Deimos trailing close behind. Her head spun and part of her swore the flowers on the wallpaper were dancing. She swayed on her feet and Deimos placed sturdy hands on her shoulders and pressed her against the doorframe. It gave her the support she needed, and she gazed up at him with hazy joy. Their near kiss left her with a deep ache in need of satisfying.

Tansy would tell her that this was the perfect time to say something charming and brilliant. To leave him for the night with a little harmless flirtation. But all she could think of was how he'd said he wasn't sure he wanted to leave Ellamere. It sobered her slightly and moved her in a way she didn't expect. She loved her village with all her heart and had never considered leaving the home her grandparents had built. For him to acknowledge the beauty in her home, was like a personal compliment to her.

Finding her voice again, she whispered, "Thank you."

Although she was referring to the compliment, naturally he mistook her meaning and nodded toward the snoring woman. "It was no problem at all. She's going to have one hell of a headache in the morning."

Abrielle snorted a small laugh. "Aren't we all?"

Then, brushing his fingers slowly along her arm, he said, "Goodnight, Brie."

"Goodnight, Deimos." She watched him descend the stairs and leaned her head against the doorframe with a pleasant sigh. *What a strange night.*

Once the wallpaper stopped dancing, Abrielle went to bed. But this time, she didn't dream about those she'd lost. Instead, she dreamed of dancing in the town square with Tansy and Deimos. She dreamed of the living, of laughter and light, and small shadows that fluttered through her hair.

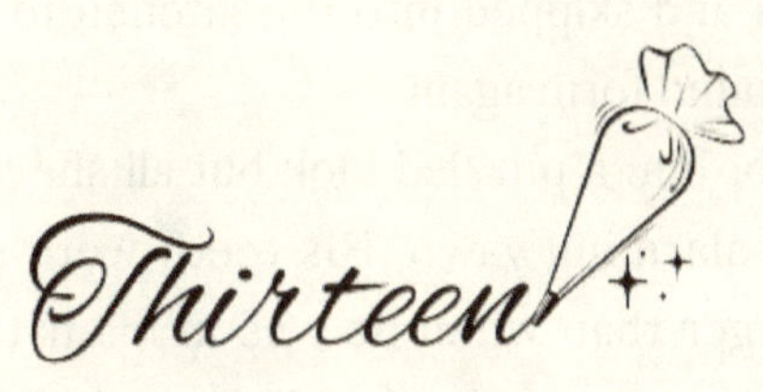

Thirteen

Abrielle groaned and cursed herself for falling victim to that second bottle of mead the night before. Cheerful sunlight drifted through her curtains, and she nearly had a heart attack when she realized it was past dawn.

She jolted upright and tripped out of the bed. Scrambling to her bureau, she tossed on the first dress she found. Its bright yellow daisies clashed with the sickly way she felt. She had slept in. Which meant the bakery hadn't been opened in time. Never in all the years that her grandmother ran the shop was it opened late.

Abrielle took the stairs two at a time in a rush to get to the kitchen. She didn't even glance at the couch to see if Deimos was still sleeping. But as she crossed the room, adrenaline rushed through her, rivaling a strong cup of coffee. The laughter and symphony of customers hammered into her head as she reached the doorway leading to the bakery. The room was packed full of friendly faces, each greeting her good morning as she wove her way to the kitchen.

Tansy was at the counter beaming at a customer who ordered an entire loaf of bread. When Abrielle caught her eye, she smiled and waved. Tinker purred as she darted between Abrielle's legs and skipped into the kitchen to join Deimos who was in hound form again.

Abrielle shot him a puzzled look but all she got in return was a rather alarming yawn. His teeth were razor sharp, and much larger than when he was in his natural state. A nearby customer gave a shocked little gasp. When Abrielle looked their way, they forced a tight-lipped smile and busied themselves with a few jars on the shelf.

It seemed Tansy and Deimos had taken it upon themselves to open the bakery that morning. Fear snaked through Abrielle's chest as she lifted the parchment covering the freshly baked loaves of bread. They were golden brown and smelled delightful. She breathed a sigh of relief.

Tansy rested her chin on Abrielle's shoulder and said, "Don't worry, I didn't let him touch any of the food."

Deimos gave a short, low growl as he laid down and plopped his head on his paws in a pout. Abrielle laughed awkwardly and turned to Tansy. "You didn't have to do all this. You should have woken me."

Tansy took Abrielle's hands and said, "It was no bother. I owed the two of you for getting me up to bed in one piece."

Abrielle blushed, thinking of the moment with Deimos in her room. Thank the fates Tansy had been there. Both she and Deimos had been drunk, and a kiss would have complicated things immensely. The curve of his lips so close to hers flashed through her mind and heat bloomed across the bridge of her nose. Trying to avoid looking in his direction, she focused on Tansy and joked, "Admittedly, it was touch and go there for a minute. Luckily Deimos is better with stairs than I am."

Tansy giggled and returned to the counter to hand out another order. Abrielle threw on the nearest apron and busied herself wrapping the palace order and putting each parcel into its designated wicker basket. Her head was still throbbing. What she really needed was some thick sliced bacon and an egg with runny yolk.

She peeked back at Tansy who was ushering the last of the morning rush out the door. Now that things had slowed down, Abrielle decided to make them all a big breakfast. One that would help them recover from their long night.

Deimos' ears perked up at the sound of bacon sizzling in the pan and Abrielle scolded him, "You really should have woken me up."

He huffed in response, but it was Tansy who spoke. "We were perfectly capable of handling things down here."

Abrielle cracked a few eggs in another pan and argued, "My grandmother always opened the shop herself."

Tansy plucked a blueberry from a bowl sitting on the windowsill. "You are not your grandmother."

"Don't I know it," Abrielle mumbled under her breath. Only Deimos seemed to hear as he tilted his scraggly head at her in a questioning sort of way.

Tansy grabbed a piece of parchment and plucked a few crispy pieces of bacon from the pan. Grease blotted the brown paper as she wrapped it up. Then, picking up the baskets for the palace, she said, "I'm delivering these today."

Abrielle opened her mouth to argue, but Tansy held up a silencing hand. "You have your hands full here. The festival is in a few days, and you still don't have any idea what you're entering into the competition, do you?" She nodded toward Deimos. "And then there's that little scoundrel to deal with. I will take the palace delivery and on the way back I'll start asking about the author."

"But—"

"Please don't argue with me. Just let me do this for you."

Abrielle gently grabbed the baskets from her, but firmly stated, "No. I've got it."

Tansy frowned but relented. "Fine. I will go start my scavenger hunt for the mysterious Mable. But please don't overwork yourself while I'm gone." She kissed Abrielle on the cheek and skipped out the door.

Abrielle let out an exasperated sigh as she plated their breakfast and set it on the table. She headed to the door to lock up just in case any customers wandered by while they ate. She could open again after just in case anyone wanted to stop by for lunch.

Deimos shifted and dressed when she wasn't looking, so he was back to his alarmingly handsome self. They sat across from each other at the table and Abrielle focused on the food in front of her. She would have to eat quickly if she was going to make it to the palace on time.

Deimos also ate quickly, though she suspected the hangover might have something to do with it. It was odd how well he had fit in with her and Tansy the night before. Laughing and talking to them as if they were all old friends.

Did he have many friends back in Selanthia? He was charming enough and she couldn't imagine it being just him and the shadows. A wave of loneliness washed over her. She'd experienced plenty of her own shadowy nights alone—though it wasn't quite the same since the shadows *she* was used to didn't think and act on their own accord.

Deep down, she wanted to ask him if he'd meant what he said last night or if it was just drunken ramblings. Did he truly think about staying? It would be impossible, even if he did. His magic was a danger to Ellamere. He knew that. So, he couldn't have meant it.

Besides, what would he do in Ellamere? Thomaz was always looking for farmhands to help. But making the sheep pass out repeatedly would be a problem. Paddy would probably jump at the chance of having someone with Deimos' physique apprentice in the blacksmith shop. But customers would be wary of him at best. At worst, they would demand the King banish him.

She sighed. Regardless of how much she was willing to accept his presence, the same likely couldn't be said for the other villagers in town. Deciding it was best not to dwell on the subject, she kept her questions to herself. If he didn't bring it up, then there was no need for her to.

Deimos finished clearing his plate and wiped his mouth with one of the dishtowels. Clearing his throat, he asked, "What's the plan?"

"Plan?" Abrielle hadn't thought that far. She was just grateful that the breakfast was soaking up the nausea.

"For today. I guess there isn't much we can do until Tansy finds Mable."

"Right..." Abrielle took the plates to the sink. "Well, I have the palace delivery. And Tansy's right, the festival is only a few days away. I need to start getting things ready for the feast and then there's the matter of the contest." Her chest tightened and it was becoming hard to catch her breath.

There was so much to get done. What had she been thinking wasting time drinking? She should have been focusing on the menu and what she was going to bake for the contest. Sending Deimos home was a priority, but so was keeping up with the bakery. In the last few days, she had missed orders, failed to open the shop on her own, and fallen horribly behind schedule.

Deimos inched closer to her. "Are you alright?"

Abrielle pressed at her temples. "No. Everything is going wrong."

He shuffled his feet, and she sensed his hand lingering over her shoulder, though he made no move to touch her. His voice was gentle as he said, "One thing at a time. What's first on the list?"

Abrielle took a steadying breath through her nose and blew out through her mouth. "The palace delivery."

"Then let's get to it. The sooner we drop it off, the sooner you can get to the next thing on your list, right?"

Abrielle nodded and grabbed the baskets. She paused, looking down at the sorry apron which was covered in yesterday's flour. "Maybe I should lose the apron."

"Really?" His voice was gruff as he said, "I rather like it."

Heat flushed from her face to her chest. She reached behind to untie it and fumbled with the double knot. Deimos moved behind her and placed his hands on hers. He softly moved them away from the tie. As he undid it for her, his fingers brushed along the small of her back, making her lower stomach tighten. When he stepped away, she found herself wishing the moment hadn't ended so soon.

She mumbled a thank you and set the apron on a brass hook. In a matter of seconds, Deimos was shifted into hound-form. She was sure the scruffy canine would still horrify her neighbors, but he was growing on her. The sight of his shifted state was less jolting than before.

They hurried together out the door and up the hill to the palace. Although the rain from the night before had left the divots in the cobblestones wet and muddy, villagers were out in droves. Some were tending to their gardens in an effort to enjoy them before the first fall chill came. Others could be seen through their shop windows. Tansy's father looked up and waved from his seat with a leather shoe and hammer in hand. Most of the townspeople were outside, enjoying the sunshine and cool morning air. Some tipped their heads to Abrielle or raised a teacup to her in a passing greeting.

Nothing seemed particularly out of the ordinary this time. That is, until they reached the palace gate. The lush grass along the path to the kitchen was a bluish-green hue. Like someone had spilled dye on it.

Erik was already there waiting for her with bags under his eyes. He yawned as he greeted her. "Good morning."

"Is it?" Abrielle stared at the grass, dumbfounded. "What happened here?"

"Who knows." Erik shrugged and signaled for her and Deimos to follow him. "It started yesterday. At first, I thought I was seeing things, but as the day went on it was clear it was changing color."

"But it's not dead." Abrielle thought of the pestilence magic that Deimos' family wielded. The grass had certainly changed where he walked the previous morning. But it hadn't died. If this was *his* doing, wouldn't it have withered? This lawn still looked thick and healthy. Just... blue.

Deimos' snout twisted as if he was trying to work it out in his head, too. There was no way she could ask him about it now, so she went about her business. Erik walked into the kitchen and held the door open for her. Before she could step inside, Deimos released a choked whine.

To Erik, she said, "Go ahead, I'll be just a moment." Then she knelt and pretended to tie her boot. As she fiddled with the leather laces that were already tied in a neat little bow, she asked Deimos, "What's wrong?"

She nearly yelped when he spoke. His snout moved as a dog's would, but a man's voice came out in a hurried, husky whisper, "Compliment his uniform."

"What?" she hissed back.

"Compliment him. Mortal men love that sort of thing."

"I am not taking dating advice from someone who licks his own butt!"

Indignantly, he responded, "I do no such thing!"

Abrielle shoved him away lightly and stood, smoothing out her gown and hoping Erik hadn't noticed anything amiss. Luckily, he was staring at something in the kitchen. Or rather, someone. The pretty lady's maid from before was fluttering her lashes at him from across the room.

Deimos snuffed behind her, and she shut the door promptly with the heel of her boot. Her face burned with embarrassment. He clearly thought she was hopeless when it came to romance, or he wouldn't be butting his large snout into her business.

His advice probably wouldn't work, anyway. Just to prove him wrong, she smiled sweetly at Erik and said, "You look particularly dashing in your uniform today."

He blinked at her in surprise. "Thank you, Abrielle. I just got it back from the tailor. They added a stripe for my service to the King."

"It suits you."

She didn't wait for a reaction as she marched over to the counter and unpacked the baskets. So, he had thanked her. Big deal. That was simply the polite thing to do. It certainly didn't mean Deimos was right. Still, as she walked back outside, she couldn't help but notice Erik's intent gaze following her. Something fluttered in her stomach like butterflies, but they died the moment she caught Deimos' dark glittering eyes watching her, too.

Abrielle and Deimos walked silently back down the hill. She couldn't shake the unsettled feeling in the pit of her stomach. For a while now, she had fancied Erik. But in her drunken state the night before, there had been a spark of something between her and Deimos. Or was it just the effect of two bottles of potent mead?

Even if she *had* kissed Deimos when she had the chance, it would have been nothing more than a silly whim. His presence was temporary. If Mable did in fact still live in Ellamere, then they would find her, and she would help them rectify Abrielle's mistake.

Before she could dwell on it further, a man wearing an attendant's uniform from the palace with the King's crest on the arm nearly bumped into her... He was rushing up the hill with a stack of papers piled high in his arms and the chancellor following close behind. The attendant veered out of her path and stumbled into Deimos' hound-like body.

"Oh my!" the man exclaimed.

The chancellor grabbed hold of the man's elbow to steady him and reached up to keep the mountain of documents from falling. Then, stopping and peeking around the stack, he smiled warmly. "Miss Grainwick, how nice to see you!"

"Good morning, Chancellor. You two appear to have your hands full." In truth, it seemed only the attendant had been tasked with carrying the load. The chancellor instead held an open box with some sort of dessert inside. She eyed the treat as she asked, "Can I help?"

The King's chancellor was especially disheveled this morning, and he pushed his slipping spectacle's back up his nose. He shook his head vigorously. "We're fine, dear. Just getting these documents back to the palace for King Vasiri to look over."

"As long as you're sure," Abrielle answered skeptically.

The chancellor tipped his head to her and took a large bite of the sticky, crispy treat before turning to walk away. Curiosity nagged at her, and she couldn't help calling out to him. "May I ask where you got that?"

The chancellor stopped abruptly, and she immediately regretted asking. It was none of her business. Maybe a friend had made it for him as a gift. But the golden crackling dessert was like nothing she had seen before. The attendant stopped, too, and wobbled with the stack of papers dangerously close to tumbling to the ground. Oblivious, the chancellor turned back to her with a mouthful of the crispy treat.

Through the bite, he said, "Oh, I got it from a charmingly odd fellow on the way to the market. Word is the newcomer plans to enter the contest. I must say, he is quite talented." He joked lightheartedly, "Might give everyone a bit of a challenge."

She knew he meant no harm in the jest, but her stomach plummeted with the million thoughts whirling in her mind. She stared down at the treat.

As if she didn't already have enough on her plate, now there was a mysterious challenger being added to the mix. Who was it? Were they a random passerby or someone who specialized in baked goods? And what if this unnamed newcomer decided to open a bakery of their own?

She took a deep breath and willed her anxious mind not to get ahead of itself. Deimos inched closer to her and leaned against her side. Her heartbeat returned to normal, and she placed a hand on his back gratefully.

Quickly, the chancellor amended, "I didn't mean to worry you."

"Oh, I'm not worried. I welcome the challenge," she lied.

"We will be looking forward to seeing what you come up with."

With a tight-lipped smile, she responded, "I can't wait."

Her grandmother would truly have welcomed the challenge, so why couldn't Abrielle do the same?

"We have no doubt in our minds that you will rise to the occasion. Everyone deserves a chance, do they not?"

She couldn't argue with any of that. But it was easier said than done, of course. Without knowing who her competitor was and what they were capable of, it was hard to tell who would win. But she was a Grainwick girl after all, just like her grandmother, and wouldn't give up so easily.

Setting her shoulders back decisively, she replied, "It will certainly be an interesting night." To be safe, she would need something exceptional to present to the judges for the contest. Her nerves inflated, making her feel like rising dough. This was a disaster.

Fourteen

Abrielle and Deimos were drenched in mud by the time they made it back to the cottage. The storm had done a number on the road through town and because Deimos had taken the journey on all fours, he had received the worst of it.

With worry about the contest still gnawing at her, she drew a warm bath for him with fumbling hands, then paused. He was still in his hound-form and for a moment, she wondered if he might expect her to bathe him like a domesticated pup. Her eyes flitted from him to the door, and he made a noise as if clearing his throat.

Then, with his strange bark-like voice, he said, "I need to shift."

In other words, *get out unless you wish to see me naked again.* Her eyes went wide, and she yelped, "Of course! I'll leave you to it then."

A small part of her considered staying to sneak a peek, but the sensible side of her was what had her moving to her feet. Drowning in embarrassment, she fled the washroom and left him to his own devices. While he bathed himself, she changed into a fresh dress and stockings. It made her feel brand new and ready to get to work.

There was no use in dwelling on the naked man upstairs or the mystery competitor she'd heard about in town. Better to keep busy and start coming up with something to wow the judges. She spent the rest of the afternoon tending to the bakery and putting together a few dinner items for customers who wandered in throughout the day. Deimos promised not to enter the bakery without shifting first, but so far there had been no sighting of him.

Abrielle hummed to herself as she worked on a particularly large batch of pie crust which she would store in the icehouse until the day before the festival. If she had all the dough and crusts prepared ahead of time, then all she would need to do is pop them into the oven the day of. Thankfully, the festival always began in the evening, so that left her plenty of time to get everything baked and packed up to go.

Next, she worked on fillings for the pies and pastries. She stirred fresh berries over the hearth with a hefty helping of sugar. The smell was divine. It was the perfect mix of sweet and tart, just like the taste would be.

As the berry mixture bubbled, she racked her brain for an idea that would win her the contest. Her grandmother had always opted to try a new recipe. But Abrielle clearly didn't have that sort of talent or creativity. She thought sadly of the crumble she had tried to serve Paddy the other day. She couldn't shake the look of uncertainty that had flashed across his face when she presented it to him.

If only she could figure out how to make it look more appealing. Her crumble was always delicious when topped on a pie, but if she could make it equally as good on its own, then it would be an easy dish to serve. She could make it a sort of special in the bakery after it won the contest.

She was getting ahead of herself. Whoever the mystery competitor was, she would bet they were going to do something to really impress the King and the other judges. Of course, there was always the option of using one of her grandmother's recipes, but she would also bet that the competition would be using recipes they had created themselves.

Removing the berry mixture from the hearth, she gazed up at her grandparent's portrait. All she needed to do was emulate what her grandmother had done. It had built the bakery into a success and doing things her way would ensure that it *remained* a success. If Abrielle simply followed her grandmother's path, then what could possibly go wrong?

Deimos tapped on the doorframe and peeked his head inside. His hair was still dripping wet from the bathroom and curled at the tips of his ears. A few strands fell into his face as he asked, "Is it safe to come out?"

Abrielle rolled her eyes. "If it wasn't, then you'd have given yourself away, anyway."

He ducked under the doorway and into the bakery. "I made sure I couldn't hear any voices. Besides, it's dinnertime. Isn't everyone at home with their families?"

She'd been so consumed with preparations that she hadn't noticed the time. The floor was cold—felt even through her wool stockings—as she padded over to the door and locked it. A chill had remained after the storm, and she shivered now.

Deimos shrugged off the cardigan he was wearing and draped it over her shoulders. It no longer smelled like her grandfather, but instead like the fresh soap Deimos had just bathed with. She drew it close around her as she watched him go into the kitchen. He clapped his hands together. "How can I help?"

"You can't," she drawled. "The dough... remember?"

"Right."

Was she imagining things, or was he flushing with embarrassment? Maybe he wouldn't feel bad if she gave him something else to do. She pointed to the creaky window frame. "I think a nail may have come loose there. If you're good with a hammer, you could fix it for me."

He perked up at that. "I've never held a hammer, but I'm sure it can't be any harder than summoning locusts." He chuckled.

Abrielle raised an eyebrow at him. "Was that a joke?"

"An attempted one." He shrugged.

Abrielle hefted her grandfather's trusty old toolbox from under the sink and handed it to Deimos. He took it as if it weighed no more than a leaf. When he opened it, she pointed to the hammer which still had her grandfather's initials, RG, carved into the handle.

Deimos ran a finger along the engraving.

"Robert Grainwick," Abrielle explained, "that was his name." Her eyes burned slightly as she stared down at it.

"It's a nice name." Deimos shifted uncomfortably, then asked, "The window?"

"Ah, yes!" Abrielle pointed to the loose part of the frame. "If you can fix it then that's one less thing for the handyman. Saves me a bit of money, so it would be a big help."

"I'm happy to do it." Deimos leaned over to inspect the loose nail.

Honestly, it was something Abrielle could have taken care of if she had the time. But the bakery was busy work, and she wanted to dedicate the same time and effort her grandmother had to it. If she won the contest, perhaps she could use the prize to hire someone to come fix things up. She bit her lip in embarrassment. Acknowledging that she might not be able to balance both the upkeep of the cottage and running the bakery felt like admitting defeat.

She made two simple sandwiches for them to eat for dinner, using some of the berry mixture she had simmered and a bit of apple butter she had left over from the fall. Deimos took bites in between hammering.

He seemed content, so Abrielle decided to revisit the crumble again. In a small pan, she stirred together oats and brown sugar. It turned a sticky golden color, and just before removing it from the heat, she added in a dash of powdered cinnamon.

Deimos stepped away from the window, which now hung perfectly tightened, and sniffed at the air. "That smells incredible."

"Really? It's something new I wanted to try. I just can't seem to find a way to make it truly special."

He leaned over her shoulder and inhaled deeply. "Smells pretty special to me."

His chest pressed against her shoulder and a warm shudder passed through her body. She was almost inclined to lean into him. *Almost.* Instead, she stepped to the side and asked, "Maybe you could be my taste tester?"

"I'd be glad to."

They both reached for the spoon and the open jar of cream sitting on the counter was knocked over. It tumbled into the crumble, completely drenching the dish. Abrielle gasped as Deimos clumsily reached for the bottle. His knuckles dipped into the pan and instantly, the cream changed before their eyes. It thickened into something white and fluffy like a cloud.

He cursed out loud and pulled his hand back quickly. "I'm sorry, Brie, I'm so sorry."

She squinted and leaned in to get a closer look at the cream. It was so soft and fluffy, and she had the deep urge to poke it. When she did, the cream stuck to her finger. She pulled it back, watching it string along like a spider's web.

"Interesting," she whispered in awe. Then she lifted the dish to her nose and sniffed it. Unlike the bread dough, it still smelled sweet and heavenly. What if...

An idea dawned on her and she rushed to the pantry to pull out the vanilla extract she had gotten at the market a few weeks ago. It was incredibly expensive to get vanilla in that form, but she was too excited to care if she wasted it.

After splashing a small bit of it onto the cream fluff, she mixed it gently. The fluff stuck to the wooden spoon, and she did her best to scrape as much as she could back over top of the crumble. She licked the spoon and her eyes widened in a pleasant surprise.

She shoved it toward Deimos. "Try this!"

His eyebrows rose, but he obeyed, opening his mouth so she could place the spoon on his tongue. When she pulled back, he smiled. "That's good!"

She didn't need good. She needed great if she was going to win the competition. The heat of the oven itched at her back. "Wait a minute."

Deimos dodged her as she fretted around the kitchen. Using a piece of parchment tied onto the end of the fire poker, she lit it in the oven and spun around with it. Deimos shouted, "Woah!" as he ducked out of her flaming path.

Before the fire could grow too big, she held it over the dish, aiming for the cream on top. Soon it was browning into beautiful golden bubbles and a dazzling aroma filled the air. She pulled the makeshift torch away from it and stared down in awe. Deimos plucked the poker from her hand and dumped it into a bucket of water sitting by the door.

When he returned, she quickly shoved a spoon into the dessert. Turning to him with hope bubbling up in her chest, she said, "Try now."

His reaction was all she needed. As soon as the gooey crumble met his mouth, a delightful moan rumbled from deep in his throat. "It's incredible."

Abrielle squealed and took a spoonful for herself. He was right. It was the best thing she'd made in a long time. The crumble stayed crisp and the fluff on top was the perfect combination of strange and delectable.

Deimos stepped to her side and leaned in close enough that she could feel his breath on the nape of her neck. "This is what you should make for the contest."

She turned her head toward him slightly, looking at him from the corner of her eye. "You really think so?" Her voice was soft and unsure. As good as it tasted, she wasn't sure it was as good as her grandmother's recipes.

Deimos placed a hand on her shoulder and tugged her to face him. "I do. I think you have a gift for creating things. For someone like me who only ever seems to destroy, it's fascinating to watch."

"You don't destroy everything." She offered a lopsided smile. "You fixed the window."

He scoffed. "By hammering it into submission."

Pointing at the fluff, she added, "And without you, I would have been missing the new key ingredient."

"*That* was an accident."

Abrielle put a hand on his chest. "Deimos, I couldn't have done this without you."

He placed his hand over hers and tilted his head slightly. "You would have found a way to make something amazing.

What you do, Brie, is a thing of beauty. Why do I get the sense you're doubting yourself?"

It hadn't always been that way. When she was with her grandmother in the kitchen, she had always felt sure. Had known exactly what needed to be done and if she didn't, she had the comfort of knowing that all she had to do was look to her grandmother for answers.

Her gaze dropped to Deimos' hand on hers.

"I can't fail." She blinked back tears threatening to fall. "There are so many things that could go wrong. If I don't use the right recipes..." her voice cracked. "If I don't do things the right way, then I could lose everything."

Deimos placed two strong fingers under her chin and tilted her head up so their eyes met. He furrowed his brow as he suggested, "Did you ever consider it's not the recipes that are the problem, but rather that you miss having someone to experience them with?"

Tears trailed down her cheeks, and she wiped them away with her apron. The lace itched her face, and she feared she might be a red, blotchy mess now. But she didn't answer him. She didn't think she had to. He'd been with her the last few days. It must have been painfully obvious how much she tended to isolate herself.

Deimos' frown deepened and his shadows danced in a nervous jitter just behind his head as he said, "Tell me something. What will do you do if you win the contest?"

The question startled her. But the answer was simple. "I could pay for repairs so I can focus on the bakery. This place isn't what it used to be, and I'm afraid that under my care it might fall into disrepair."

"No." Deimos' voice was firm, but kind. "What would you *like* to do with the money?"

Abrielle bit her lip. In her heart of hearts, she longed for more excitement. More noise. She thought of the cheerful voices each morning during the rush and how it made her feel alive. Then the truth hit her.

"I would make a place where no one would have to be lonely again. Where they could stay and eat and enjoy themselves. Where they could meet with friends and family they haven't caught up with in a while."

She realized they had been on the subject of *her* hopes and dreams for a while now. So, she asked him, "What about you? What do you wish for?"

Deimos' nose flared as he inhaled deeply. "I've never thought much about it. Never had many options or the time for dreams. But what you speak of sounds nice. I've never had a place like that. Where all were welcome and accepted. It shouldn't come as a surprise, but back home, my kind are outcasts. I've only ever had my brothers." His shadows pecked at his shoulder, and he laughed. "And my shadows."

He straightened and took a step away from Abrielle, leaving her suddenly very cold. She fought the urge to follow him and remained where she was with her hands balled in her apron.

Deimos raised his chin. "So, are you going to use this new creation of yours to win that contest and expand your bakery?"

Abrielle blushed so deeply she thought it must be reaching her chest. First, she corrected him, "*Our* creation." Then, she continued, "And I don't know that something like the expansion would work. What if nobody came? And besides, this is how my grandparents left the place. I don't know that I could ever change it so drastically."

Deimos bit his lip. "Brie, I didn't know them, but I think they would have wanted you to follow your heart. It seems to me that was what they did when they built this place and when they raised you."

This time, he stepped toward her and placed a hand on her cheek. His voice was husky as he said, "If you trusted your gut more, like you did with that dessert just now, you would be unstoppable."

A deep longing rumbled in her chest as he spoke. It wasn't the pang of loneliness and the longing for her family that she had become so accustomed to. This was something more passionate. She leaned into his hand. When they first met, she would have thought she would shy away from his touch.

He had reminded her of the midnight hour when the sun was long gone, and the air was crisp. Cold and forbidden. Lonely. But he wasn't like that at all. He was compassionate. Even as he lifted her hand to his mouth to kiss the back of it, his lips were as warm as a midsummer's day. Heat stirred in places she hadn't yet explored. But more than that, it felt as if her heart was so full that it might expand right out of her chest.

She knew what he was now. Where he had come from. The sort of business his family tended to back home in Selanthia. She was slightly more aware of how much power he held, yet it didn't stop the butterflies from growing wild in her stomach. But somehow, that's what made it all the more terrifying.

Fifteen

Abrielle was finally back in her normal routine. Aside from Deimos' steady presence, she would have thought everything was finally falling back into place. She had a recipe for the contest, which loosened the knots in her stomach about the new competitor. She'd taken care of preparations for the Star Crossed festival, which was a mere three days away. And she had gotten through the morning rush smoothly.

With all of that done, she busied herself with putting together a few piping bags for the icebox. Carefully, she mixed powdered beets into the vanilla frosting. With precision, she added in just enough to turn the topping red without allowing the beet's flavor to show through.

Deimos hadn't come into the bakery yet and she wondered if he was feeling as confused as she was after last night. There was no denying that they had shared a moment. But she wasn't sure what to make of it.

Maybe she was being foolish. Why open up to someone who wasn't going to stick around? Rumors were growing about the strange occurrences in town. Customers speculated all morning about a long-lost witch coming back to Ellamere. Or a problem with the water in the stream that ran through the village. No one could quite figure it out, but Abrielle knew the truth.

Deimos' summoning was the only real connection between it all. That and the fracture in the gemtower behind her home. Just that morning she had peeked at it when she'd gone to collect mint from the garden. The fracture had turned into a significant crack. Panicked, she'd run inside to stir up some frosting using pigment from flowers that would match the wintery color of the stone.

She felt foolish about it now. The gemtower wasn't one of her cakes. Covering something like that up with frosting wouldn't do anything but attract ants. And all it would take was one good rain to wash it away. But what else could she do? Her heart raced the more she dwelled on it. Would things get worse? So far, the occurrences were strange but miniscule. They hadn't done any actual harm. But was that because Deimos was holding back? Suppressing his power as he said. What if it was his use of magic when he shifted that was making the crack worse? And what happened if he lost control or if dampening it became too difficult for him?

The bell rang as Tansy walked in. She was smiling brightly and had a baby blue kerchief on her head. With her arms spread open in a grand show, she boasted, "I am a master of espionage."

Abrielle snorted, "Is that so?" Then realizing she could only be referring to the Mable search, she gasped. "Did you find her?"

Tansy clucked her tongue against her teeth. "Not exactly."

Abrielle's smile fell.

Tansy held up a finger. "But I'm close!"

Deimos strolled in and leaned lazily against one of the shelves. "What does close mean?"

"Thomaz's cousin works in the archives, and he got me in. There was only one Mable listed in the town registry. She must be at least eighty years old by now, and I'm not sure the address listed is current. I'm going to do some more digging and see if I can track her down."

"We can do that," Deimos suggested.

Tansy wrinkled her nose. "If you go pawing up to her front door while you're shifted into that beast of a thing, then you'll give the poor thing a heart attack."

Deimos grimaced. "I would hardly call her a *poor thing*. Don't be fooled just because she's elderly. A witch's power can be strong no matter what age she is."

Abrielle narrowed her gaze. "They can't all be dangerous. You said yourself that many used their gifts to help their community."

He went silent at that. Perhaps he'd had bad experiences with them, but Abrielle saw first-hand that not all magical beings harbored ill-intent. Deimos had shown her that in their short time together.

Tansy shrugged. "Either way, I've got it handled." She jabbed a finger in Deimos' direction. "You just need to focus on keeping a low profile." Next, she pointed at Abrielle. "And you need to ask Erik to the festival."

Abrielle's eyes darted to Deimos before she could stop herself. His gaze locked on hers with an intensity she didn't expect. Not even after last night. She bit her lip and said, "I don't know…"

Tansy must not have noticed the exchange because she kept encouraging her. "It can't hurt to ask. Thomaz and I will be going together, and Luna is even thinking of asking one of the guards who keeps finding reasons to come into her father's shop."

"I'll think about it," Abrielle blurted just to appease her friend.

It seemed to work because Tansy bid them farewell and bounded out of the house.

Deimos chuckled. "She's having way too much fun with this Mable mystery."

Abrielle laughed lightly. "She likes to help."

He followed her into the kitchen while she gathered up a few canvas bags to take to the farmer's market. Thursdays were always reserved for shopping. The palace didn't require a delivery on these days, so Abrielle had the chance to grab new and interesting things from the market.

Sometimes merchants would set up—stopping in while they passed through Ellamere's port. It was always exciting to see what other countries were using for their delicacies, even if she was too afraid to try them herself most of the time.

Tinker sidled up to Deimos, and he scratched her under the chin. A few gray hairs fluttered in the air, swirling with the shadows, which were inching closer to the cat. Abrielle could have sworn the stubborn feline was smiling as she tilted her head up to the ceiling to give him better access.

Deimos perked up as Abrielle untied her apron and asked, "No palace delivery today?"

"Nope." She readjusted her lacy trimmed blue skirt and added, "The farmer's market is today, so I thought I'd pop in and grab a few things for the festival."

He stood and walked to her side. Each step he took toward her filled her with an excitement she wasn't used to. It was like her nerves were telling her to flee, but also holding her in place with the anticipation of having him near.

She glanced at the corner near the window. That would allow her the space she might need in order to keep a clear mind around him. She swallowed heavily and said, "I just need to feed my sourdough, first."

She slid next to the glass jar housing the yeast mixture that she often used for her bread. She scooped a small portion from the top and disposed of it. The sound of Deimos' footsteps carried through the room as he followed.

With his body pressed against her side, he peered down warily. His nose crinkled in distaste and Abrielle stifled a laugh. The man was a powerful magical being, yet the yeast might as well have been a monster the way he was watching it.

Skeptically, he asked, "You *feed* it? What sort of creature is that?"

Abrielle choked with a laugh. As she added a bit of flour and lukewarm water from the bowl beside the sink, she explained, "Uh, it's not a creature... it's for making bread."

Deimos took a decisive step back and said, "I don't understand."

Patiently, she explained, "It helps the bread rise. But you have to make the bubbles appear first. By adding flour and water."

"I see." He waited for her to finish mixing it and then said, "Ready to go?"

Abrielle hesitated. He'd already gone out in town with her a few times now, but were they pushing their luck? With Tansy so close to locating the mysterious spell writer, it might be best to keep the lowest profile possible.

As if sensing her hesitation, he exclaimed, "I've been working on my glamor. I think I can appear a little less... well, you know." He shrugged awkwardly and then called on the nothingness.

As it circled him like a tornado coming to claim everything in its path, Abrielle leaned away. Though she had experienced the magic of that particular darkness before, it still made her woozy. Deimos' shadow friends drifted to her side. Even *they* appeared to be wary of the power that the void held.

When it dissipated, Deimos was in hound form once again. Only this time, the fur had a glossy sheen to it. He wasn't nearly as scraggly as before and almost looked as if he'd been to the groomer recently. Abrielle's heartbeat steadied as she circled around him.

"Impressive," she said. But he was still quite large, and his fangs were protruding from beneath his lip. There was no hiding the ferocity and power the canine held. Whatever effort he was putting in to keep his glamor under control was working to make him look less wild. But he most certainly did not look like a typical mortal realm hound.

She bit her lip as she gazed into his large, hopeful eyes. Then she relented, "Okay, you can come."

He loped to the door and nosed it until she turned the handle. The sun was beaming today, much to the little shadow tendrils' dismay. They tucked themselves well into Abrielle's canvas bags. She gave them a comforting pat and headed on their way.

To Abrielle's relief, the town appeared the same as ever. Each home they passed had neatly trimmed grass and unique decorations on the lawn. Paddy had an anvil at the end of his pebble drive, Tansy's father had little stone gnomes scattered by a cluster of trees beside his walkway, and Miss Rita had a lovely new sign over her bookstore.

Abrielle stopped for a moment to admire the brightly painted wooden sign. The one outside of her own shop hadn't been changed in many years. Not since her grandfather had presented it to her grandmother. It read: *Trish Grainwick's*

Bakery. But after all this time the lettering had begun to fade, making it difficult to read.

Not that anyone needed to be told what the little cottage housed. Even travelers passing through could guess that it was a bakery just by the delightful scent drifting through the door and the many customers streaming in and out during the busy hours.

There were times when Abrielle considered commissioning a new one. The only problem was she wasn't sure whose name to put on it. She could put her own name, but would that be betraying her grandmother's memory? Deep down, she knew her grandmother wouldn't mind. But she kept putting it off, nonetheless.

Abrielle kept a close eye on the crowds ambling through town. Each new face came with suspicion. Was her new rival amongst them? The chancellor had described him as a charming, odd fellow. Being with Deimos the last few days had her questioning her own definition of that. Would the competitor stand out in the crowd, or would she pass by him oblivious to who he was?

Soon the farmer's market came into view, with its stalls topped with colorful canvas to keep the summer sun at bay. Cheerful faces littered the square—some familiar and some newcomers from out of town.

Luna shouted from two stalls down. She had a bundle of wildflowers in hand and waved to them enthusiastically. She jogged over easily thanks to the pants she wore. While other girls in town always opted for traditional skirts and dresses, Luna preferred to do things differently.

When she reached Abrielle and Deimos she chuckled. "Cute... dog?"

"Thanks." Abrielle ignored the uncertainty in her tone. "Here with your father?"

"Yeah, he's over there talking to Tansy's father. I just grabbed these from her flower stand. No roses, today, though." She gave a little pout.

Both women waved at the two older men, who stopped haggling over a pair of leather boots long enough to shout a greeting. Then Luna turned her attention back to Abrielle. "You'll be at the festival, right? Are you going with anyone?"

Abrielle suppressed a sigh. Why was everyone so interested in her love life? Or lack of one. Still, she answered, "I'll be there, but I don't have an escort."

Luna winked. "They're overrated, anyway. Everyone acts like we women always need some man beside us. But let's be honest, they usually just get in the way."

Deimos let out a strangled laugh and Abrielle hoped Luna wouldn't notice.

She didn't seem to as she went on. "One of the palace guards asked me, but I think I'll go solo this year."

"That sounds—"

Abrielle was interrupted by a familiar wind-chime voice. "I agree! Who needs them?" Princess Greer strode toward their small group with a broad smile on her face. Her shining blonde hair was drawn into a braid with flowers intertwined in it. She was the very epitome of royalty, though Abrielle knew better than to underestimate her.

The Princess was a storyteller. She delighted in drawing people into her stories and loved to play pranks. Even in her twenties, she had not grown out of her antics. Not that she needed to as the youngest of her siblings. The King held her at a much lower standard than her older brother, who was in line for the throne. That's why Abrielle also wasn't surprised to find her at the farmer's market wandering around barefoot like a girl raised in the countryside.

She knelt in front of Deimos and squinted as she studied him. "*What in the Otherworlds?*"

Abrielle's heart leapt into her throat. "W-what did you say?"

"This is the biggest hound I've ever seen!"

Abrielle breathed a massive sigh of relief, realizing Greer was using the Otherworlds as an expression and not because she had instantly figured out their secret. When she rose, she put a hand on her hip.

"Does he belong to you?"

The question caught Abrielle off guard. Deimos was a person. Well, maybe not a human person, but he was his own being. He didn't belong to anyone. But she didn't want to confuse the women standing in front of her, so she opted to say, "He's staying with me for a little while."

Luna and Greer seemed appeased by that because they began chattering amongst each other. Meanwhile, Abrielle excused herself and made her way along each of the stalls.

Each person handling a stand smiled hopefully at her as she walked by. Awkwardly, she walked up to every single one, feigning interest in their wares. She had a few stalls that were her favorites, where she could find new ingredients and her favorite items. But with so many beaming smiles, she couldn't just stroll by without a glance at what they had to offer.

At one stand, she stopped to compliment a woman on the interesting socks she had strewn about. It was a chaotic setup with socks hanging from lines above Abrielle's head and laid out on three long tables. There were polka dots and zig zagged stripes as far as the eye could see. Although it wasn't Abrielle's style, she still admired the dedication and craft that went into making such things.

Ahead, one of her favorite stalls was set up. Armana, a woman from the southern isles, waved merrily. Abrielle greeted her pleasantly and beelined for the delicate soaps the woman made with oils from her home country. The scent was dazzling, reminding Abrielle of sunshine and the sea. She grabbed several and paid Armana.

With a heavy accent, the woman said, "What an interesting beast. Perhaps he would like a treat?"

Without waiting for an answer, she pulled out a sliver of dried fish. It was briny with a heavy stench from sitting out in the morning heat. Deimos took an alarmed step back and sneezed. Abrielle apologized. "We appreciate the offer, though," she added before dipping out of the stall with Deimos in sync beside her.

"Sorry about that," she whispered to him.

Across from Armana's stall were the farm stands. Crates were filled to the brim with the best that Ellamere had to offer. Abrielle turned a pomegranate over in her hands admiring the bright red color of it. The seeds would be a nice addition to the feast table and perhaps she could even use the juice from another for a refreshment.

Erik stepped up next to her and picked up a large, spiked fruit with an interesting yellow color. She wasn't sure why, but she tensed immediately. It was an unwelcome instinct and made her feel incredibly silly. When she was younger, it had been the same old story. She would get all clammy and say something embarrassing or do something clumsy when a cute boy was around.

She groaned internally. Why couldn't she relax and interact with Erik like she would any other person? Like she did with Deimos. With him, it was effortless. To be honest, she had been more open and at ease with him than she had been with anyone in a long time. Maybe it was because he wasn't human... or because she knew he would be gone soon.

A weird weight settled deep in her stomach and her chest tightened. She was so focused on the feeling that she hadn't heard what Erik said. He was staring at her with a puzzled look plastered on his face.

The pomegranate slipped from her hand and fell to the ground. Quickly, she bent down to grab it and clashed with Erik as he moved to do the same. They both went tumbling back into the dirt.

Abrielle squeezed her eyes shut wishing this was just a bad dream. When she opened them to reality, she apologized profusely. "I'm so sorry. I don't know where my head was."

Erik laughed lightly, picked up the pomegranate, and offered a hand to help her up. "That's alright. I was just asking if you were enjoying your morning."

"Oh, yes, I am very much." She paused, searching for something more to say—anything to make up for her fumble just now. Then, recalling Deimos' advice, she said, "That sword is nice. Is it new?"

The blade's hilt gleamed in a thin ray of sunlight. Erik placed a hand on it proudly and said, "Yes, the King commissioned it for me. Paddy does fine work."

"Always," she agreed.

"King Vasiri says I'm the finest guard he's seen since Galhane."

Galhane was one of the King's most trusted guards and in Erik's world she supposed it was a high honor to be listed amongst his name.

"That's amazing," she said, mustering false awe. Truthfully, she'd rather be talking about anything else.

Erik puffed out his chest.

The conversation wasn't going terribly after all. Maybe Deimos' advice was working. She took a deep breath and was about to ask him about the festival like she'd promised Tansy, but something tugged at her skirt. She yelped and looked down to find Deimos with his canine teeth latched onto the delicate lace.

"Deimos!" she shouted and pushed him back. He released his hold on her and shook his head angrily.

She had half a mind to scold him, even in front of the large crowd, but a loud crash from behind made her gasp. Erik grabbed her by the arm protectively, as if to draw her away from the unknown danger, but Deimos jumped between them. He pressed his body against her legs, pushing her away from Erik and whatever was happening across the way. It was difficult to see through the crowd which had gathered, so she inched closer, forcing Deimos forward slightly.

The villagers surrounded Thomaz's vegetable tent where the canvas roof had caved in. Something rather large shifted underneath and the crowd collectively stepped back with a gasp as the creature which had taken out the entire stall revealed itself.

The toad that wiggled out from the canvas flaps was as big as Tinker. Its skin was green and slimy, though, and it let out a croak that was as loud as a hog's squeal. Murmurs spread through the villagers' ranks. Some called it unnatural. Some claimed it was a bad omen. Others fled the scene altogether.

Abrielle's gaze fell on Deimos, but he wouldn't meet her eye. Erik and some of the other men helped Thomaz lift the poles of the stall, so she took the opportunity to slip away. She'd lost her appetite for pomegranates and anything else she might have found at the farmer's market.

The villagers were right about one thing. The toad was most certainly not an occurrence brought about by anything natural. And perhaps it *was* a bad omen. One that was trying to show them the horrible mistake she had made. Toads falling from the sky could only be compared to something plague-like. Something *Deimos-like.*

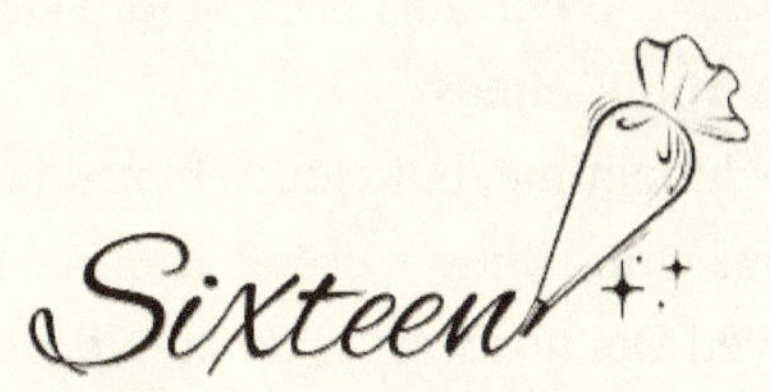

Sixteen

A brielle and Deimos walked back to the cottage in silence. He shifted the moment she shut the door. She took her time locking it to give him a chance to put on clothes and didn't turn around until she'd heard sufficient shuffling.

When she turned to him, he had his back to her. The muscles in his back were visibly taut through the light linen shirt he had on. It pulled at the seams, and she was surprised it hadn't yet ripped from the strain.

In all the days they had spent together, she had seen him worried, remorseful, and wistful, but never mad. Never lost in a seething anger like this. His hands were balled into fists on the counter, and she racked her brain for something to say.

Daring a step closer, she whispered his name. "Deimos? Are you alright?"

When he turned to her, purple shadows swirled in his black eyes. Through clenched teeth, he said, "I'm fine."

"You're lying." She crossed her arms. What happened to being honest with each other?

He shook his head and stomped into the living room. She followed, drawing the curtains back before sitting down on the sofa across from Deimos.

It was nearly lunchtime, but clouds blotted the sky. A vast difference from when they were at the market moments ago. Abrielle eyed Deimos warily. Could his mood affect the weather? She hoped not, considering the way he was brooding in the armchair. It could mean a torrential downpour.

His demeanor was unusual. Since coming to Ellamere, he had mostly been easy going. Even taking his summoning with a grain of salt. So, what had him so frustrated now? Her eyes flitted to her skirt where he had tugged her away from Erik.

"Was it something with Erik?" she asked. Though she couldn't see why their conversation would have sparked anger in Deimos. It was he after all, who had given her the advice in the first place.

The sky darkened even more, casting shadows in the room. Abrielle leaned forward to light a few candles on the small table between the sofas.

Deimos snorted with disdain. "What would make you think that?"

Abrielle shrugged. "Well, for starters, you interrupted us. I don't know why, though. Your advice was working. I thought, if anything, you'd be feeling very smug about that."

He scoffed. "Of course it worked. Mortals like him love talking about themselves."

Abrielle scrunched her nose. She might not have been well versed when it came to men, but she knew a spark of jealousy when she saw one. Was that what had caused the toad's appearance?

She switched gears. "Well, if it's not Erik, then was it the toad?"

Deimos leaned forward, hovering his hand over one of the candles. The flame flickered in his presence as he said, "I was reminded today just how vulnerable this realm is to my existence."

"We already sort of knew that though, didn't we?" She had been on edge since learning what he was and the sort of effect he could have on her world. Maybe she had become too comfortable around him, and it *was* making her forget the dangers involved. Why else would she be less concerned about the toad than he was?

Deimos pinched the flame between his fingers. His gaze followed the smoke as it snaked up to the ceiling, but Abrielle kept her eyes trained on him.

His throat sounded tight as he said, "Magic doesn't flow freely here in Ellamere. You have no idea how much effort it takes to control myself because of that. I should be master to my power, not the other way around. Someone could have been hurt."

"But they weren't," she blurted it out instantly. It was the truth. Thomaz's vegetables were sure to have some bruising, but none of the villagers had been injured in the fall.

Her assurances seemed to fall flat, because he huffed. "It's taking too long to send me back." His eyes fell on her. "What if I hurt you? It seems no matter how hard I try to contain my power, it finds a way to seep through and do what it was meant to."

His hand still lingered near the candle, and Abrielle reached out to take it. She gave him a light squeeze and said, "I might not understand your power, but if you had *meant* to harm anyone then you would have done it by now. Accidents happen. What matters is that you keep trying to do the right thing."

His brow furrowed, but he didn't pull away from her. Raindrops began to fall outside. They tapped softly on the window in a steady rhythm that matched the way Deimos' shoulders rose and fell with each breath he took.

Abrielle pulled back and looked out the window. A few of her neighbors ran by with jackets over their heads to shield them from the rainfall. *At least it's not frogs.* She bit her lip. Maybe what Deimos needed right now was space. Besides, she needed to clear her mind.

Silently, she went to the kitchen to find comfort in baking. Perhaps some chocolate chip cookies would lift his dark stormy mood. And the methodic steps of making the dough would help steady her nerves. She pulled out the parchment that had her grandmother's recipe written on it and followed each step.

The chocolate morsels were her favorite part and when she was younger, she would always sprinkle in a few extra when her grandmother wasn't looking. As she took them from the small canvas sack, she peeked up at her grandparent's portrait. Then, with a cheeky grin, she dumped in an extra handful. That was a sure way to cure any sour mood.

Soon she was so focused on stirring and rounding out the smaller balls of dough that she hardly noticed the rain pitter pattering on the roof. Nor did she notice Deimos until he was standing at the back door.

"What are you doing?" she asked, noting his hand on the handle.

"I just wanted to get a little air."

"Do you think it's wise to go out like that?" She bit her lip. Paddy and Luna had most likely returned from the market by now. They had probably shut the whole thing down for the day due to the weather.

He pointed out the window and said sullenly, "There's no one out there. Your neighbors are probably curled up by a fire right about now, trying to dry off."

"Okay…" Abrielle teetered on uncertainty, but she didn't want to control what he did. He was his own person, and it wasn't her place to keep him locked away.

Deimos shut the door gently behind him and Abrielle couldn't stop herself from peeking out the kitchen window every few seconds. Every once in a while, she would catch sight of him meandering in the garden. And after a bit, she stopped checking. She took a deep breath. Everything was fine. It was fine.

She lost herself once again in the familiar scent and peace of baking. Two trays of cookies had been baked into warm, soft, perfect circles. She stacked them on a round wooden display, smiling softly to herself, until muffled voices grabbed her attention.

Her heart skipped a beat as she ran to the back door. Sunlight once again drifted through the window. When had it stopped raining? And where was Deimos? She threw open the door and nearly tripped trying to get outside.

Paddy's voice boomed cheerfully. "Miss Grainwick!"

Abrielle's heart was racing as she took in the scene before her. Deimos was standing face to face with Paddy and Luna. Their secret was completely and utterly exposed. Or at least that's what she thought until she got a closer look at Deimos.

His eyes were still dark with a purple hue to them, but there were now whites in them much like her own. When he smiled, it wasn't pointed like it usually was, except for two canines which were sharper than a mere mortal's would have been. He looked more human than she was used to, but if she focused hard enough, she could see through the guise to find that same otherworldly quality about him.

The father and daughter duo, however, did not seem to notice. Deimos smiled nervously at Abrielle when she joined them.

Paddy said, "We were just getting to know your friend here. Nice lad."

"Yes," Abrielle said slowly, "he's..." She wasn't sure how to finish that sentence. They had no clue how close they were standing to magic.

She locked eyes with him. What was he thinking right now? The rain had stopped, but he'd been seen. There went their plan for keeping a low profile.

Luna cleared her throat and cast them both an amused smile. "Well, we'll let the two of you get back to the rest of your day."

She grabbed her father by the arm and tugged him out of the garden and back to their home. Once they were gone, Abrielle shook out her sweaty palms. By the fates, now her neighbors would think that she was having a man stay in her home. An eligible bachelor as far as they could tell who was incredibly handsome. Staying with an unmarried woman. Her magical mistake might not have been revealed, but this was sure to stir up some gossip if they told anyone.

"It worked," he chuckled in awe.

Abrielle's mouth gaped open. "It worked? You let them find you on purpose?"

"No," he answered quickly. "I didn't expect them, but they saw me from their window rooting around in the garden and came to see if I was trespassing."

"And the glamor? Is that what you're using now?"

"I was testing it before they came outside. Trying to see if I could take control and keep anything like this morning from happening again."

Abrielle's gaze flitted to the tree line where the gemtower was tucked away. What would this mean for the fracture? Still, she couldn't help but be amazed at Deimos' trick of the eye. She peered closer at him. At first glance, he did look like a mortal man. Still much taller, and broader than most, but if you looked closely, there was an air of something ethereal. She wasn't sure how Luna and Paddy had missed it. And yet, they hadn't raised any alarms. They had simply introduced themselves and then went on their way.

Tinker mewed from the doorway and Abrielle was reminded of the third batch of cookies in the oven. To Deimos she said, "I have to get back inside."

"I'm going to stay out here a while longer if that's alright with you." The clouds had officially lifted from over his mood and Abrielle didn't have the heart to tell him he still needed to be careful.

As she walked inside, he called out to her, "Could I borrow your grandfather's toolbox?"

"What for?"

Deimos hesitated, then said, "I thought I'd fix up a few things out here. If that's alright with you."

"Sure." Abrielle grabbed the hefty box from under the sink and handed it to him. She studied him for a moment, wondering what sort of projects he planned to tackle, but she certainly didn't want him to think she was ungrateful for the help. So, she went back inside to do the one thing she *was* certain about. The thing she relied on to soothe her soul. She baked.

Abrielle was exhausted by the time she cleaned the kitchen. She'd been at it for hours. Worry for Deimos and the secret they held about how he had ended up there to begin with left her in a haze. Before she knew it three trays of cookies had turned into four trays, five apple tarts, six blueberry crumbles, several loaves of bread along with more to bake in the morning, and a hearty beef stew.

She was literally cooking and baking her troubles away. Deimos must have been doing something similar, but with a hammer instead of a whisk. He had only come inside once for a tall glass of fresh squeezed lemonade. Abrielle had tried to bring it out to him as a peace offering to show that she wasn't upset with him about the run in with Paddy and Luna—she was just worried. But he had abruptly stopped her at the threshold and ushered her back into the house, claiming it was too muggy outside to enjoy the lemonade.

Instead, he chugged the refreshment in the kitchen, then ducked back outside before she could question him. She supposed there was plenty for him to do. The gutters were in desperate need of a cleaning with all of the rainy days they'd had lately—including the mood induced one she suspected Deimos had caused earlier. There was also plenty more to keep him busy; other odds and ends like loose stones and the creaky door to the icehouse.

Deimos seemed perfectly content to lose himself in the work and Abrielle could relate. Now she had plenty to offer customers in the morning. People from all over Ellamere would be pouring into the small village for the festival. The inns were already booked solid and rarely offered anything other than porridge for breakfast.

As Abrielle began packing a few things for the festival—jarred goods she had wrapped with neat little bows for people to take home and enjoy afterward—Deimos came inside. The sun was going down and he looked as tired as she felt.

His shirt was off now, revealing tight muscles covered in sweat and dirt. He wiped at his brow with a calloused hand and her knees nearly gave out. The same feelings she'd had whenever he was near enough to touch her returned and she sucked in a nervous breath.

Although she was inexperienced, she knew what it was like to want someone. Erik for starters. But Deimos... He made her stomach do somersaults. She wasn't sure what to make of it. Nothing could be done. He would be leaving as soon as they tracked down Mable. But it didn't change the fact that he was standing in front of her at that moment.

He sent a lopsided grin in her direction. "Dinner smells amazing."

Abrielle blinked rapidly, snapping out of whatever lustful trance he'd had her in just now. "Your timing is perfect." She ladled a large helping into a stone-fired bowl and set it on the table for him.

Instantly, he took a big chunk of beef from it and shredded it, placing it under the table for Tinker. She purred in thanks. The two of them were becoming fast friends. Nothing like good food shared to warm even the crankiest of hearts.

The air around Deimos seemed much lighter than earlier. He spoke between bites. "I like your neighbors."

"They're good people."

"Seems like they really care for you." He stared at her over his bowl with an intense gaze that warmed her to the core.

Abrielle shifted in her seat. Paddy and his family had lived next door since she could remember. The old blacksmith had been a good friend to her grandfather. But once her grandfather had passed on, it was difficult to be around him. Accepting his help when he offered it meant having a constant reminder of what she was missing. She didn't need any more of those than she already had.

When Abrielle said nothing, Deimos changed the subject. This time, his smile fell slightly. "I'm sorry about earlier. It wasn't fair to expose you to that side of me."

Abrielle chuckled. "Deimos, we all get a bit down sometimes. I've had my fair share of moody days."

"Yes, but do yours usually stir up rain clouds?"

No, they did not. She pressed her lips together.

Deimos continued, "I've been practicing, and I think I have a handle on it. As long as I focus."

"You need to go easy on yourself." She almost couldn't believe the words had slipped from her mouth. How many times had Tansy and even her grandmother said something similar to her, encouraging her to take a break and not worry so much? Even Deimos had told her as much. Maybe it was time he took his own advice. She could see how hard he was trying.

Deimos shrugged. "I like this town. I like the people." His gaze fell heavily on her as he set his spoon down. "I just don't want to be the reason anything bad happens."

Abrielle wondered how many times in his life Deimos had tried to be *good*. Had attempted to change or ignore who—or what—he was. She reached across the table and took hold of his hand. His callouses scratched her skin, but it brought her as much comfort as it seemed to be bringing him. The color of his cheeks brightened. And for a moment while they sat hand in hand, it was as if the rain had washed all the badness of the day away.

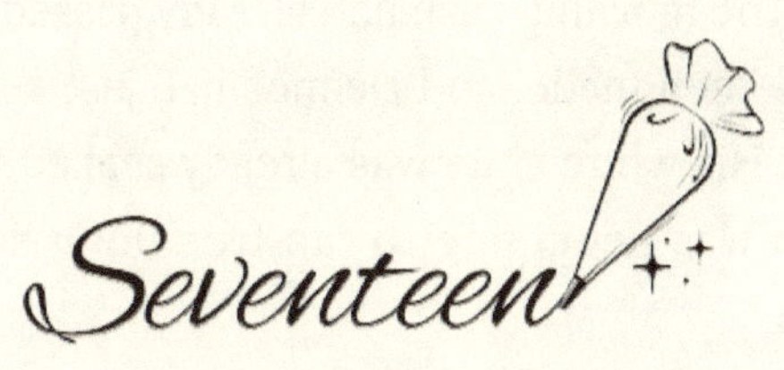

Seventeen

The next two days flew by. Abrielle was so busy keeping up with the many villagers and travelers pouring in early in the mornings and with last minute preparations for the festival that she'd hardly had any time at all to relax.

Deimos, too, was preoccupied during daylight hours. Abrielle wasn't sure how she had let the cottage fall into such duress, but it seemed he had found plenty to keep him hammering away at all hours of the day.

Whenever she tried to venture out back to sneak a peek at his projects, he would shoo her away, insisting that he wanted her to wait until he was finished. Although she appreciated a good sturdy nail on a board as much as the next, it wasn't exactly a marvel to behold so she wasn't sure what he was so excited about. Eventually, she assumed he was just proud of a job well done.

Since the day with the toad, they hadn't spoken any more about Erik or the events of that morning. Instead, they had focused on other things. Like taste testing the creation she'd been practicing for the contest or checking in with Tansy about her progress in finding Mable.

It was actually at that moment that Tansy strutted into the bakery. The morning rush had already passed, the palace delivery had been made, and Deimos had just come in for a quick break. His white shirt was already soaked with sweat, and his skin was beginning to tan from long hours in the summer sun.

Tansy whistled when she saw him. "Wow, you look…"

He smiled slyly. "It's the glamor. I think I've finally mastered it."

"Right." Tansy drawled as her eyes roved to his chest. When he turned to set his glass in the sink, she mouthed scandalously to Abrielle, *he's gorgeous.*

Abrielle's face instantly flushed. Of course, she'd noticed how handsome Deimos was when he disguised himself as a mortal, but she preferred him in his true form. Blackened eyes and all. It was more natural seeing him that way. More fitting. But she wouldn't deny how good he looked with that shirt unbuttoned at the top.

Tansy hopped onto the table in the kitchen and swung her legs. To Abrielle, she said, "How much do you love me?"

Abrielle gasped. "You found her, didn't you?"

Tansy jutted out her bottom lip. "No fair, you didn't play along."

"You know I love you dearly. Now please, tell me."

Tansy tilted her chin up. "I found her."

A glass shattered in the sink and both women stared wide-eyed at Deimos. He cursed and shook out his hand, which had been nicked by a shard. Abrielle rushed to his side and fussed at the cut. She dabbed a clean washcloth in some fresh water and pressed it to the side of his hand.

He griped at her. "I'm fine, Brie. It's just a little cut."

She ignored him, grabbed a jar of healing herbs from a cupboard and pressed them on his injured hand as she said, "Just hold still."

He hissed slightly. *Big baby.* And then she wrapped it in some fresh dressings. Tansy watched silently, waiting for them to finish. Something ruffled Abrielle's hair and she side eyed the shadowy tendrils that were peaking over her shoulder.

When she was done, she turned to face Tansy but remained at Deimos' side. Tansy glanced between the two of them with narrowed eyes. After a beat, she said, "Yeah, so I found the last known address for Mable. I didn't want to go marching up to her house by myself, so I left a note requesting that she meet us at the festival." Tansy held up a folded piece of parchment. Then giddily added, "She responded!"

Abrielle's throat tightened. "She's going to meet us?"

"Yes." Tansy's curls bounced as she nodded excitedly.

Deimos' voice was rough as he asked, "Tomorrow?"

"Yes. After the contest at the festival." Tansy crossed her arms over her chest, crumpling the letter. "Why don't the two of you seem more excited? This *is* what you wanted, right?"

"Of course," Abrielle said far too loudly.

Deimos chimed in, less enthusiastically. "Yeah, of course."

Tansy shot them a skeptical look. "Alright, then. I'll see the two of you tomorrow." Before she bounded out the door, she turned to Abrielle who was following closely behind so she could lock up and asked, "Did you invite Erik to the festival?"

Abrielle glanced at Deimos over her shoulder. He was already headed back out to the garden and didn't seem to be listening in. Somehow Erik had become a touchy subject. After Deimos' reaction at the farmer's market, she couldn't help but wonder why he cared so much. Especially when he would be gone soon.

"No. I haven't. I thought I would just see him there."

"If you say so." Tansy gave her a halfhearted smile and said her goodbyes.

Once she was gone, Abrielle leaned with her back against the door. Tinker padded in her direction and rubbed along her stockings. Abrielle slid to the floor, pulling the tabby cat onto her lap. The comfort of the grumpy feline's fur under her fingers brought little comfort. Tinker squirmed. Abrielle released her hold and allowed the tabby to jump off her lap. She didn't run off, though, instead she let out a long, depressing meow.

"Same," Abrielle said as if she understood the cat. Tinker had become accustomed to Deimos. Just last night, Abrielle had made fun of him for letting Tinker lick his arm like he was a fellow cat that needed grooming.

Tansy's news should have been welcomed by all in the little cottage. Instead, Tinker was whining, and Abrielle was left with a sense of emptiness. It was awfully close to the loneliness that often settled over her prior to his arrival.

Deimos wasn't her family, but he *had* grown to be her friend. They'd shared enough with one another to earn that title. But they had both known it couldn't last. Even if he was getting better at hiding who and what he was, it was no way for him to live. He couldn't go the rest of his life pretending to be something he wasn't. No one deserved to live that way.

There was a soft rapt on the back door and Abrielle stood quickly to find him standing in the doorway to the garden. He looked down at the floor sheepishly, then back up at her. She crossed the room to see what was wrong, but when she reached him, he smiled.

The purple in his eyes glinted in the soft rays of light seeping through the window and door as he said, "Brie, I wanted to ask you something."

He took hold of her arm gently—the one she had injured that first night when he'd appeared in her house. His thumb grazed along her bare skin, tickling the sensitive part of her wrist. He shook his head.

Abrielle bit the inside of her cheek. A million thoughts ran through her head. Was he going to ask to find Mable sooner? Maybe he didn't want to wait another moment. Perhaps he was tired of fighting so hard to suppress his magic and disguise himself.

He cleared his throat and said, "I admit, I've enjoyed my time here with you. It's been nice watching someone *create* rather than destroy." He ruffled his hair with his free hand. The glamor had dropped now, and he was back to the same familiar Deimos she had grown so used to.

His thumb continued to trace small loops along her wrist as he said, "I've told you about my family's business. How the natural order demands that we use our power for destruction. But these last couple of days I've fixed loose stones and tightened stray boards and I've..." He was speaking rapidly and sucked in a long breath. "I've *fixed* things and I've made things. Beautiful things. I'm finally doing something good rather than ruining everything."

Abrielle's heart warmed. She appreciated all the hard work he'd been putting in, even if she hadn't had the chance to see all of it yet. But she wasn't sure what she could say. She wasn't sure where he was going with any of this and part of her—the part she had walled off after the loss of her grandparents—dared to hope. Though, she wasn't sure what she could hope *for*. Their situation was out of the ordinary. There was no recipe to help her navigate it.

He chuckled. "I'm rambling. What I want to ask is if I could escort you to the Star Crossed festival?"

Abrielle's heart leapt into her throat and butterflies bloomed to life in her stomach. He wanted to go to the festival? *Together*? That was something couples did... What did that mean for their meeting with Mable?

His smile grew taut as he added, "As a final farewell."

Her heart sank a little. *Oh.* It was a simple goodbye and nothing more. She hesitated, unsure of how she felt about the whole thing. She had planned on going alone—deciding not to approach the subject with Erik again because she had so much on her plate. But she supposed Deimos would have to come either way to meet with the witch.

Before she could gather her thoughts, he exclaimed, "Don't answer yet. I have something to show you first."

Abrielle wasn't in a joking mood, but she attempted one anyway. "If it's a nail or a piece of wood, I have to say it's really not my thing. I'm more of a pretty new teacup or hand-woven blanket, kind of girl."

"It's not a nail and wood. At least, not exactly."

With a kind tug, he pulled her outside with him.

She wasn't prepared for what she saw. Beside the garden, the space had been utterly transformed. Beautiful glittering stones were laid flat to the side of the cottage in view of the cobblestone street. Carefully crafted wooden tables and benches were strategically placed throughout, allowing enough room for people to maneuver around the space. There were emerald green and white striped canvases propped on a pole by each table offering shade from the beating sun.

And above it all, attached to the roof was a sign. It was hand carved, and the bold black letters were painted with excellent handwriting. It read:

Brie's Bakery

Come and Sit a While

A warm tear drifted down Abrielle's cheek. Deimos wiped it away with a calloused finger. She was left speechless and unable to take her eyes off of the sign bearing her name. She wasn't sure how long she stood there awestruck at the care that had gone into creating the patio, but she was incredibly aware of Deimos' steady presence at her side. In just a couple short days, he had brought her dream to life.

Finally, she spoke. "It's incredible."

Incredible didn't even cover it. Once she found the ability to move her feet, she walked to each of the tables. Each had a metal vase sitting on top and was filled with wildflowers from the outskirts of her garden.

Deimos followed closely behind and explained, "The vases were Luna's idea."

Abrielle glanced up in surprise.

He continued, "She and Paddy helped a bit. I told them I wanted to do something nice for you after all the kindness you've shown me since I've been here."

Tears threatened to choke her as she said, "But, Deimos, it's my fault you were forced here in the first place. If it weren't for me and my foolishness, then you wouldn't have been stranded here, forced to glamor yourself and made afraid of what you might do."

How could he have put so much effort into thanking her when he should have been blaming her?

Deimos stepped close to her and placed a hand on her cheek. He wiped away more tears as they fell and said, "Fool-ish is the last word I would use to describe you. There is no recipe for life, Brie. The only thing we can do is keep trying different things until we get it right. You're not the only one who has made mistakes. I've made many myself. More than

I care to admit. But how can things ever change—ever get better—if we don't give something new a chance?"

She hung her head. "My grandmother always made it look so easy. Sometimes I wonder if I didn't inherit that same talent."

"I don't believe that for a second. And I think if she were here now, she'd tell you that you're wrong. You spend so much time trying to live up to her memory that I think you might have lost sight of her belief in you. She entrusted this bakery to you. Her life's work."

Abrielle looked around at the patio. At the thing she had hoped for but had been too afraid to actually create. But Deimos hadn't been afraid. He had brought her dream to life.

He tilted her chin up. "Don't you think it's time you stopped living in someone else's shadow and stepped into the sunlight?"

His shadows—which were tucked beneath his arms flickered almost in protest to the mention of the sun. Her own heart fluttered, too. Until now, she always thought of the bakery as her grandmother's. Like it was something Abrielle was just tending to until the true owner returned. But her grandmother was gone, and she knew that Deimos was right. The tender, encouraging woman wouldn't have wanted Abrielle to remain trapped in time like that. Instead, she would want Abrielle to feel as if the bakery was in fact hers to keep.

What Deimos had done here was the greatest gift she had ever received. A deep sadness washed over her as she realized how much she wanted him to stay. There was no denying that. Not anymore.

"I'm going to miss you," she whispered.

He didn't respond, and for a terrifying moment she thought maybe she'd overstepped. She began to pull away, eager to put distance between her and the embarrassment, but he grabbed her hand.

In one swift movement, he drew her in and put his other hand on the small of her back. His dark eyes bore intensely into hers, and his lips parted slightly. But he didn't lean in. Made no move to press his mouth to hers.

What are you waiting for? She wanted to groan out loud. Her body buzzed with excitement and her limbs grew stiff with anticipation.

As if taking their cue, his shadows took it upon themselves to wrap around the two of them and push them further together. *Time to step into the sunlight,* Abrielle said to herself as she reached up on her tippy toes and kissed Deimos.

As their lips met, it was like a thousand tiny stars burst in her head all at once. His hand went to her hair, ruffling a few strands from the neat braid, and encouraging her to kiss him more deeply. His lips were soft and warm. She reached up, placing her hand on his jaw and brushing against the slight stubble that had grown over the last few days. Her heart raced as she lost herself in his embrace. Who needed a recipe for life when you could craft something this wonderful without one?

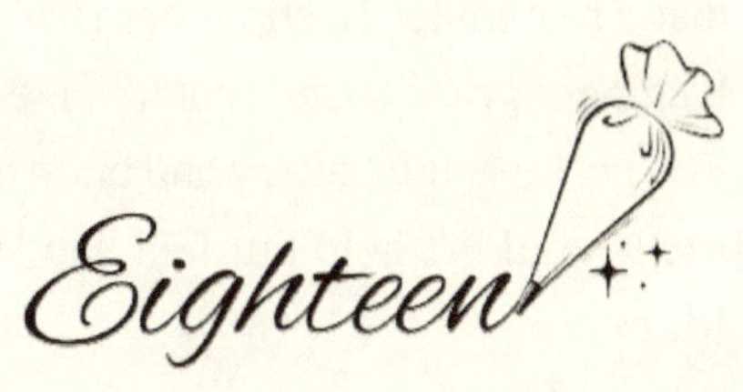

Eighteen

The kitchen was as chaotic as Abrielle's life. Pots and pans filled the sink, dishes and baskets with baked goods tucked safely inside littered the table, counters, and even the floor. As for her life... Well, Abrielle had gone from wishing for more excitement to getting more than she could handle.

She removed her apron and tossed it carelessly behind her. Her hand drifted to her lips, where the ghost of Deimos' touch still lingered. They had kissed. *Kissed.* No one had kissed her since two summers ago when Thomaz's gangly cousin had come to visit. And that had been nothing more than a fling.

This was... well, she didn't know what this was. It didn't feel the same as a carefree, flippant summer with someone she didn't care to ever see again. Deimos had inadvertently become her friend and confidant. And after what he'd done for her—created for her—how could she not have wanted to kiss him?

It wasn't just the patio and the sign. Though it was something she would cherish for a long time to come, it was the act itself. The fact that in his predicament, he had selflessly done something to make her smile. To show her that he cared.

It was something her grandfather would have done for her grandmother. The cottage and bakery had been his love letter to her. And Abrielle couldn't help but feel like Deimos' patio was the same for her.

The rapid beating of her heart rose and for a moment, she allowed herself to imagine what life would be like if Deimos did stay. He'd been working so hard to get a handle on his magic. One thing she was realizing was that if he put his mind to something, there was a good chance he'd be able to do it. Would it even be possible to convince him to stay, though? Maybe the kiss hadn't meant to him what it had meant to her, after all. It was likely just a goodbye kiss. He hadn't mentioned it all day. Perhaps the grand gesture yesterday was simply a thank you for hiding him and not turning him over to King Vasiri's guards.

She jolted as Deimos called for her from the living room, "Ready to go?"

"R-ready," she stammered, smoothing down her hair, which she was wearing in loose waves today. The sound of Deimos rummaging around in the other room echoed through the bakery, and Abrielle quickly adjusted her flower crown. With all the preparations, she hadn't had a lot of time to dedicate to it. She'd thrown it together late last night in her room as she replayed the kiss with Deimos over and over in her mind. One small red poppy dangled from the green garland, and she hastily tucked it back in. It didn't matter that the crown didn't quite match her dress, which was a flowing sky blue with butterflies embroidered on it. The delicate winged creatures trailed from her hip, across the bodice, and up to her shoulder. Luna's mother, Nia, had a way with embroidery and the butterflies looked as if they were fluttering carefree in the wind.

But there were more important things than what she was wearing. The contest being one of them. The prized dessert was resting on the counter in separate pieces. If she put it all together now, then it might arrive at the festival soggy and sad. Instead, she had the crumble placed in a delicate dish painted with bluebirds and yellow butterflies to match her dress. It was one of her grandmother's favorites and warmed Abrielle's heart to know she was bringing a little piece of her along.

The fluff, which Deimos had helped with earlier that morning was safely secured in a glass jar, ready to be plopped on top when the time came. It was as ready as it was going to be. All she could do now was hope that it would be enough to wow the judges.

Deimos finally made his appearance in the bakery, and the breath that escaped Abrielle's lips when she saw him would have been enough to blow out a thousand candles. Nia had generously offered to make him something to wear at the last minute. According to Deimos, he had explained to Luna that his luggage had been lost on his journey to Ellamere—Abrielle still wasn't sure where he was telling people he had traveled from—and Luna had insisted he allow her mother to make him something for the festival.

The outfit fit him effortlessly. The pants were made of a fitted lightweight linen without being too snug. His white linen shirt was unbuttoned at the top and on the collar, Nia had embroidered a moth. Its body was a pattern of black and gray zigzags and swirls. It faintly reminded her of his shadows.

"Wow," she breathed. "You look..."

"Like a mortal man?" Deimos set his shoulders back proudly.

Actually, he did, with his glamor set in place. Her nerves grew taut. This could be their last night together, and it saddened her to know that he couldn't fully be himself for it. There was nothing to be done about that, though. As much as she preferred his true appearance, it wouldn't be safe for him to show it to the entire town.

He took a step toward her, and she noted the boots he was wearing. "Paddy?" she asked, pointing down at them.

"Tansy, actually. Her father had a spare pair in his shop." There was a twinkle in his eye. "Your friends are incredibly generous."

"That they are." She rubbed her arm uncomfortably as he came close enough to touch her. They hadn't been this close to one another since their kiss. Every part of her felt heavy. She ducked her chin, hoping to hide the uncertainty in her eyes.

Deimos' voice was low as he said, "About yesterday—"

The bell at the door chimed, and Tansy and Luna waltzed in with their arms linked. Abrielle took a large step back and forced a broad smile as she greeted them. Both women were dressed in their best, wearing gowns that were worthy of their beauty. Their floral crowns were detailed with wildflowers and expertly braided together.

Abrielle adjusted her own and wished she had put more effort into it. Deimos seemed to notice because he pulled her aside as the other women fussed over how delicious everything looked and smelled.

He leaned down and pulled something from under the counter. "I wasn't sure if you had your own. Luna mentioned the custom, so I thought I'd offer..." He straightened and held out a flower crown as he finished, "this."

Abrielle stared down with her mouth open wide. It was stunning with a twisting pattern of blue and yellow flowers. The same ones in the vases on her patio tables. It must have taken an excruciating amount of effort for him to handle the delicate flowers without wilting them. Her palms began to sweat. Yet another gift from Deimos. So many kind gestures, yet she had done little to deserve them.

"If you'd rather wear yours, then I understand." Sweat was beading on his temple and Abrielle wasn't sure if it was from nerves or from the strain of holding his glamor.

"No," she said quickly. "I would love to wear yours."

Her body buzzed as Deimos plucked her crown from her head and put his in its place. Although it was dainty and light, it weighed heavily on her, along with the deep longing in her chest. The words were on the tip of her tongue. *Stay in Ellamere.* But she couldn't find the courage to say them out loud.

Tansy drawled, "Let's go! I want to get your things set up before the dancing starts."

Abrielle inhaled deeply through her nose. "Alright, let's go."

The four of them loaded baskets and trays onto the little wagon Abrielle's grandfather had built years ago. The wood was old and creaked under the weight, but it did the job. Deimos gallantly pulled it along as Abrielle and the others walked side by side down to the lake.

The water glittered under the warm glow of the evening sunlight. Blankets were laid out along the edge in the grass, each already occupied by groups of people—couples, families, friends—all smiling and chatting amongst themselves.

A few had taken it upon themselves to set tall tree branches against one another like makeshift tents, creating a little triangle shaped haven. Small twinkling lanterns were already lit throughout the clearing, offering extra light.

Long oak tables had been placed strategically to the side. The King's staff had worked tirelessly to lay out a wonderful fare. Trays of turnips, fruits, and dried meat were scattered along the pink table runners. Fish, with citrus fruits adorning them, laid amongst bowls of sauces and sides. Roasted potatoes, meat pies, figs, and nuts were also present. And everything smelled heavenly.

Beside the tables were large cauldrons of stew—beef, vegetable, and pork—all kept warm over a fire. And on the other side of those was Abrielle's designated table. It was already topped with a pale pink muslin runner.

She nodded to it, and Deimos began unloading the cart. Abrielle joined him, starting with the pies. Tansy and Luna reached to grab a few things, but she stopped them.

"Go and enjoy yourselves. I can do this." There was no reason that they had to miss the beginning of the festival when she could easily unload and organize the table herself.

They both argued for a moment, but Abrielle didn't budge. Eventually, they gave up and loped off to join Thomaz and a few others from the farm. Deimos returned to the cart to balance a few trays on his arms, careful not to touch the food itself. They both knew the consequences of him and the food mingling.

As he set them on the table, Abrielle offered, "You can join them if you'd like. I really can handle this on my own."

"You can, but you don't *have* to." Deimos brushed by her to grab the fruit tarts.

"Yes, but it's your last night here." She bit her lip to quell the ache in her heart. "You should go and have a good time."

"The sooner we finish here, the sooner we can both go and have a good time." Stubbornly, he continued to unload.

Abrielle gave up and got to work. By the time they finished, the table was stuffed end to end with desserts and breads. Abrielle strategically placed a few jars of spreads—strawberry jam, fig preserves, hot pepper cheese, and others—along the table. Then she added a few flowers from Tansy's garden to fill any spaces that were left.

It was a job well done, in her opinion. As it should have been, considering she had learned from the best. She waited, expecting the familiar pang of loneliness to rise, but it didn't come. As much as she still missed her grandparents, she didn't feel the unbearable heartache this time. Rather, she was excited to go and join her friends.

Deimos set the cart far off to the side and offered his arm to her. She took it and the butterflies in her stomach went wild. As she looked out at the growing crowd of people surrounding the bonfire that was being started, her nerves twisted.

Before they started walking, Deimos reached for her shoulder and dusted it off. With a smirk, he said, "You have a little flour there."

Abrielle snapped her gaze to her dress so fast that she stumbled back. Deimos caught her and steadied her with his hands resting on her back. Their bodies were pressed together, and she nearly melted in his arms. Heat blazed across her face.

"Is it gone?"

"Yes, you're perfect."

Her blush deepened. "I don't know about that but thank you."

Deimos's shadows poked their tendrils from the canvas bag they had been riding in to hide from the sun. Now that dusk was nearing, it seemed they wanted to come out to play. Abrielle gestured for them to come. They took her cue and tucked themselves close to her and Deimos, blending in with their actual shadows that were cast onto the ground.

Music began to play, summoning whoops and hollers from everyone in the clearing. Couples hurried to join the group near the bonfire. Soon, they were a blur of twirls and jumps as the people lost themselves in the dance.

Abrielle tensed. Dancing was a struggle when her feet rarely did as she commanded.

"Maybe I should prep for the contest."

Deimos gazed down at her intently. "If that's what you want."

"But if I do it too soon, it might not be as good." Her heart was about to beat out of her chest and Deimos was standing so close she couldn't gather her thoughts.

He shrugged slightly. "Okay, let's go."

"But maybe we shouldn't."

Her grandmother's encouraging words echoed in her mind. If she was there with Abrielle right now, she would have said, *Go. Dance with the boy.* She could almost picture her grandparents standing before her, gesturing for her to go and have some fun.

Deimos chuckled. "If you—"

Decidedly, Abrielle said, "Okay, maybe just one dance."

One little dance with Deimos wouldn't hurt, right? It certainly wouldn't hurt her chances in the contest, which wasn't until later that night once everyone had eaten their dinner. But as Deimos drew her toward the fire and into his arms, it felt as if the world was closing in around her. What would it be like when he was no longer there to steady her?

Now, the loneliness returned. It hit her so hard that she gripped him tighter for fear of crumpling under the intense pressure of it. His face darkened with something resembling worry, but rather than pressing her to talk to him as she expected he would do, he ran a comforting hand through her hair and pressed his other to the small of her back.

Even his shadows snuggled up closer. And for a moment, Abrielle felt as if she was quite literally wrapped in love. She wanted to hold on to that, but worried that after tonight, she would instead find herself buried under regret and sadness.

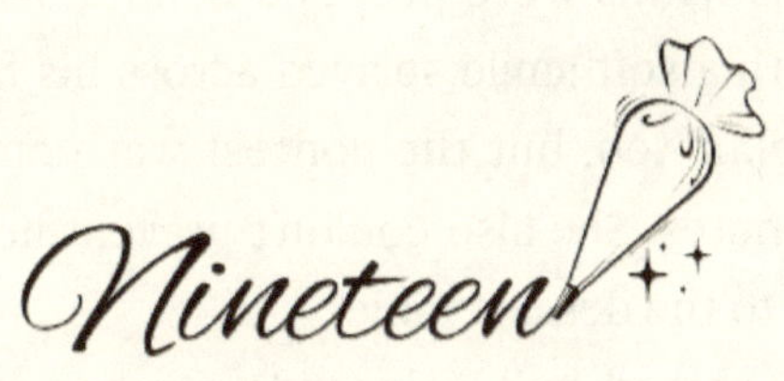

Nineteen

The grass tickled the bottoms of Abrielle's toes. She'd kicked off her shoes somewhere between the third or fifth dance with Deimos and the others. Now the group sat on an enormous white cotton sheet that was laid out under the stars.

Light twinkled down on them and was made greater by the lanterns they had scattered around them. The entire lakeside was much the same with villagers and guests broken off into smaller, more intimate groups.

Thomaz had joined them when they took a break from the dancing and he and Tansy were leaning in close, whispering to one another. Luna was flanked by two very handsome gentlemen, each of whom seemed to be vying for her attention. Neither seemed to be having any success.

Abrielle, Deimos, and Tansy didn't dare bring up the subject of the witch. There would be no tactful way of explaining it to the others. But Abrielle knew that at least for herself, it weighed heavily on her. Would Mable have the answers they had desperately been seeking? If she did, then how many hours did Abrielle have left with Deimos?

Deimos was lounged out with one long leg crossed over the other. His hands were propped behind his head as he stargazed with a soft smile splayed across his face. Abrielle wanted to relax, too, but the contest was coming up in a matter of minutes. She also couldn't prevent her gaze from drifting over to the dessert table.

Everyone seemed quite pleased with her work. Dishes were disappearing in the blink of an eye with each horde of people that came and went. Was the mystery baker for the contest amongst them? She wouldn't blame them for wanting to scout out the competition.

With a lazy drawl, Deimos said, "Stop checking on them. Everyone loves what you brought."

Abrielle blew a stray strand of hair that had fallen in front of her eye. "I'm just making sure. That's all."

A woman was scraping the cherries off the top of a piece of pie with her mouth twisted in a grimace.

"Oh, come on. If she doesn't like cherries she should be trying the custard instead."

"She'll be okay, Brie." Deimos chuckled with his eyes still trained on the night sky.

Abrielle bit her lip. "I'm just going to go let her know. I'll be right back."

No one stopped her as she scrambled up and walked barefoot to the table. With a polite smile, she picked up a slice of custard pie and handed it to the woman. "Here, I think you'll enjoy this, instead."

The woman blushed. "Oh, thank you."

"If you don't like that either, it's okay!" Abrielle added quickly, not wanting to pressure the woman.

When she took a bite, her face lit up. "This is divine."

Abrielle's entire body warmed from head to toe. This. This right here was why she loved baking. The woman walked away and Abrielle took note of everyone digging into the goods she had brought. They chattered while filling their plates. A couple at the end fed pillowy bites of cake to one another. A mother handed a piece of baked apple to her toddler, who reached for the table with a chubby eager hand.

Being able to bring so many together like this made all the hours in the kitchen worth it. This is what she craved. It was why the patio meant so much to her. Having a place all her own where families, friends, and even lovers could take time out of their busy lives to reconnect. Even if just one person used it to stave off their loneliness, that would be enough for her.

She spotted Erik amongst a group of people from the palace staff. When she caught his eye, he raised a glass to her. She awkwardly raised her hand to wave, but instead the back of her hand smacked into an unfortunate villager's cheek.

He let out a yelp and she spouted off apologies. When he stormed away, Erik joined her. His eyes were glazed over, possibly from too much ale. But he smiled brightly. This time, no fluttering appeared in her stomach. No blush heated her cheeks.

Erik set his drink on the table and said, "It's nice to see you out and about. Looks like you were having fun out there."

He pointed to the bonfire where people still danced with reckless abandonment under the full moon.

She tucked her hair behind her ear. "Yeah, it's been nice to get out of the bakery for a while."

"I bet. So, I was thinking, maybe we could—"

Erik was cut off by Deimos. "Hey, Brie, I think the contest is starting."

He barely glanced at Erik and didn't bother to acknowledge or greet him. Abrielle shifted on her feet awkwardly. To her relief no toads fell onto her dessert table and the grass seemed to remain green—although it was a bit difficult to tell under the orange glow of the lanterns.

"Sorry, Erik, I really should prepare." Abrielle was already grabbing the crumble and fluff from its designated spot in a crate of ice Deimos had rigged for her. "I'll see you later tonight."

"Of course," Erik said with a strange look on his face.

Was that a sneer he just shot in Deimos' direction? Abrielle shook her head and started walking away from the table. Deimos followed beside her, and she caught him glancing back at Erik one last time with a snarl threatening to show on his lips.

"What is going on with you two?" She scoffed.

"I have no idea what you mean." Deimos graced her with a charming smile.

"It's just..." Abrielle sighed. "We'll be meeting Mable after the contest. And with the possibility of so little time left together, I'd rather not spend it watching you and Erik making funny faces at one another."

Deimos stopped walking and Abrielle turned to face him. She clutched the dessert close to her. It might not matter to him how they spent their last night together, but it mattered to her. And even if it embarrassed her to say it out loud, she feared holding it in would make her feel much worse.

"That's just it." Deimos tilted his head. "I'll be gone soon, and I can't stand the thought of you being left with the likes of him."

Her heart did a little flip at the mention of him going home. She couldn't blame him for being ready to leave. He'd been there far longer than she had imagined he would. But still, it stirred something in her that felt frighteningly close to anger.

If he was leaving, then what did it matter to him who she was around? "What's wrong with Erik?" She scrunched her nose. He was no prince charming, even if he did look like one. But he was nice enough and hadn't done anything to warrant suspicion as far as she could see.

Deimos sneered. "He just seems sort of... flighty. Like a ratawilly ready to spook at first light."

"Okay, first, I have no idea what that means. And second, you hardly know him." She wasn't in the mood to defend Erik when she had the contest to worry about, but she also didn't want Deimos to spend the entire night worrying about it.

"Well, rattawillies are notorious for hating sunlight, you see, and—"

Abrielle held a hand up to stop the nature lesson. "Deimos, the contest..." She nodded toward the tent.

"Right!" He gestured to her to take the lead.

She bee-lined for the contest tent across the lawn. It was already set up with a long table for the judges. They were sitting and chatting amongst each other eagerly with the King in the center.

A simple crown of steel rested on his salt and pepper colored hair. Though he wasn't as spry as he used to be, King Vasiri was an athletic-built man who nearly always had a genuine smile on his face. More often than not, he could be found telling stories of his younger days at these events. He was much like his daughter in that respect. An entertainer. A charmer.

When Abrielle approached, he scratched his beard and leaned forward for a better look at what was in her hands. The other judges, who were picked at random each year to give everyone a fair chance at the fun, craned their necks to see as well.

King Vasiri's voice boomed above the noise of the crowd that was gathering. "Abrielle Grainwick, it is so good to see you!"

"You as well, your Majesty." She dipped into a very small curtsey, afraid if she went too low, she would topple right over.

The King leaned back in his chair and patted his stomach—which did not match the roundness of most men his age—and said, "I look forward to your deliveries every morning. If I'm not careful, I'll end up looking like my father before me."

King Vasiri's father had been a lover of sweets as well, though in him, it had showed. Abrielle blushed and set the dish down on the table. She chanced a side glance to see who the other entries were, hoping to catch a glimpse of the mystery competitor. To her surprise, she only saw familiar faces. The only people standing beside her were an older couple who entered the same fig foldovers every year, a young woman by the name of Dina with a cake in the shape of a heart, and a bearded man she recognized from the docks who had a grand, towering creation resembling a volcano that was made up of candied lemons and oranges.

The bearded man went first. Attendants placed a special table a good distance away from the judges. Once the towering dessert was in place, the man signaled for one of his friends. They brought a torch to him.

Some of Abrielle's confidence deflated. Dessert and a show would certainly leave an impression on the judges. It was what she had planned to do with her own, only *her* fire would be on a much smaller scale. If his dessert tasted as good as the show that he was putting on looked, then she might need to worry about him instead of the mystery contestant.

The man proudly said, "Stand back, everyone!"

As soon as the torch touched the top of the dessert, bubbles began to form. At first, they were small, like suds in a sink. But then they grew. And grew. And grew. And grew. The crowd swept back, and amused murmurs spread.

Abrielle racked her brain to figure out what sort of dessert would bubble up like that. Soon a thick yellow mixture began to follow the bubbles. It was the consistency of a custard. And Abrielle couldn't take her eyes from the intriguing sight.

The man boasted, "My special mixture of lemon pudding, baking soda, and a dash of vinegar gives it the effect."

Deimos whistled low under his breath. "And here I thought I was the one who needed to stay away from the kitchen."

Abrielle swatted at him. "It's certainly… different."

When the dish was cut and presented in front of the judges, their eyes widened in unison. The smell emanating from the plates was sharp and faintly resembled the lemon cleaning mixture Abrielle used in the bakery.

Still, they each took a bite. Their lips puckered and one judge even smacked his lips together with a confused look on his face. Abrielle suppressed a laugh. The last thing she wanted to do was make the man feel bad.

Seemingly unphased by their reaction, he chuckled, shrugged, and said, "It's not for the faint of heart. Takes a sophisticated palate to recognize its true potential."

King Vasiri dabbed at the corner of his mouth with a kerchief and smiled. "Thank you for your entry. It was most entertaining and for that, we appreciate you." His smile matched his eyes and Abrielle had a feeling he truly meant what he said.

With a grin that spread ear to ear, the bearded man bowed and walked away. The other contestants took their turns with far less of a show. The judges seemed to enjoy the desserts, though Abrielle imagined anything would taste good after that opening entry.

There was still no sign of the stranger the chancellor had mentioned, so that meant it was her turn next. With a slight tremble in her step, Abrielle approached the table. Using the wooden spoon her grandmother had brought to the festival every year—the one with a heart carved into the handle—she scooped a bit of the crumble onto each judge's plate. Next, she topped each portion of the mixture with the fluff Deimos had helped with.

King Vasiri grabbed his fork, but before he could dig in, Abrielle pulled his plate back. "Sorry, your Majesty. Just one more thing."

Deimos was already prepared beside her with a branch no thicker than his finger. It was about the length of a candle and much less impressive than the first contestant's torch. But it did its job as Abrielle took it and held it over each dessert. The fluff began to melt slightly under the heat, and soon an even coating of golden brown covered the dessert.

Abrielle took a step back and gestured to the King's plate. "Now, it's ready."

They each took a small bite. Abrielle held her breath. Then one after another, the judges took a bigger bite. The King rumbled in delight. They liked it! Abrielle spun to face Deimos. But instead of watching the judges like everyone else in the crowd, he was watching her. Only her. He gave her a wink and his smile grew.

There was something familiar about the way he watched her. She had seen her grandfather look at her grandmother like that countless times before. In moments when she was baking, and didn't realize he'd come into the kitchen. In the morning, when she gardened, and he took a moment to glance up from his woodwork.

Abrielle was so consumed with the way Deimos was looking at her, she almost didn't notice the little man waddle up to the table next. He carried a picnic basket on a slender arm and placed it on the table. Without a word, he pulled out a dark bar of chocolate.

He appeared fairly young—no older than she was—but there was a mature quality to him. Like that of a man who had seen the world and only wanted to prop his feet up and rest with a good book by the fire. Abrielle couldn't explain it any other way.

There was a large sack on his back, and he pulled it off effortlessly. It was nearly the size of him, and it was a wonder that he hadn't toppled over with it on. The crowd moved in closer as he pulled a large metal contraption from it.

It had a spout like a teapot, but a small canister on the bottom was what caught Abrielle's curiosity. The man took a container of milk from his sack next and poured it into the teapot. She, too, found herself leaning in close to watch as he pulled a short stick from a box and swiped it on the table. A tiny flame appeared like magic and the crowd murmured in awe.

The stranger placed the flame near the canister and steam flowed upward from the contraption. King Vasiri leaned back in his seat warily. A judge at the end of the table scratched their head curiously.

Once the teapot appeared to be good and heated, the little man opened the top and plopped the chocolate bar in. After a few moments, he poured the creation into ice-filled, frosted cups that had been set out by one of the attendants. A thick, creamy fountain poured from the spout and into each cup.

The judges eagerly picked it up and drank it. Calm, merry smiles spread across their faces and Abrielle could understand why. The scent of the drink was rich and inviting. Her own mouth watered in longing to try it.

The judges set their drinks down and stood, congregating in a huddle together. As the contestants waited to hear the judgment, Deimos placed a comforting hand on the small of her back. After a few minutes, King Vasiri clasped his hands together. Abrielle could hardly concentrate as he gave a grand speech about how they look forward to the contest every year and how each and every year, the villagers never disappoint.

Win or lose, she was proud of herself. Proud of what she and Deimos had made together. And she knew in her heart that her grandmother would have felt the same in that instant.

King Vasiri puffed out his chest and said, "It's a close call. Our runner up is Miss Abrielle Grainwick with her interesting campfire dessert. But tonight, the award goes to our visitor, Sir Peakbottom!"

The crowd cheered wildly. Abrielle waited for the disappointment to come, but it didn't. Sure, her pride was a little hurt. But the man—or Sir Peakbottom as he was called—had outdone her. Not only was his presentation intriguing and entertaining, but his treat was one of a kind. She clapped and let out a loud whoop with the crowd.

Deimos leaned in close and whispered in her ear, "Are you alright?"

She turned to him, their foreheads almost touching, and said, "I tried something new, and it didn't completely blow up in my face. I might not have won the contest, but in a way, I still feel like I came out on top. So, yeah, I'm more than alright."

Deimos wrapped an arm around her shoulders and hugged her tight. She leaned into him, resting her head on his chest. She could have let the loss get her down. Before Deimos' arrival, she might have. But as Sir Peakbottom collected his prize, all she could think was that she *really* wanted to taste that concoction for herself. And with a little time left before meeting with Mable, that was *exactly* what she was going to do.

Twenty

Sir Peakbottom was a curious sort of man. He was smaller than most Ellamere villagers and his clothes, though worn and a bit tattered, were handwoven from things in the forest—leaves as big as her hand were tied over his leather shoes and bark was layered on the vest he wore. It reminded her of Deimos' attire when he first arrived.

As Abrielle approached Peakbottom, he faced her with fiddling hands. His contraption had been packed up snuggly in the sack, but a few cups sat filled to the brim on the table. A few of the villagers shoved in to try the frosted chocolate concoction for themselves.

She offered a friendly smile, which he returned as he said, "Well done, Miss. I wasn't sure I would win..." he drifted off and shuffled his feet in the dirt shyly.

"I wanted to wish you congratulations." She nodded to the drink. "Would it be alright if I tried it for myself? I run the bakery in town and I'm in awe of your innovation."

Sir Peakbottom nodded eagerly and handed a cup to both her and Deimos. He began talking about how the intricate kettle worked as Abrielle lifted the cup to her lips. The chocolate was pleasantly cool. The rich drink felt like velvet on her tongue, and she shivered in delight. It wasn't as thick as she expected. Not quite like the melted chocolate she used in her desserts. The milk offered it the perfect balance. This was quite possibly her new favorite drink in the whole world. In *any* world for that matter.

Deimos narrowed his eyes as he looked down at the man. "You're a forest dweller, are you not?"

Abrielle gripped the cup in her hands. Her grandfather had often whispered tales of garden fairies or gnomes who guarded the forest, but she had never seen any for herself. She wouldn't even know what to look for. But there *was* something unique about this man. She waited for his reaction.

Sir Peakbottom nodded eagerly with a bright smile. "Me ma twas' rumored to have some forest elf blood in her. Pa was a mortal man, though."

Deimos hummed in response, then asked, "And they chose to stay in Ellamere when the gemtowers were created?" There seemed to be a hint of skepticism and awe in his words. His brows knitted together, and he rubbed the back of his neck.

"Aye." There was a sad glimmer in Peakbottom's eyes. "When talk of magic being expelled from the land started makin' the rounds, many returned to the Otherworlds before the gemtowers could be erected. Me ma choose to stay with me pa. Gave up all her magic and the ties to the land, she did. All fer love."

Abrielle's chest tightened. It never occurred to her that the gemtowers had separated families. Had forced them to choose. It was heartbreaking. She couldn't imagine having to choose between her family and the one she loved. Nor could she imagine leaving everything she'd ever known behind. But she didn't blame Peakbottom's mother for choosing to stay, even at a cost.

A solemn quiet fell over the three of them until Sir Peakbottom forced a smile and said, "You know, that dessert of yers was quite imaginative."

"Thank you." Abrielle placed a hand on Deimos' arm. "I had a bit of help."

"You know, I twas' thinkin'..." Peakbottom approached her dish which still had a serving left in it. "May I?" he asked with an eager twinkle in his eye.

Abrielle's curiosity rose. "Of course!"

Peakbottom quickly pulled out a bar of chocolate he'd used for his drink and broke a few morsels off. Then he turned to Deimos. "Would ye mind lightin' a branch?"

Deimos did as Peakbottom asked, handing a small torch to the man, who was nearly vibrating with excitement now. He placed the chocolate in an empty mug and hovered the flame over it. Soon the chocolate was smooth and melted. Then, he poured it over the fluff and crumble mixture, creating a delightful design that resembled a star.

"Fer star-crossed lovers," he explained with a whisper. Then he handed the dessert to Abrielle.

She took a bite and hummed as the flavors burst in her mouth. It was more incredible than her version had been. The chocolate added to a symphony of taste, adding just the right amount of sweetness and bitterness.

Deimos quickly tried a bite, too, and growled with pleasure. Abrielle swatted at him playfully. If he wasn't careful, they'd wonder why he sounded so much like the hound that had been shadowing her the last few days.

To Peakbottom, she said, "This is brilliant! You truly have a talent, sir."

He dipped his head with a blush on his cheeks. "I thank ye for yer kind words. Tis' been a rough go of it lately. Me Ma and Pa have both passed on and I suppose I've been searchin' for my new place in this world."

A deep pang struck Abrielle's heart. "Is that what brought you here?"

"I thought maybe I could find a fresh start. Everyone in Ellamere knows about the festival and when I found out about the contest and prize money, I thought it might be me chance to get back on my feet, so to speak."

Abrielle pressed her lips together. She didn't know what to say. Part of her wanted to offer this man some assistance. But what could she do? What did she have to offer? She stared down at the crumbs left over from her dessert. He really did have a talent.

Then she gazed up at Deimos who was staring intently at her. She had given *him* a chance. Had let him into her life and look at what had come of it. Sure, a few patches of discolored grass and animals behaving incredibly out of character, but there was no denying the friendship that had formed.

Someone shouted Sir Peakbottom's name from one of the other tents and he excused himself. As he walked away, Deimos leaned in and whispered in her ear. "You should invite him to the bakery."

"You think?" She bit her lip. The idea of having someone else in her kitchen twisted her nerves. "I don't know. How would I be able to pay him?"

Deimos nudged her in the side. "You have a brand-new patio, remember? If you have customers sticking around throughout the day, you'll need help. And you'll be bringing in more business. It might be nice to have someone around when..." he drifted off and she knew he meant *when he was gone.*

The ache in her chest returned. And before she knew it, she was calling out to Sir Peakbottom. He turned and lifted his chin as if straining to hear her. She approached, taking a deep breath and said, "You know, I own the bakery in town. And we recently expanded." She grinned gratefully at Deimos, then turned back to Peakbottom. "Perhaps you would be interested in bringing your contraption sometime to serve your drink to my customers?"

Sir Peakbottom beamed. "I would love nothing more!"

"Great." Abrielle reached out to shake his hand. "You are welcome to come by any time you'd like."

He shook her hand wildly and said his goodbyes in between many thanks. When he wandered away, Deimos pulled her to his side with an arm around her shoulder. "You did a good thing just now."

"I think my customers will really enjoy it."

"I mean a good thing for you."

She pulled away slightly and studied his face. "It won't be the same, you know."

"It's alright to surround yourself with friends, Brie. I know you miss your family, and it won't be the same as when they were around but—"

A rush of courage swept through her and she interrupted, "I meant, it won't be the same as it is having you here."

"Oh." Deimos' face fell, and he broke eye contact with her, his gaze dropping to his feet. His shadows tightened around him. Abrielle reached out to touch him, but someone shouted her name.

She spun around, to see Tansy at the edge of the lake pointing wildly at the moon. It was nearly at its peak and the witch would be waiting for them on the outskirts of the lake. She'd been so overcome with adrenaline from the contest and had been so focused on her talk with Sir Peakbottom that she'd nearly forgotten.

Deimos took her hand gently, lacing his fingers through hers. They took a few steps, but she slowed, hesitating. *I want you to stay.* The words were on the tip of her tongue, but they would not come. She swallowed the lump in her throat and started walking again. All the while, Deimos said nothing.

If he wanted to stay, he would have found a way. Abrielle was not so foolish to believe that he would be willing to leave behind everything he had ever known. It wasn't the same as it was with Sir Peakbottom's parents. They had made a family together. Had committed in their love. What she felt for Deimos was powerful, but was it love? She wasn't sure.

As they walked, she played memories of her grandparents in her mind. They were the one couple she had always known loved each other more than anything in the world. They weren't just husband and wife. They were *partners*. But isn't that what Deimos was proving himself to be? He had supported her and assisted her even when she didn't ask. And had made her feel as if she could lean on him without hesitation.

When they reached Tansy, Deimos fell behind them walking a few paces back. Abrielle glanced over her shoulder but found that his shadows were hovering close to him like a mask. She sighed as Tansy bumped her shoulder.

"I noticed Erik looking your way all night long." Tansy smiled and swayed slightly as if she'd already dipped into the good wine that Thomaz always brought with him.

Abrielle fiddled with the skirt of her dress, twisting her fingers into the fabric as if it were the tether to a kite. If she let go, she might fly away. Every step they took was one step closer to saying goodbye to Deimos.

She shook her head. "I'm not sure I'm interested in him anymore. I—"

"Have feelings for Deimos," Tansy guessed.

"I don't know..." Abrielle launched into the story of what he did for her with the patio and how much it reminded her of her grandfather building the cottage for her grandmother. How an act like that had to mean *something*.

Tansy's voice was low as she said, "But he has to go home, Abrielle. You know that." She glanced over her shoulder and then leaned in closer to continue. "What happens if you get caught by the King? If they find out what he is? He can't hide it forever."

Abrielle became lightheaded and her limbs tingled. For a moment, she wondered if her fear of floating away was about to come true. The last thing in the world she wanted was for Deimos to get hurt.

Before she could respond to Tansy's doubts, a young woman came into view. She had a wild mane of red hair and rosy cheeks. Abrielle glanced around. This couldn't be the woman they were looking for. Mable would have been no younger than her own grandparents would have been if they were still around.

Tansy's voice dripped with confusion, too, as she said, "Hi there, we were looking for someone. Her name is Mable."

"I'm Mable." The girl lifted onto her tippy toes with her hands clasped neatly in front of her. When she came back down on her heels, her hair bobbed. "You must be Tansy."

"Yes," Tansy hesitated and stared wide-eyed at Abrielle and Deimos before continuing. "And these are my friends. The ones I told you about in the letter."

"Ah, yes. It was a rather cryptic note. You said they found something of mine?"

Abrielle took a step forward. "There must be some sort of mistake." She reached out to Tansy to take the bag they had brought with them, and pulled the old recipe book out. "I came across this book. It belonged to a Mable. But you can't be…"

The Mable they were looking for would have been around during the time the gemtowers were erected. This girl was no older than she and Tansy were. It wasn't possible that this was the woman they were searching for.

The girl stared hungrily at the book. "It belonged to my grandmother. I am named for her."

"Oh," flitted from Abrielle's lips in one swift breath. "Where is she now?"

"She passed some time ago." Mable reached out and brushed the book with her fingertips wistfully.

Abrielle glanced at Deimos. The muscle in his jaw ticked and she couldn't tell what was going through his mind. Disappointment? Distrust? It certainly didn't appear to be a relief that his one sure way home was no longer alive.

Abrielle hugged herself tightly. "Do you happen to know anything about her spell work? Would you know how to reverse one of her spells?"

Perhaps young Mable had learned from her grandmother just as Abrielle had learned from hers.

Mable shook her head vigorously, giving Abrielle a strange mixture of dismay and relief.

"May I?" The girl opened her hand, palm facing up.

She placed the book in Mable's hands, and the girl flipped through the pages. "It is nice to find a piece of her after all this time."

Abrielle's stomach twisted. Here she was searching for relief on Deimos' face and ignoring the pain this girl must be feeling in the absence of the grandmother she loved. After all the loneliness Abrielle had been burdened with, how could she be so thoughtless?

"Would you like to keep it?" she offered. She and Deimos had sifted through the spells countless times. There was nothing in there for them. It was why they had resorted to tracking the original Mable down. Just because it was a dead end for them did not mean something nice couldn't come from it. Offering this girl a piece of her family and heritage was the right thing to do.

The young girl hugged the book tightly to her chest. "Thank you. Thank you all."

"You're welcome." Abrielle gave her a half smile. Truthfully, she just wanted the whole exchange to be over with. To figure out what their next step was. And to take a moment to sort out the relief she was feeling.

When they parted with the girl, Tansy went on ahead and left Deimos and Abrielle to walk side by side. Neither of them spoke until they reached the edge of the bonfire. The festivities were still in full swing, and couples danced close to one another. Some had filtered off to blankets of their own, huddled in close as they shared secrets that they likely wouldn't be confident enough to share in the daylight.

Deimos cleared his throat. "Look, Brie. I don't really know what to say or do here. All I do know is that the moment that girl said her grandmother was no longer around, I felt like a weight had been lifted off my chest."

"Really?" Abrielle's heart raced as she allowed him to take both her hands.

"Maybe this is just the way things were meant to be." He leaned in close to her and she tilted her head up to him. His breath was warm on her face and smelled of chocolate as he said, "What are the chances I would end up in your kitchen that night? That book drew you to it just as that spell drew me to you."

Abrielle's lips parted, and she struggled to maintain steady breathing.

Deimos spoke softly. "This festival celebrates lovers that are drawn together by the fates. Maybe we were brought together in the same sense. As if the stars demanded it?"

Taking a bold step toward him, Abrielle tilted her head up and all doubt faded away. He leaned down, but just as their lips touched, a scuffle broke out nearby. Two men were shoving each other and shouting.

Deimos and Abrielle followed the growing crowd and several villagers attempted to part the men before someone got hurt. Deimos released his hold on her hand and leapt between them, gently pushing one away from the other. One of the men—emboldened by too much ale, judging by his unsteady gait—swung at Deimos, hitting him in the jaw with a thud. Simultaneously, the large, healthy oak tree above them gave a thunderous crack.

Abrielle gasped, and her hands flew to her mouth. She stepped toward Deimos, but one of the massive branches fell to the ground. Shocked cries spread through the crowd as people scrambled back. The tree itself split in two as if struck by lightning and a sickening crunch echoed through the chaos as both pieces fell.

People leapt out of the way, and a few of them hit the ground with shouts. In the chaos, Abrielle lost sight of Deimos. A flood of relief flushed through her when he jumped over the branch and grabbed her arms.

"Are you okay?" he asked breathlessly.

"Fine." She placed her palm on his cheek and moved his face gently to the side. A nasty bruise was already forming in a blend of red and purple. "Are *you* okay?"

Deimos glanced back at the mess of what was left of the oak tree. Pieces of it were scattered every which way and stunned villagers murmured to one another excitedly. Thank the fates, no one was harmed, but the same couldn't be said for Paddy's cart which had been parked nearby.

One of the wheels had been knocked clean off, leaving it toppled over. The handles were splintered, and useless. Beside it, Luna rubbed her arm and winced. Paddy was fussing over her in a frenzy. She and Deimos jogged over to them.

Abrielle's breath caught in her throat when she reached them. "Luna, are you hurt?"

"Just a little bruised. It's no big deal." She shot a pointed look at Paddy. "Something my father is unconvinced of."

Paddy's cheeks were blazing red and sweat beaded at his temples. "Damned tree came out of nowhere. You could have been crushed!"

"But I wasn't," Luna argued. Then to Abrielle and Deimos, she assured, "I'm fine, really. I just landed on my arm when I jumped out of the way. Go and enjoy the rest of your night. I promise, I'm okay."

When Abrielle turned to Deimos, he was as white as a wraith. Under his breath, he said, "This is all my fault."

Abrielle shot a nervous glance back at Paddy and Luna, afraid that they might have heard him. But both were fussing at one another, arguing about whether or not she should see the healer.

"Come on," Abrielle said gently, tugging Deimos by the sleeve.

Once they were away from the crowd, he pulled away. He clenched his fists and shook his head. "I could have killed someone."

"It wasn't your fault." The words fell flat. She knew he hadn't meant for any of that to happen. It was like a reflex. Like when the healer taps your knee, and your leg kicks out. When the man hit Deimos, his power had reacted. That didn't mean it was his fault.

She reached for his hand, but he snatched it away with a furrowed brow. "This is wrong, Brie. *I'm* wrong."

Her heart ached at the raw emotion in his words. More than anything, she wished to go back in time to just before the fight broke out. Strained, she asked, "What about all those things you were saying about fate and us being drawn together?"

Deimos' eyes darkened, casting out the purple flecks, and his shadows pulsed at his shoulders. "It was a naive dream, nothing more."

"How can you say that?" As afraid as he was, he couldn't pretend like whatever was growing between them was nothing more than a dream that was out of reach. Not after he had said all of those beautiful words to her.

"How can you ignore the danger I pose to you and your people? Do you truly believe I belong here?"

She winced, and irritation reared its ugly head. "I am not ignoring it. Nor am I naive." The words felt empty. Deep down, she knew he had a point. No matter how much her heart had yearned for more moments with him, the words wouldn't stop pouring from her mouth. "I don't know what to believe. This... us... I just don't know what the right thing is here."

"Maybe I should just go."

Abrielle opened her mouth to argue. To tell him that's not what she meant. Her reluctance was for his own safety, as much as it was for her village.

"Abrielle, is everything okay?" Erik's ruddy face came into Abrielle's line of sight. He sized up Deimos with an air of suspicion.

Abrielle forced a polite smile. "Now isn't really a good time, Erik..."

Deimos released her hands and brushed a strand of hair from her face. "Go and dance. Maybe we just need a bit of space to think."

He stalked off to the tree line and she took a step to follow him, but Erik swept her into his arms. "Just one dance?"

She sucked in a sharp breath. Deimos wanted space, and she needed to give it to him. So, she allowed Erik to spin her slowly around the bonfire. For a while, she was able to keep an eye on Deimos, but soon he sulked out of sight.

Did he think she'd been ready to tell him she agreed that he should leave Ellamere? Was that why he had been so eager to run off?

Erik said something in her ear about long days at work, but she didn't pay much attention. Not until he said, "...chaos in town. King Vasiri intends to investigate it."

"He does?" She immediately began scanning the crowd for Deimos. If he was in danger of being found out, then she needed to warn him. There was no sign of him, though, so she took the chance to dig deeper. "Does the King have any leads?"

"Not really. If he did, I'm sure he'd have shared the information with the guard."

"Right..."

"I was thinking. Would you care to join me tomorrow for a picnic?"

Abrielle's feet instantly froze, and Erik nearly tripped over her. Not so long ago, she would have said yes without a second thought. But now, all she could think was that she needed to find Deimos. To tell him that she wanted him to stay. To find a way to throw the King off his scent and keep their secret.

But before she could do any of that, a horrible scream tore through the air. It overwhelmed the festival, forcing the music and dancing to a stop. There was another scream, and it was coming from the direction where Deimos had wandered. Abrielle broke away from Erik and ran.

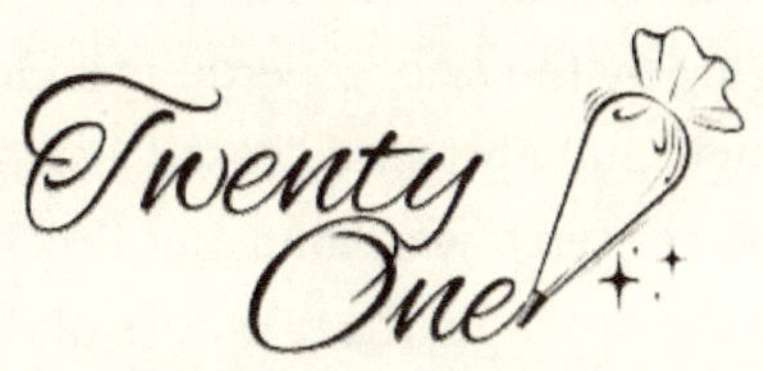

Twenty One

Abrielle couldn't remember the last time she ran this fast. Hours spent in the bakery had resulted in quick whisking, but it had not translated to her feet. But the scream that had torn from the tree line near the lake undoubtedly belonged to a man. And she still hadn't spotted Deimos since he stalked away while she danced with Erik.

She should have never let him walk away like that with so much between them left unresolved. Erik and others ran alongside her, determination in their eyes as they headed into the darkness. The bonfire's light didn't reach the clearing they came to. Only the moon high overhead and a blanket of stars lit the scene before them.

Abrielle didn't need direct light in order to spot the gem-tower that stood on this side of the village. It appeared untouched, but scorched earth surrounded them in a circle, giving a wide berth around the tower. Littered on the ground like an outlined border were numerous wilted flowers. Their once beautiful green stems were laid limp, brown, and broken. The ground beneath the dead flowers bubbled like the dirt was being boiled. It was a jarring sight. But what was worse, was the lump lying in the middle of it all.

A man, judging by the size, covered in a cloak. There was no blood, though, and Abrielle released a sigh of relief as he stirred. She took a step toward him, but Erik stopped her.

"Let me and the other guards take care of this." He went to the man and drew the cloak away from his face.

Her heart thudded with relief when she realized it wasn't Deimos. The man was vaguely familiar, a guard from the palace and someone she'd seen Erik speaking to on a few occasions. His face, however, was covered in bright pink polka dots. He reminded her faintly of the socks she'd seen at the farmer's market.

When he sat up in a daze, his hands flew to his cheeks, and he said in agonizing despair. "It itches!"

One of the townspeople snickered at the dramatic way the guard sobbed. Abrielle felt sorry for the man, but the spots appeared to be harmless. Nothing that a topical cream couldn't fix. That is, until they began to rise. They bubbled up in an irritated fashion the more the man scratched at them.

While the villagers and guards focused on the man and the bizarre set up in the clearing, Abrielle searched the shadows for Deimos. He had to be there somewhere. The burnt earth and ruined wildlife surrounding them made her suspicions rise.

Someone whispered, "Sacrificial altar." And their companion shushed them angrily. A few murmurs wove through the crowd and made Abrielle cringe.

She couldn't blame them for panicking. It was like a plague had swept through. Like *Deimos* had swept through. Off to the side, a few villagers ran with buckets of water from the lake to put out a few sparks that had caught on the trees. They worked quickly to keep the fire from spreading further.

Her stomach recoiled. She had yet to witness something this destructive from his magic, but she knew that was only because he had been suppressing his power. Had he lost control? Or had he made a grave error in his desperation to get home?

A few shadowy tendrils beckoned her from a thicket of trees far from the scene of the crime. She knew those shadows well by now, and guessed Deimos wouldn't be far from them. The moment she stepped foot into the thicket, someone yanked her into them.

Deimos' voice was panicked and husky as he said, "Are you alright?"

"Me?" she whispered back, matching his panic. "What about *you*? What have you done?"

"Brie, I didn't mean for this to happen. You have to believe me."

Locking eyes with him, Abrielle said, "Deimos, if you caused that circle out there, then you need to tell me. Were you trying to find a way home on your own? If the guard caught you and tried to bring you in, you can tell me. If you didn't mean to do that to him—"

"*If?*" Deimos snapped. "Of course, I didn't mean to do that to him." He gripped her shoulders tightly. "It was an accident.

He found me by whatever that is out there... the flowers and the ground... and he tried to arrest me. I lost control. I would never have hurt anyone on purpose."

"No. I didn't mean it that way. But did you destroy the earth? Did you make that... altar or whatever it is to try to break through the gemtower?" Her heart was sinking by the second. How could they fix this?

"You think I would try to cast a spell in the middle of a festival? Do you really believe I would destroy all that life without a second thought? I would never intentionally destroy one of your King's towers without knowing if it would release more magic into your land." Desperation dripped in his voice, and he reached up, placing a gentle hand on her head. "More than that, how can you think I would leave without saying goodbye?"

Abrielle's pulse raced. Of course, she didn't think he would cause all this mayhem with ill intent, but after what she'd just witnessed—the chaos of the scene—she wasn't sure what to do. He had alluded countless times to how dangerous and volatile his magic was. At how important it was that he keep it under control in her world. How could she not be worried?

Her voice broke as she said, "We're in over our heads. I wouldn't blame you if you were trying to go home... I won't turn you in, but maybe it was a mistake to hope that you could stay." By the time the words were finished pouring out of her mouth, she felt like a flame about to sputter out. She shuttered and wrapped her arms tight around herself.

"I wasn't trying to find a way home on my own." He released his hold on her and straightened. "But maybe I should have. If you had never brought me here in the first place, none of this would have happened. We both knew I didn't belong. The minute you couldn't send me back, I should have found my own way home."

The shadowy tendrils had been cowering behind him, but now they grew. They rose above him like the wings of a hawk, and Abrielle took an alarmed step back.

He continued, "Perhaps that is what I will do now." He turned away from her, going deeper into the wooded area.

Abrielle reached out but couldn't find the strength to follow him. "Deimos, please." She wasn't sure what she was asking of him. Didn't know whether to stop him or encourage him. Tansy was right. He was right. This was not his world. And it was only a matter of time before the whole thing blew up in their faces.

Deimos stopped and said over his shoulder, "You belong with someone who you can trust to keep you safe. It was never going to be me."

When he faded from view, folding into the shadows of the forest, Abrielle reached up and tore the floral crown from her head. Through tear-filled eyes, she stared down at it. The flowers were no longer blooming and vibrant. Instead, they had wilted and withered under his touch when he'd placed his hand on her head. Most of the petals had fallen, leaving only sad, crumbled stems in their wake.

Numb, she wandered back to the clearing where guards were cleaning up the mess and arguing over what to do about the bubbling muddied ground. She wiped vigorously at her tear-soaked cheeks and attempted to regain her composure. When Erik approached, she summoned a sad smile.

Clueless as to why she was truly upset, he assured her, "We'll find out who did this. All will be well."

All she could do was nod. There was no way she would give Deimos up. Besides, he was gone. Off to find his own way home. She simply hoped no one else would get hurt.

Erik rubbed her arm gently and said, "You should go home, where it's safe."

Bitter sarcasm brought a grimace to her face. If only he knew that she was the cause of the danger. That Ellamere was no longer safe from magic because of her and the secret she'd been harboring in her home. She should have never allowed herself to get distracted. To get close to Deimos. Now all she was left with was regret and guilt.

Erik offered his arm to her. "May I walk you home?"

She looked up at the gallant man standing in front of her. The mortal, non-magical man. The one who protected the kingdom and served his King loyally. Was Deimos right? Did she belong with someone else? Someone like Erik? The thought left a bitter taste in her mouth.

The festival had cleared out by now. Tables, blankets, and lanterns were left behind as if they had all left in haste. Even the streets were dark and abandoned. Having Erik pulling the cart by her side did little to comfort her. He rambled on about this and that and for the most part she tuned it out. It was impossible to concentrate when every shadow and sound had her whipping her head around, expecting to see Deimos. Yet, there was no sign of him.

When they reached her door, Erik waited patiently while she unlocked it. She turned to him and dipped her head in thanks. "I appreciate you walking me home." In truth, she could have made it back just fine on her own. One thing she was still sure of was that Deimos was not a threat to *her*.

Rather than say goodbye, Erik lingered a moment.

She tugged at a strand of her hair to keep her nervous hands busy and said, "Well, goodnight." She opened the door and stepped inside.

Erik placed a hand on the doorframe and put one foot on the threshold. "About that picnic. I know things got a little out of control tonight, but I have no doubt we will track down whoever was responsible. For all we know it was just some grotesque prank."

"Perhaps..." Abrielle hoped he didn't notice the quake in her voice. If the King decided not to pursue the matter further, then Deimos might be safe until he got himself home. Or at least, until he escaped over the Ellamere border. Maybe he would flee after tonight. The prospect made her eyes sting with the threat of tears.

"So, would you? Care to join me for a picnic?" Erik's crystal blue eyes were wide and hopeful. He added, "You'll be safe with me, I promise."

"I don't know..."

"Is it because of that man I saw you with? I didn't recognize him, but I had assumed you were unattached."

Abrielle's heart leapt into her throat. The last thing she needed was Erik asking questions about Deimos. Especially when half the village now believed there was a rogue witch running lose. Would they lay their accusations on any stranger passing through for the festival?

"No, he's..." A *friend*? It no longer felt like the right word. It had felt like so much more than that lately.

"Oh, well if he's not the problem, then will you join me?"

Abrielle wasn't sure what tomorrow would bring. As of this moment, a picnic sounded mundane and useless. As angry and scared as she was, part of her still wanted to know where Deimos had gone. And how he planned on finding his own way home. The official crest on Erik's vest caught her attention. If the guard caught Deimos, Erik would be the first to know. Would he find it suspicious if she asked him about the investigation during a picnic? If Deimos didn't turn up by the morning, it might be her only option for answers. To be sure he had gotten away.

She bit the inside of her cheek and summoned a pleasant smile. "That would be lovely."

Erik's face lit up in the moonlight. "Wonderful. I will come by at noon."

"Perfect," she responded, ignoring the pang in her heart.

As soon as Erik was gone, she shut the door and leaned against it. Tinker was there in an instant, meowing incessantly at her feet, but Abrielle ignored her. The bakery was empty and nearly pitch dark with only a thin veil of moonlight drifting through the curtained windows.

After the night she'd had, all she wanted to do was crawl into the armchair with her favorite blanket and drift off into oblivion. When she had woken up that morning, she had a feeling she would be saying goodbye to Deimos that night. But not like this. Their farewell had been filled with heated words. And with no way to know if he would be successful in returning home on his own, she was left with nothing but knots in her stomach.

She pushed herself off the door and reached for the lock. Stopping short, she hovered over it. What if he changed his mind or needed to seek refuge from the guard? Decidedly, she left it alone and walked to the living room.

When she stepped into the dark room, she half expected to find the quirky tendrils of shadows waiting for her. Or to find Deimos with his feet dangling over the arm of the sofa. But there was no one. The home was utterly empty. *Painfully* empty.

With a plop, she dropped into the armchair. Her eyes burned and hot tears streamed down her cheeks. Who was she kidding? He was gone and he wasn't coming back. She had doubted him when she saw that altar. But if it wasn't him, then who? He was the only one with that sort of power in Ellamere. Maybe he had lied to her tonight.

So why was she hit now with intense loneliness? Why did she want someone like him around. Always worrying that he might lose control at any moment. As she curled up, pulling her knees to her chest, horrible thoughts warred in her mind.

The toad, the patch of grass at the palace, and the strange effects on the livestock. What if Deimos had done all of that on purpose? Had she been naive in thinking he didn't want to do those things to her world when it was all he had ever done in his? He said it himself; it was all he'd ever known. Truthfully, she didn't believe any of that. Her heart wouldn't allow her to.

Tinker snuggled in beside her and she pulled the blanket over them both. She shut her eyes and let the tears fall. Allowed herself to grieve the moments she and Deimos had shared. The bottom line was that he was gone. He made his choice and left. She needed to let it go. She needed to let *him* go.

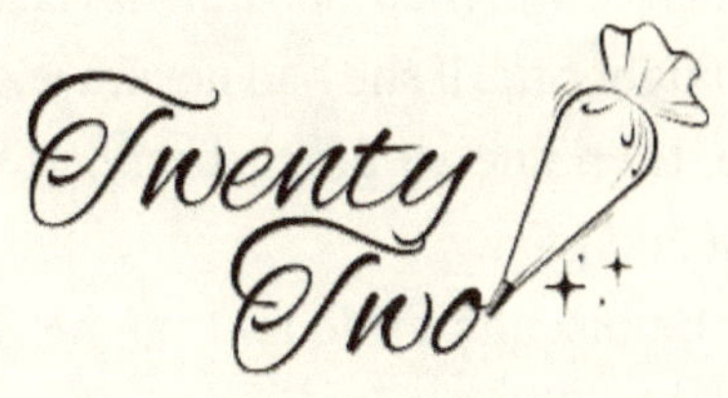

Twenty Two

A brielle woke before dawn to Tinker purring against her face. The vibrations tickled, and she rolled away with a groan. Her eyes were sticky and sore from a tear-filled night and she wiped them groggily. Although normally, she would be waking to prepare for the day, her limbs were as heavy as her heart, and she couldn't find it in her to even light the oven.

Instead, she kept the curtains drawn and hung the closed sign outside the door. She poured a warm cup of breakfast tea and despite her poor appetite, grabbed a few biscuits from a tin with little stars painted on it. Then she wandered out back to the patio. It was as pristine as she had left it with the little vases of flowers still bloomed. She slumped into a wrought iron chair and waited for the sun to rise.

She could barely see the fractured gemtower through the weeds at the tree line, but she felt its presence. It was there, broken, and alone. Just like she was. With a groan, she sank deeper in the chair and ran her hands through her tangled hair.

Even outside in the fresh air, Abrielle felt stifled. It was as if a heavy blanket weighed her down, veiling any sort of light or joy she might find. If she had never welcomed Deimos into her home, then she wouldn't be filled with so much disappointment and pain.

She pushed the biscuits aside and ran her hand over the grooves in the table. If things had gone differently last night, she would be opening the patio up to her customers any moment now. But instead of being surrounded by cheerful voices, it was quiet. It was the sort of silence that seeped into one's bones and settled in with a chill. It served as a reminder of everything and everyone she had lost. And all the things she may never have.

With a heavy sigh, she returned to the cottage, leaving Deimos' parting gift behind. Although she had forgone the morning rush and palace deliveries, she supposed she should get out of the cottage for a bit. It hurt too much to remain. So, she got dressed, choosing a burnt sienna linen day dress with yellow roses embroidered on the bodice.

Erik would be arriving for the picnic soon, and she tried her best to make herself presentable in hopes that it would trick her spirits into lifting. Outside her window, she could see villagers going about their day as usual. It seemed the excitement and fear from the night before had worn off enough for them to venture out into the streets.

She rested her elbows on the windowsill as she watched. After what she'd witnessed, it was odd to see everyone lost in their own little worlds. None would ever suspect that magic had been walking amongst them only hours ago. If Abrielle watched them long enough then maybe she, too, would start to believe that their world was still guarded by the gemtowers. That Deimos and his summoning had been nothing more than the dream of an overworked, grieving woman looking for a change in her life. A woman so desperate to honor her grandmother's memory that she hadn't realized she was also searching for someone—*anyone*—to share the special moments with.

Time went by and she continued to watch her neighbors. It wasn't until someone knocked on her bedroom door that she stirred with a jump.

Tansy ran to her with open arms. "Thank the fates, you're alright!" She wrapped Abrielle in a hug, but a chill still remained in her bones.

She pulled back quickly. "Has something happened? Has Deimos been caught?"

"No. No," Tansy assured her. "As far as I can tell, everything has returned to normal. There's no sign of him or anything like that bizarre scene last night."

Abrielle twisted a strand of hair around her finger nervously. He hadn't been caught. That was good. But it also meant he was out there somewhere all alone... or that he was gone. Maybe he had found a way home.

Tansy studied Abrielle with concern drawing her face down. "Are you okay?"

"I'm not sure I even know what okay is anymore." Abrielle led the way downstairs.

Through the light muslin curtain on the bakery door, Abrielle spotted the shape of a man. Her heart leapt to her throat, and she ran to it with Tansy close behind. When she opened it, her heart sank back down. Erik was standing there with a bouquet of lilies.

"Good morning, ladies." He tipped his head to Abrielle and Tansy.

Tansy's eyes bulged. "Oh, hello."

Erik held up a wicker basket. "Are you ready?"

Abrielle smoothed down her skirt and nodded. As she stepped outside, Tansy shot her a look of confusion and mouthed *what is going on?* Abrielle swatted at her in response and ushered her out the door.

She closed it behind them and said to Tansy, "I'll see you later."

"Sure," was all her best friend said in response.

Erik led the way to a hill near the palace. Normally the view would have wowed Abrielle, reminding her of the vast beauty of their village and the land surrounding it. The forest was a wonderful mixture of varying shades of green and the rolling hills were healthy and filled with an array of crops. Each cozy cottage could be seen from where they were sitting, and she could make out several of her neighbors in the distance.

But her heart wasn't filled with any sort of joy or appreciation. Instead, it was empty. A void as dark as Deimos' magic when he shifted. Her melancholy only worsened when Erik put his hand on hers.

"I'm glad you decided to join me today." He gave her a lopsided smile.

Not so long ago she would have been elated to be sitting there with Erik. But nothing about it sent butterflies fluttering around her stomach. After her time with Deimos, being around Erik felt similar to when you take a bite of bread after having enjoyed a delectable buttery croissant with melted chocolate. This just... fell flat.

She snapped to attention when Erik handed her a glass of something bubbly and she realized he'd still been talking. With her eyes trained on a wolfhound chasing birds at the bottom of the hill, she tuned back in to what he was saying.

"I'm glad Tansy suggested it when I ran into her last week." he said.

That caught her interest. "Suggested what?"

"That I ask you to dance at the festival," he replied simply, taking a long drink from his glass.

Abrielle held in a snort of laughter. So, it had been Tansy's matchmaking and not Deimos' advice that had finally made Erik notice her. For a smug moment, she couldn't wait to tell Deimos that he wasn't as smooth as he thought, until she remembered she likely wouldn't get the chance to tell him anything ever again.

Her stomach sank as Erik reached for the hand she had resting on the blanket. He rubbed his thumb along her knuckles, and she pulled away pretending to be interested in a fruit plate he had laid out. She grabbed a particularly small grape and popped it into her mouth. The juice burst as she bit down, and she winced at the tartness.

Erik must have mistaken her silence for lingering nerves from the night before, because he said, "I know that nasty business last night left many in the village shaken."

She furrowed her brow and set her sights on the villagers who seemed rather unbothered by the whole thing. There were quite a lot of people out and about. Travelers were ducking into shops with broad smiles on their faces. Down by the stream, groups of friends and couples holding hands picnicked or skipped around with one another. Perhaps they were confident in their King's protection. Or maybe it wasn't as bad as she had played it up in her mind. She guessed the former, since the latter seemed more like wishful thinking.

Erik continued, "Rest assured, the King is taking strong measures to prevent anything like it from happening again. It's being taken care of as we speak."

That piqued her interest even more. This was precisely why she had accepted his invitation.

"How so?"

"The crown has hired someone who is an expert in these matters."

Abrielle tensed. Who in town would be familiar with magic, let alone be an expert in it? Was there another witch they had overlooked? She hadn't even considered trying to find someone else who might have been around when the original Mable had written her spells. Maybe that was where Deimos was. But if the King had hired that person to track him down, then he would be walking right into their clutches.

Someone needed to warn him. She pressed her fingers to the bridge of her nose. There had to be a way to find Deimos. To get him out of Ellamere one way or another before the King's new hire found him. She needed to leave. Now. But how could she do so without drawing suspicion?

She sucked in a loud breath and fluttered her eyes while putting a hand to her chest. Erik swiftly scooted to her side and grabbed her elbow to steady her. It was working. She inhaled deeply through her nose and apologized.

"I feel a bit faint. Perhaps last night took a bigger toll on me than I thought." She stood on unsteady feet. Though, she didn't need to fake that part. The urgency to find Deimos made her legs tremble.

"Let me walk you home," Erik offered.

But Abrielle shook her head vehemently. "Oh, no. I'll be fine, really. I just need a warm cup of tea and a bit of rest."

He narrowed his eyes. "Are you sure? You look a bit pale."

"I'm sure. Really, it's just been a long few days." She forced a tight chuckle.

Erik raised a curious eyebrow.

Not wanting him to turn his suspicions back on Deimos, whom he'd asked about more than she liked, she added quickly, "What with all of the baking for the festival and what not."

"Oh," he said slowly, "Okay, well I guess I'll see you later then."

"Definitely!" she said over her shoulder as she hurried down the hill and far away from Erik and his picnic.

The further she went, the faster her pace picked up. Once she reached the bottom of the hill, she glanced back to find that Erik was still watching her. She ducked behind one of the shops, bumping into a few passersby. Spouting off apologies, she slipped between the shoe shop and butcher. Erik wouldn't be able to see her now. That was her opening. She took off at a sprint.

There was no telling where Deimos was. Or if he had already been caught by whoever the King had sent to hunt him down. He was a newcomer. Perhaps he had gone to the inn just as any other visitor would have done. But he had no money that she knew of.

She slowed now, realizing she had no idea what direction she should be running in. There was an irritating cramp in her side, and she stopped to rest against the wall of Nia's dress shop. The stone was uneven and jagged, digging into her back, but she paid no mind to it. Instead, she racked her brain for answers.

The bell on the dress shop's door chimed and a lovely, kind voice called out, "Abrielle, darling, are you quite alright?"

Nia's forehead was wrinkled with confusion. She swung a piece of peony pink fabric over her shoulder and clasped her hands together. Luna's mother was petite and had the look of a cute little house mouse. But her honey brown eyes were kind and comforting.

Abrielle didn't want to worry her, so she said, "I was just resting a moment." Not a complete lie.

"Perhaps you should hurry home, dear. It's been an interesting couple of days for everyone. Might be best to go home and get some rest."

Rest was the last thing she could afford. Even so, Abrielle smiled sweetly and said, "I will, don't worry."

She pushed off the wall and stepped back onto the cobblestone street.

"Oh," Nia called out, "You may want to cut through the alley here. There seems to be a commotion of some sort up the road."

"A commotion?"

Nia's eyes widened. "Oh, yes. Thomaz stopped in to let me know that there is an overgrowth of carnivorous plants that sprouted up. No one knows how it happened. One minute the road was clear as ever and the next, little green plants with bright pink centers and needle point teeth popped up a foot high. They're eating any bug that comes close."

Full grown plants sprouting out of nowhere was strange in itself. But *bug eating* plants with *teeth*. That was a very Deimos-like occurrence. He was still in town. And he was close. He had to be.

Gleefully, Abrielle exclaimed, "Thank you, Nia!"

Nia's mouth popped open. "Um, you're welcome?" she said with open uncertainty.

Abrielle waved to her as she bounded across the cobblestones. It didn't take long to find the source of the excitement. A crowd had gathered around, and several men were standing in the middle bent over the odd little plants. There was a whole garden full of them poking out in between each stone on the road.

Each time one of the men reached down to grab one and pull it up from the root, the plant nipped at him. One man yelped loudly and drew his hand back with a pin prick of blood on the tip of one of his fingers.

No one seemed to be in any particular sort of mortal danger so that was a relief. But there was also no sign of Deimos in the crowd. If he was on the run, then he might not even know the effect his magic was having on the town.

Across the street, someone's dog was walking on its hind legs. It appeared to be tap dancing its way toward a woman who had just left the butcher with a large cut of meat wrapped in her hands. The others seemed too preoccupied by the gobbling plants to notice.

Deimos was leaving hints all over town. But it was so sporadic, it was impossible to tell if he had been through recently. The village was quaint, but it wasn't so small that she could search it quickly on her own. Shoved in with a few of the bystanders were Paddy and Luna. They craned their necks to get a better look at the nibbling plants.

There was Abrielle's answer. What she needed was help. People she could trust. What she needed were her friends.

Twenty Three

It didn't take Abrielle long to gather everyone. Paddy and Luna hadn't even asked her to explain when she approached them and said she needed their help. With the father and daughter duo in tow, Abrielle headed for Tansy's cottage at the edge of the forest. Now they all sat in the beautiful little home, gathered around the hearth.

Paddy and Luna were side by side. It wasn't until the two of them were together that one was able to see the similarities between them. Both wore open expressions—ready for anything Abrielle was about to throw at them.

Tansy and Thomaz—he had simply stopped by for tea and had no idea what he was actually walking into, poor guy—stood at the other side of the room nearest to the door. And Abrielle in the middle. Surrounded by the people who had been encouraging her to depend on them for years. Neighbors and friends who always said they'd be there for anything she needed.

Flowers from Tansy's garden filled the room and their sweet scent wasn't helping Abrielle's lightheadedness. She clenched and unclenched her fists in anticipation. Tansy gave her an encouraging nod. They had all agreed to come simply because she had asked. Without any explanation, they had dropped what they were doing and showed up for her.

Abrielle inhaled slowly and willed her courage to come. "I-I did something. Something foolish." She chuckled awkwardly and fiddled with a statue Tansy had on the mantle. The great winged beast was carved from wood with wings spread wide as if it was in full flight. Its head was that of a bear, but it had the body of an eagle. Its strangeness made her smile, reminding her of the first time she had seen Deimos shapeshift.

He needed her help. It was time to swallow her pride. "Okay, so I accidentally summoned a man from the Otherworlds. His family peddles in... well, plague, pestilence, and whatnot. His magic is apparently out of control, and I don't know what's going to happen next."

Paddy's jaw dropped, a grin spread across Luna's face, and Thomaz turned as white as one of his sheep. Tansy, of course, already knew everything so she simply crossed her arms and leaned against the wall watching everyone's reactions.

Abrielle continued, "But he's not a bad man. At least, not intentionally. That part is a little fuzzy for me right now. But what's *not* fuzzy, is that this was all my fault to begin with. I let things get out of my control. I brought him here and I hid it because I thought I could handle it on my own. But the truth is, I can't."

She rolled her eyes at her own stupidity. "I need help. I've probably needed help for a while now but was too stubborn or shortsighted to realize it. Since my grandparents passed,

I thought I could handle the bakery. I thought if my grandmother could do it then so could I. And when Deimos showed up in my home, I figured that situation would be no different. But I was wrong."

"Yes," Paddy said as crossed his arms. "You were very wrong."

Abrielle winced, ready for a lecture.

But instead, he continued, "Your grandmother was never afraid to ask for help. She relied on the community that surrounded her. Me, Nia, and her friends. But most of all, your grandfather. This village is special. Because we come together when one of our own is in need."

"He's right," Luna reached out and touched her arm. "Your grandparents stood with this community many times. Trish, especially. Whether it was to help a traveler down on their luck or helping my mother sew last minute orders in her spare time. And she wouldn't have hesitated to reach out now for help."

Paddy chuckled. "She also sure wasn't frightened of failing." He elbowed Luna in the side. "Remember that time she asked us over to try that pepper cherry pie?"

Luna seemed to turn green at just the thought of it. "Oh, it was awful. I don't know that I'd ever seen her laugh as hard as she did when she saw our reactions to trying it!"

Abrielle laughed with tears welling in her eyes. She remembered that, too. They'd had an abundance of peppers that year and her grandmother had concocted all sorts of wild recipes with it.

Her heart filled with appreciation for the reminder. More memories flooded in of all the times her grandmother had failed with a smile on her face. She never let it deter her. Instead, she took it all in stride. Didn't Abrielle owe herself that same grace?

Thomaz spoke for the first time. "I knew something was going on when the sheep started fainting." He chuckled. "But I never would have guessed it was this. That it was you."

"I'm so sorry, I really am. I thought as long as he could control his power then no one would get seriously hurt. But the gemtowers hindered his magic. I'm afraid the more effort he puts into controlling it, the more it goes awry."

"Don't apologize," Thomaz said with a smirk. "There was no harm done, truly. The flock is fine. But I saw that mess last night. It was pretty intense. Is Deimos dangerous? What's the plan for when we find him?"

Abrielle hadn't thought that far. She'd spent every day since Deimos arrived trying to figure out their next move. She raised her chin. "All I know is we have to get him out of town before the King's expert finds him."

Tansy pushed off the wall and set her chin in the air. "Alright, so where do we start looking?"

Abrielle shook her head. "He could be anywhere. Last I saw, he was in the woods down by the lake. But I can't imagine he would have stayed there long."

Paddy scratched at his beard. "If he's struggling to keep control of his magic, then it could be likely that he's leaving us a trail, right? Those little buggers in the cobblestones are evidence enough of that.

"Yes!" Abrielle exclaimed. "That's precisely what I need help with. We should be looking for things out of the ordinary. You know, wilted flowers, animals behaving out of the norm, things like that."

Luna announced, "Great, so we have a plan. Let's go—"

A deep rumble shook the entire house, jostling Abrielle into the fireplace. Another quake came, harder this time. The impact threw the wood sculpture from the mantle along with all of Tansy's flower vases. They shattered on the ground and the bear's head rolled into Abrielle's foot.

Paddy cursed loudly and helped Luna up from the couch she'd stumbled into. Thomaz and Tansy clung tightly to each other. And Abrielle took a moment to look at each of their frightened faces.

Tansy trembled as she said, "Now *that* seems rather unordinary. Deimos?"

"There's only one way to find out." Abrielle bolted for the door and the others followed closely behind.

Villagers were gathered on the streets, shaken from the sudden upheaval of their afternoon. Other than that, though, the houses seemed to be fine; rattled, but structurally sound. Paddy helped to calm a few panicked neighbors while Abrielle stepped into the street.

From there she could see the bakery down the road. Her grandmother's sign was still swaying from the quake. Worried there might be damage, she jogged with the others following behind. When she came closer to her family home, her gaze flitted to the sign hanging on the side of the cottage above the patio. It appeared to be unphased by the sudden impact a moment ago which struck her as odd. If the cottage had been shaken, then why was she only seeing its effects in the front and not the side or the back?

Her gaze rose above her house where dense, dark clouds formed. They spread slowly, creeping through the afternoon sky. Inching toward Paddy's house and the others on the block, they blotted out any sunlight making it seem as if the night was approaching when, in fact, the evening was still hours away. The pit in her stomach grew and she called for the others who were surveying any possible damage on Paddy's home. Something was wrong. Not just in their town, but in her own backyard.

The crowd on the street had already begun to disperse. Worried eyes watched the sky as they all prepared to take cover for what they likely assumed was a coming storm. It gave Abrielle and her friends the opening they needed to sprint for her garden where the brunt of the storm was gathering.

Abrielle was the first to reach the patio. The moment she stepped foot on it, she sensed something wasn't right. There was a chill in the air that rivaled the worst winter day. Frost coated everything. Spread in a thin, glistening layer on the tables and the flowers.

Her own breath came out in a steamy white cloud as she stepped into the garden and gasped. Everything was ruined.

The beautiful, full greenery had wilted into nothing but sad brown stumps. Strawberries, tomatoes, peppers... they were all rotten and frozen over with ice.

It was as if a plague had run its course only to be hit with a hoarfrost immediately afterward. Footsteps behind her crunched on the icy ground and Tansy whispered her name, but Abrielle barely registered it. It was like she was underwater, and out of her friend's reach.

She followed the path that led to the trees. Her dress was far too thin for the change in weather. By now the frost had spread into Paddy's yard, icing the roof of his blacksmith's workshop. If it continued this way, it would spread to the rest of the town and maybe even further. The crops that their people relied on would be destroyed. It would be catastrophic for Ellamere's people.

In her heart, she couldn't believe Deimos would do something like this on purpose. But if he was hurt or frightened... or captured, then there was no telling what his reactions would do to his magic. The guard last night was proof of that.

Abrielle crossed the garden at a pace that matched her quickened pulse. The wood at the back of the garden had rotted. What was once strong and sturdy, was now spongy and had a strong musty scent that she could smell even from where she stood.

The gemtower came into view as she neared the forest. She stepped over the fallen fence and into a clearing that resembled the one at the festival. The grass was sopping wet, and Abrielle's feet sank into it like a marsh. There was no sign of wildlife. No cheerful chirping birds and nothing rustling in the tall weeds. Only Abrielle and the sad, dead wildflowers she used to pick for her grandparents when she was just a girl.

In the middle of it all, was Deimos. And behind him, with raised hands and shimmering shadows between them was the girl from the festival with wild flaming tresses. Mable.

Twenty Four

Abrielle couldn't bring herself to move. If she didn't know any better, she'd have thought the frost had seeped into her own body and frozen her in place. But it most definitely had more to do with the girl who had somehow forced Deimos to his knees.

His shadowy companions whipped around Mable's head trying to tear her away from him, but she swatted them away with sparks of light as if they were nothing more than flies. If Abrielle could just reach them... offer assistance... She stepped forward.

The young woman who had teared up at her grandmother's spell book—who Abrielle had felt a deep connection with through their shared grieving—hissed at her now, "Don't take another step."

Tansy and the others stopped in their tracks. Abrielle raised a hand to them, signaling not to make any sudden movements. The woman was clearly unhinged. If she was strong or clever enough to force Deimos into submission, then there was no telling what she might do if they disobeyed.

Deimos growled, "Get out of here, Brie."

"No." Abrielle met his eyes. There was no glamor in place. He was the same Deimos she knew and cared for. His eyes were dark pools, but she could make out the worry in them. He was frightened. But she wasn't sure if it was fear for himself or for her.

To Mable, she said, "Let him go. No one has to get hurt."

The girl cackled. "Now, why would I want to do that?"

For a moment, Abrielle swore she saw lines of age on her face. And when she moved, there was a slump in her back and a slowness to it that came with years of wear on one's body.

Mable sneered. With a clenched fist, she drew her arm back roughly. The shimmering shadowy magic drifting between her and Deimos grew taut, and he growled in pain. It was as if she was ripping the magic from his body.

With disgust, Mable asked, "Why do you care what happens to this creature?"

"Deimos is not a creature. He's my friend. And you need to release him." Abrielle took a bold step forward but stopped as the woman pulled Deimos by the hair, lifting his chin further in the air.

He spoke through a grunt. "Go, now, Brie." His nostrils flared as he said, "Mable is the witch. It was she who made the altar last night."

Abrielle gritted her teeth. It hadn't been Deimos after all.

While guilt washed over her, her friends gasped. None of them had ever faced a witch before. At least, not as far as they realized. Only hours ago, Abrielle had stood face to face with

Mable believing she was a grieving granddaughter. Never did she imagine this was the Mable they had sought all along. That this young girl was, in fact, the elderly witch who had written the spells in that cookbook.

"What do you want?" Abrielle asked. All Mable had to do was name her price.

"Stupid girl. I want *him.*" The witch gave her a sickly smile, flashing a row of crooked teeth yellowed with age. But it was the malice in her eyes that disturbed Abrielle the most.

Abrielle raised her hands with a determined shrug. "Well, you can't have him." What else could she say? She had no magic. No threats to wield at the witch. But she simply could not have Deimos. That's all there was to it.

Mable rolled her eyes. "It's too late, dear. In a few short minutes, I will have harvested his power to add to my own. I would have had it last night if that guard had not stumbled upon Deimos before I could ambush him."

A nagging part of her wondered if Deimos' magic being gone would truly be a bad thing. He could stay in Ellamere without risk. But if he did, then Abrielle would spend whatever time they had together wondering if it was *his* choice to stay. She would forever wonder if she had been enough reason or if he simply had no other choice. Besides, she wasn't familiar enough with magic to know what would happen once someone's power was completely drained from them.

No. She had to get him out of Mable's clutches. And fast. Abrielle wrinkled her nose. "You're a witch. And you have your book back. Don't you have power of your own?"

Mable let out an exasperated sigh. "I have gone *decades* being unable to do even the simplest of spells."

Deimos signaled with a faint tip of his head toward the gemtower. Though the air was freezing, heat pulsed from the crack in the large structure. The fracture had doubled in size. Whatever Mable was doing to cause Deimos' magic to act so erratically, it was opening the gate.

Abrielle had to keep her distracted until they could figure something out. Out of the corner of her eye, she noticed Luna inching around the perimeter with a metal flowering can in hand. Although Abrielle didn't like the idea of bludgeoning this woman in the head with one of her gardening tools, it might be their only option.

So, she kept talking. "There must be some magic left over from before. How else would I have been able to perform the summoning spell?"

Mable's cheeks flushed a deep red, and she bared her teeth. "Do you have any idea how embarrassing it was to find out that a young baker was able to perform my spell when I myself could not? I don't know how you did it, but I'm going to take what I'm owed."

Through gritted teeth, Deimos said, "It did not work for you because you did not have the right intention for it. Brie deserved to get what she wanted. You, however—"

Mable cut him off as she forced his own magic into his mouth; stuffing it in like it was nothing more than a sock. Abrielle had never felt anger like she did right now. She moved toward them, but Deimos held up a hand to stop her.

The witch wasn't doing any real damage, but Abrielle's rage built, nonetheless.

Mable shrieked, "Years of draining my power just to stay beautiful and then you two waltz in. It was fate. A gift just for me."

Abrielle released a heavy breath, then said, "Alright, Mable. I get it. Your power has been slipping away for years. Trust me, I know what it's like to feel like everything you have ever known and cared about is being wrenched away from you one bit at a time."

Mable stilled and drew away from Deimos slightly.

Abrielle continued, "But one thing I've learned is that you need to find others to rely on. You need to know when to ask for help. So, what if I offer mine? Hm?"

She took a careful step forward. She was close enough now that if she leapt, she would reach Deimos. But she held steady. Mable's eyes were wild, and she swallowed heavily. She was so distracted by Abrielle that she didn't realize the others were slowly beginning to surround her. Each held whatever item they could find nearby. Thomaz with a rotten frozen tomato in each hand, Paddy with a garden hose, and Luna wielding a rake.

Mable said thoughtfully, "It has been a long time since I have worked with another..."

"Then tell me what we have to do. Surely there is a way that doesn't involve draining Deimos of what is rightfully his. A path where we can all find a way to be happy."

She met Deimos' gaze, and he gave a small shake of his head, but she ignored him. This would not end with him being harmed. No one was going to get hurt if she could help it.

Mable shifted back and forth on her feet. "You expect me to trust you?"

"I saw the recipes in that book," Abrielle said as she thought of the detail and care that had gone into the spells. The handwriting and notes were that of a woman who was passionate about what she was doing. She continued, "There were healing spells, love spells, things that could help people. You are not a monster, Mable. You don't have to be the thing that the late King feared. We can do this without hurting anyone."

For a moment, Abrielle thought she had succeeded. But Mable kicked Deimos hard in the back, sending him to the ground. As she raised her hands higher and began to chant, Luna and Paddy flanked her. A bright white light bloomed to life around Mable's hands and slammed into Abrielle's friends, sending them flying into the trees.

Deimos' shadows rushed to them. They circled each one and nudged them awake. Then they clung to them. It shook Abrielle to see them as frightened as the rest of them were. It likely meant Deimos was just as scared about their situation.

When the light faded, there was no sign of the young bright-eyed girl from before. Mable's true form was showing, and she panted heavily as if strained. Her white hair cascaded around her in a flurry and dark circles surrounded eyes that sagged from years of age.

She snarled at Abrielle, "I don't need your help."

Again, she raised her hands above Deimos and chanted more vigorously this time. He groaned loudly and clutched his stomach in pain as he writhed on the ground. Abrielle stood paralyzed with fear as his power—the void he used for shifting—tore from him and flowed through Mable then into the gemtower. With each word, the nothingness grew, blotting out any sight of her friends across the clearing.

When the power met the gemtower, lightning cracked into a nearby tree. The ground quaked once more as the fracture grew. It burrowed from top to bottom, then into the earth itself. As the gemtower tore into two, the land rocked so hard that Abrielle fell into Deimos.

On the ground, the two of them clung to one another.

Mable's voice rose above the thunder and lightning. "With all of the gemtowers destroyed, magic will be released, and I will finally give this kingdom something to truly be afraid of!"

Deimos choked and looked Abrielle in the eye. He pulled her close until their foreheads were touching and said, "The door is opened. We could send her there." His gaze darted to the gemtower which was split in two and glowing an orangish-red.

Abrielle hesitated. She certainly didn't want to hurt anyone. Not even after all that Mable had just done. Perhaps banishment was what she deserved.

"What if she comes back through?" She bit her lip with uncertainty.

"What choice do we have?"

They could try to reason with her one last time. Abrielle shoved her hair from her face. Mud coated her hands, reminding her of her childhood. After particularly rainy days, her grandmother would encourage her to play pretend in the garden. Rather than jump in puddles like most children her age, she would make mudpies and pretend to serve them in the backyard to her imaginary customers.

Everything she had ever needed had always been there. And everything she needed was there now. *Everyone.* She couldn't let anyone threaten that.

With Mable seemingly too consumed by the power within her grasp, she didn't notice the fat tabby cat who had somehow gotten out of the bakery. Tinker waddled up to them like an oblivious bystander strolling onto a battlefield.

Deimos moaned again in pain. The veins in his neck were strained. Abrielle wasn't sure how much more of this he could take. Boldly, she faced Mable and said, "Please, be reasonable. We can go to King Vasiri. Maybe together we can make him understand that not all magic is bad. That we can work together to use it for good."

Mable took a step back, dangerously close to the round old housecat. Abrielle winced, but the witch didn't seem to notice.

Paddy and Luna inched closer, low to the ground, and tried to catch the cat's attention—wiggling their fingers enticingly—but she seemed intent on investigating the strange newcomer who was causing a ruckus in their backyard.

Tansy and Thomaz looked to Abrielle for instructions, but she had none to give. Mable wasn't listening. Deimos' breathing was loud and erratic now. Then, another quake had her friends yelping in surprise. They scrambled away from Mable on unsteady feet.

Tinker mewed loudly, the hairs on her back rising. Mable's eyes went wide as she looked down to find the tabby cat hissing at her feet. Abrielle's stomach dropped and she lunged for the cat, afraid that Mable would do something terrible.

Instead, the witch seemed more frightened of the feline's wrath than she was of the mortals who had her entirely outnumbered. She released her hold on Deimos' magic for a moment, giving him a reprieve from the painful spell work she was doing.

Tinker slipped between Mable's legs, and they stumbled toward the gemtower. Abrielle scrambled to keep up, reaching down for the cat in between Mable's desperate attempts to shake her away.

Mable screeched, "Get that wretched thing away from me!"

"I'm trying," Abrielle snapped. "Just hold still!"

Abrielle finally got a grasp on Tinker and swept the stubborn troublemaker into her arms. She clutched her tightly with a huge sigh of relief that the cat was no longer in danger of being trampled. In the same beat, Mable, intent on putting distance between herself and the cat, tripped on a stone and tumbled into the gemtower's opening. It swallowed Mable as easily as a person might swallow a piece of pie and then with one shrill scream, she was gone.

Deimos grunted as he rose to his feet. Abrielle ran to him. Holding Tinker in one arm, she ran her free hand over him to see that he was alright. His shadows were there, too, wrapping themselves around the two of them like one grand hug.

Placing strong hands on both sides of her face, Deimos said, "You did it, Brie."

"We did it," she replied, gesturing to their friends gathered around them.

Paddy rubbed his shoulder and groaned. But they all seemed to have fared well. Far better than Mable had. And Abrielle's backyard for that matter. She spun slowly, taking inventory of the damage. The gemtower was destroyed beyond repair. Split clear down the middle. The chill in the garden still lingered, and though it was lessening by the second, the plants were beyond saving. And her patio...

Her breath hitched in her throat. Stone was uprooted, tables overturned and smashed to pieces. And her sign. The wonderful sign Deimos made her was broken in two, with half of it dangling sadly from the cottage roof.

Devastated tears streamed down her face. Tinker leapt from her arms and marched proudly back to the house. Deimos pulled her in close and she buried her face in his chest. Then more arms wrapped around her as her friends joined them. They leaned on one another, allowing her to grieve in their steady presence, until the tears faded to sniffles.

Drawing away, she thanked them all. Without them, she never would have saved Deimos. Here she was crying about broken things, when she should be celebrating their victory. She wiped the tears from her face and smiled at them gratefully.

"Hands where we can see them!" Erik's shaky voice cut through the stillness of the moment.

Abrielle spun to face him. Several palace guards flanked him near the cottage. With his jaw set, Erik commanded, "You are all under arrest by order of the King."

A low, threatening rumble came from Deimos, but Abrielle placed a hand on his chest. Mable had spoken of fate today. And if theirs was to face what they had done—the events they had set into motion—then so be it. They would face it together.

Twenty Five

"Deimos, listen. About what I said at the festival..." Abrielle craned her neck to catch a glimpse of him as he was dragged roughly behind her.

"Save it for later, Brie." He earned several grunts from the guards struggling to contain his brute strength.

Abrielle had a feeling that if he really wanted to escape, then he would have already done so. Was he allowing himself to be arrested to stay with her? She tried not to let the hope swell too greatly. Their argument last night had practically pushed him right into Mable's clutches.

But it seemed her apology for the part she played would have to wait. Villagers lined the streets—people she had known most of her life—craning their necks to see what was going on. Some held battered pieces of wood and other remnants of sheds and things that had broken in the quake. A few shouted angry words at the guards for arresting Abrielle, Paddy, Luna, Tansy, and Thomaz. Others staggered back at the sight of Deimos in all his un-glamored glory.

It reminded Abrielle of the first night she had encountered him and how struck she was by his appearance. Since then, it had become easy for her to see past the dangerously pow-erful presence he carried with him. Even his shadows were something she'd grown used to. They clung tightly to him now. To the average eye, it would have been nearly unnotice-able.

Erik yanked on her arm as they passed through the palace gate, causing her to trip. While she tried to regain her bal-ance, Erik let out a yelp and fell to the ground, clutching his leg. Abrielle whipped around to see Deimos lowering the foot he'd just kicked him with. There was a satisfied smile on his face even as one of the other guards punched him in it.

When Deimos looked back up, the smile had turned fear-some, and shadows rose behind him like the wings of a fallen dove. The sky darkened above and even the guards had the good sense to step away warily.

None of this would help their case. Even if Deimos could take on the King's entire force, it would only serve to make their fear of him grow. The entire village might make up their minds that he was a monster and that it was Abrielle who had subjected them all to his wrath.

Desperately, she called out, "Deimos, please don't."

Instantly, the shadows dissipated, and the clouds cleared, giving way to the purple and orange evening sky. He rolled his shoulders back and raised his chin. Then without the guards urging him on, he walked right past Abrielle and the others. She watched in shock as he strolled up the palace steps and through the front door as if he were a guest and not a prisoner.

Tansy turned wide-eyed to Abrielle. Well, the King *did* want to see them. And Deimos *was* just doing as she'd hoped. With a shrug in her best friend's direction, Abrielle stepped gingerly over Erik who was still cradling his injured leg and didn't bother glancing back to see if the rest of the guards were following as she, too, strutted into the palace.

It was the first time Abrielle had waltzed through the front door of King Vasiri's palace. Few events were held within its walls, as it was easier to accommodate attendees outside. She had attended the Yuletide ball each year, but even that event was spent baking and delivering wares into the kitchens before heading to the ballroom to enjoy a night of holly hanging and tree decorating.

But now, with the guards scattering to catch up and Deimos leading the way, Abrielle wasn't in awe of the intricate beauty that dripped from each corner. She didn't take time to admire the tapestries or wonder at the delicacy of the chandelier in the corridor. Instead, she kept her sights trained on Deimos' back and her mind focused on what was to come.

The moment they entered the King's great hall, a hush fell across the crowd. Courtiers who had gathered to witness the most exciting thing to happen in Ellamere in decades shoved one another gently to get a better view of the man leading the charge toward the thrones.

King Vasiri's personal guard unsheathed their swords, drawing gasps from those standing closest to the dais. Even Princess Greer flinched at the scraping of blade against leather. The King, however, was unmoving. All good humor she had witnessed the night before at the festival's baking contest was gone. In its place was a mask of indifference.

Abrielle sidled up to Deimos. From her peripheral, she spotted Tansy and the others. But she never moved her direct gaze from the King; the man who held their fate in his hands. Abrielle dipped into a low curtsey. The sort that she had seen courtiers do many times before. When she rose again, she made sure to stay straight-backed with her head held proud.

The best strategy was to humble herself in front of the royal court, but not to show any shame. She'd been beating herself up since the summoning, but she was done with that now. It was her mistake. She could admit that. But she hadn't done any of it out of malice. There was no grab for power like there had been when Mable committed her crimes.

King Vasiri spoke loudly, his voice echoing through the chamber. "Abrielle Grainwick. You have been brought before the court for the unauthorized use of magic. Do you admit to the accusation?"

Abrielle laced her fingers together in front of her. The ropes around her wrists chafed, but she ignored it as she answered, "I admit that I tried to make a soufflé, but it didn't quite turn out as I expected."

Before, she would have said that it didn't turn out as she had *hoped*. But now, she couldn't imagine hoping for anything other than what she had. Deimos—a man she cared deeply for—and her neighbors coming together to stand with her in the face of strife. Her heart swelled with pride and love. How could she have asked for anything more?

King Vasiri raised an eyebrow. "A *soufflé*? As in the food?"

"Well, I *am* a baker, your Majesty. I didn't realize it was a spell..."

Murmurs filled the room. Some were amused while others were appalled. Abrielle ignored them all. The King's opinion was the only one that mattered. She was met with another quizzical look, so she elaborated. She started by admitting to borrowing the recipe book from his library and how she and Deimos had tried to fix things on their own. She gave a detailed account of Mable who had pretended to be her own granddaughter so that she might throw suspicion and strike when they least expected.

King Vasiri leaned back in his throne with an exasperated huff. "The witch, you say, is gone?"

"Yes, Your Majesty. She disappeared into the gemtower's crevice."

"You understand that your... *recipe* gone wrong has destroyed the gemtower behind your home beyond repair. We do not know what this means for the wards around Ellamere. The ones we rely on to protect us from those who hold far greater power than we do."

Prince Raden, the King's eldest, spoke for the first time, tossing his dusty brown hair back with a smooth hand. "You have endangered this entire kingdom. The actions that led to today nearly destroyed the village. There must be consequences for such things."

Deimos nearly roared as he said, "Abrielle and the others standing before you did nothing wrong. It was I who failed to contain the magic the witch harnessed from me. And before that, I was the one responsible for the strange occurrences in town."

Paddy piped in. "Occurrences that did not *really* do any harm."

Prince Raden chided, "Tell that to the villagers outside repairing the damages to their homes."

Tansy corrected, "You mean the ones that Mable caused."

King Vasiri raised a silencing hand. "Regardless of intent, we are faced with a serious problem. We do not know what the loss of one of our gemtowers means for this realm. If more Otherworlders," he paused and gave a sympathetic smile to Deimos and Abrielle, then continued, "ones who are less inclined to live peacefully amongst us come, then we will not know how to defend ourselves. I understand that not all who wield magic harbor ill-intent, but what of those who do?"

Murmurs of agreement spread through the room from one courtier to another. Abrielle tensed and waited for the royal response.

It was Prince Raden who proclaimed, "I say we give them the same exile as the witch. Banish them to the Otherworlds by sending them through the gemtower just as they did to this *Mable*."

It was as if he was pulling the world from under her feet. She couldn't go to the Otherworlds. Deimos might recover from such an exile, but she had never wanted to leave her home. Ellamere was a part of her very soul.

Princess Greer snorted. Her brother shot her a glare, but she ignored it as she stood and said, "Abrielle has never harmed a fly. Even when this stranger came into her home, she did not turn him away for fear of what harm might come to him."

Deimos grumbled. "Well, she did hit me with a rolling pin."

Tansy snickered, but promptly quieted as the King gave her a stern, fatherly look.

The Princess continued, "We cannot even be sure that putting someone in the gemtower's crevice would safely send them to the Otherworlds. What we need to be doing is discussing how to close the opening. Or at the very least how to prepare ourselves for the reintegration of magic in Ellamere should it come to that."

There were a couple shouts of agreement in the crowd and Abrielle was finally able to take a deep breath. If Princess Greer continued to speak on their behalf, maybe the King would listen. His face was as unreadable as the scribbled-out notes in Mable's recipe. It didn't do much to inspire confidence.

After a moment of contemplative silence, King Vasiri stood abruptly and stepped down from the dais to stand face to face with Deimos. "You have spent a significant amount of time here amongst my people."

Deimos was at least a head taller than the King and had to look down to speak to him. "Yes..."

"Do you like it here in Ellamere?" There was nothing sly about the way King Vasiri asked the question. Rather, it seemed like genuine curiosity.

Abrielle had to remind herself to breathe in and out as the anticipation built.

Deimos met her eyes as he answered the King. "I *love* it."

The King glanced over at Abrielle and his face softened. "I see." With a tilt of his head, he added, "What if I offered you a place here? If you were to pledge your allegiance to Ellamere and help us protect it from the unknown dangers that may be coming, then there may be a way to make everyone happy with the situation."

Prince Raden whispered. "Father, are you serious?"

"Hush," Princess Greer hissed.

Deimos' gaze fell to the floor and a blush crept across the bridge of his nose. "I do not know that I could promise to contain my magic."

"What if you don't contain it?" King Vasiri suggested. "What if instead, you *channeled* it to act as a strengthener for the gemtower?"

Deimos shook his head. "It might not work." The shadows creeped over his shoulders, hugging tightly to him. "What happens to me and to Abrielle if I cannot do what you ask."

"All my father is asking is that you try." Princess Greer gestured around them. "Is that not all any of us can promise to do? Magic used to be a part of us all. Rooted deep within our world. And it wasn't all bad. Perhaps the mistake was suppressing it in the first place."

Prince Raden scoffed. "I wouldn't go *that* far, sister."

She brushed him off with a wave of her hand. "This village can always benefit from a new neighbor willing to lend a helping hand. You can teach us more about your world so that we can meet any newcomers with understanding. Ellamere strives to be a peaceful and welcoming place. That should not change now. If you can promise to try to help us do that, then I do not see why you cannot stay."

King Vasiri held his hand out. "What do you say?"

Deimos locked eyes with Abrielle and she sucked in a pained breath. If he accepted he would be turning his back on his home. He would be leaving behind everything he had ever known. Trading it all to help protect a people who were not his own.

He clasped hands with the King and said, "I say you have a deal."

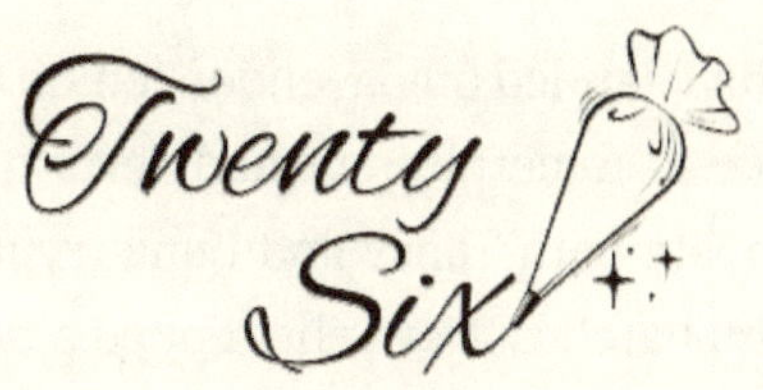

Twenty Six

Abrielle dusted flour off her dress and sat down on the stool. Tinker meowed and padded up to her, rubbing her side along the wooden legs of the table. She slipped the needy tabby a piece of dried fish. Tinker's part in defeating the witch had apparently gone to her furry little head. Since then, the tabby had been reminding them all that she was owed extra treats.

With the cat munching happily, Abrielle opened the newly bound notebook she'd picked up that morning at Miss Rita's bookstore. It was a warm, sunny day and she relished the cool breeze drifting through the open window of the cottage. Outside, hammers echoed through the village as each neighbor pieced together what had been broken. They'd been working over the last week to repair the damage Mable had caused while harnessing Deimos' magic.

Since then, things had been hectic, but in a way that Abrielle appreciated. She'd been going about her daily orders but took the time to bake a special treat for her friends and neighbors each afternoon. They worked tirelessly to fix their homes—relying on one another to get the work done—and she wanted to provide them with something extra to lift their spirits.

Today, she had handed out lavender, lemon cookies, with a citrus glaze. It was something she had never tried before and had stayed up late with Tansy and Luna trying to perfect it through several batches. Now, she dipped a quill in the little jar of ink she'd found in her grandmother's desk and put pen to parchment.

The little book she had picked up for herself was filling up one page at a time. The first recipe she had written down was the one that she had created for the contest. Over time, she hoped to have a recipe book filled with all of her own creations. None of which would include a soufflé or hidden spells.

Someone cleared their throat from the other side of the counter, but Abrielle couldn't see anyone. She stood and peeked around to find Sir Peakbottom. He offered her a beaming smile and a glass of something yellow with flowers floating in it.

"A new drink?" Abrielle took the glass eagerly.

He nodded, strolling into the kitchen and setting his things out on the counter. Then he said, "Lavendar lemonade to go with the cookies ye made!"

"Brilliant!" She sipped the refreshing drink. It was tart with just the right hint of floral.

She leaned against the counter and watched Peakbottom as he went to work making mini savory meat pies for the new afternoon rush. With everyone busy throughout the day rebuilding the town and completing their everyday jobs and tasks, they had been coming to the bakery for lunch.

There was a knock on the back door and Abrielle turned to find Deimos peering through the window. There was a hint of excitement in his eyes. She'd begun to notice that they were not just a dark pool of black, but rather glittered in the direct sunlight, bringing out more of the purple flecks.

He opened the door popping his head inside and said, "Morning Peaky!"

Sir Peakbottom didn't look up from the contraption he was setting up on the counter—one that used blades to crush ice to make a remarkably refreshing blended fruit drink—but he waved and said, "And a good one at that! I should have this up and runnin' in just a few short minutes."

"Just in time." Deimos flashed a dazzling smile.

Abrielle, however, felt like she was left in the dark, so she asked, "In time for what?"

Deimos reached in and grabbed both her hands, tugging her toward the door. She resisted. Every time she had tried to assist in the rebuild, she had just gotten in the way. Several attempts had resulted in disaster; including Paddy's broken toe, a terrible mishap with a nail and Tansy's favorite dress, and an entire day's worth of work set back. Deimos had since taken to shooing her back into the house just as she did to him when he tried to help in the kitchen.

And although she was grateful for the way things had worked out—for King Vasiri's decision to allow Deimos to stay in Ellamere and that nobody had been harmed in the chaos—it still broke her heart every time she observed the damage done to the garden and the gift that Deimos had worked so hard on.

"Come on, Brie. You'll want to see this, I promise."

"I've already seen it. I don't need to be reminded. I told you, once things are set right in town, I'll get around to replanting." It was the one thing she *could* help with, but it was better to wait until the other repairs were done so she wouldn't be in the way.

Deimos draped an arm over her shoulder and steered her outside anyway. Abrielle gasped as she stepped into the yard.

He whispered in her ear. "No need."

"You finished? So soon?" She stammered as she peered around.

The garden, which had been putrid and burned, was now laid out with fresh soil all neatly raked and replanted. A new fence was expertly standing in the back, this time, built around the gemtower to include it in her property line.

Beside her, the patio was as good as new. Its tables and canvas coverings were even better than before with little flowers hand painted on each of them. And best of all, every chair and bench were filled with her friends and neighbors.

Peakbottom hurried around to each of them, handing out glasses of his frozen drink. And soon the chatter started. Tansy, Luna, and even Princess Greer laughed loudly and openly from one of the tables. Paddy sat on a bench beside Nia with her head resting against his shoulder. And so many others were there, too. More began to gather and soon the entire patio was full.

Abrielle turned to Deimos, stunned. "I thought this would take at least a few more weeks. You did all this?"

He shook his head. "*We* did this. The town knows how hard you've been working... How hard you've *always* worked. This isn't just a love letter from me to you. It's from all of us."

Abrielle's heart somersaulted. "*Love* letter?"

Deimos placed a finger under her chin and tilted it up. "I saw the possibilities of making a life here in Ellamere, but I stayed because I fell in love with more than just the village, Brie. Surely you see that by now."

Abrielle bit her lip. The deal he made with King Vasiri did not hold him to Ellamere forever. He was free to try to return home any time he wanted. And over the last week, Abrielle had considered many times what would happen if Deimos changed his mind. If he grew homesick or tired of using his power to try to contain some of the magic that was still seeping through the broken gemtower.

"But won't you miss living in a land full of magic?"

Deimos smirked. "I don't know." He leaned closer, so close that he was only butterfly wing's length from her lips, and said, "Seems to me all the magic I need is right here."

Epilogue

"Brie! Please, don't panic." Deimos shouted from the kitchen.

Abrielle tripped and then quickly righted herself, jumping over the threshold from the back door with a tray in hand. Sir Peakbottom's drinks had become renowned in Ellamere and paired with her new recipe creations; the patio was busier than ever.

"What happened?" She panted and pushed her hair away from her sweaty temples. Despite the chilly late winter air, she'd been bustling around all morning caring for customers and prepping for her birthday party later that afternoon.

"It wasn't me this time, I swear." Deimos held his hands up defensively and took a step away from the counter.

Abrielle leaned over to see the problem and yelped in shock. The candied oranges she laid out for the day's special had little bite marks all over them. She seethed, "Fairies! Again?"

"I thought I'd frightened them all away, but I guess I'm just not as intimidating as I used to be." He shrugged.

More and more frequently, the stubborn little creatures that found a way to slip through the gemtower, had been stealing bites of Abrielle's baked goods. They were as relentless as mice in the cupboard. It didn't matter to her that they were adorable little things with glittering, translucent wings and dainty smiles. They were an utter nuisance.

Deimos wrapped his arms around her. "Could be worse," he offered with a smile.

That much was true. There had been no sign of Mable since that horrible day, and nothing truly dangerous had found its way into Ellamere. But that didn't mean the threats didn't exist. She and Deimos had to choose to look at the bright side of things.

And with the royal family's approval, Abrielle was free to be with him. Each week he met with them, giving them detailed accounts of Selanthia. Princess Greer catalogued everything she could and was absolutely enamored of the creatures who lived there. By now, Deimos had fallen into a steady rhythm and since he no longer had to focus his efforts on a glamor or suppressing his power, he'd regained his control.

Abrielle suspected that the gemtower had something to do with it as well. With bits of magic released into Ellamere through the broken tower, Deimos likely had more access to it, granting him strength he did not have before when it was simply fractured.

She leaned against him, reveling in his steady presence. A shadowy tendril ruffled her hair, and she laughed. The family she had made for herself might not be the one she had spent so many lonely nights wishing for. But it was the one she needed. And she wouldn't trade them for the world.

Deimos nodded a nearby drawer. "Maybe you could make a fairy swatter. A little cheesecloth could do the trick without hurting the little buggers."

It wasn't a bad idea. Just to scare them off. Deimos let her go and she reached for the drawer, to find a little blue box painted with little yellow stars.

Her heart sputtered as she reached for it. "What's this?"

The box was light, and her fingers trembled as she opened it to find a delicate gold band inlaid with diamonds. They glittered in the light like blinking stars.

When she turned to Deimos, he was on one knee. She hugged herself, clutching the open box tightly in her hand. Her heart drummed in her chest and tears stung her eyes.

"Abrielle Grainwick, you are more than I ever could have wished for. When I am in your presence, there isn't a moment that passes when I'm not in awe of you. Before you my life was a plague. I lived a dreary existence. The night you called me here, you saved me. It was no mistake. I have to believe that it all happened so that it would lead us here. To this." He gestured around the cozy kitchen. "Brie, will you be my wife?"

Breathlessly, she said, "Yes." *Yes, yes, yes. Always yes.*

Deimos stood, taking the box from her and placing the ring on her finger. She didn't give it a second glance before throwing her arms around him. He hugged her tightly, pulling her off the ground. Her heart soared as their lips met and joyful tears fell from her eyes.

The bell chimed, suddenly, drawing them from their embrace. When they turned, Tansy was standing frazzled in the entryway, her head scarf had nearly come undone and was barely doing its jobholding her hair back from her face.

She let out an exaggerated huff and plopped onto a stool. "Have you guys heard the news?"

Deimos laughed. "Whoa Tans, you don't look so good."

Abrielle elbowed him in the ribs.

He gave her a sheepish grin. "What?"

Tansy grabbed a chocolate chip cookie the size of her hand from the table and tore into it. With a mouthful, she said, "He's right. Some arse has been building on the property in the woods behind my house. They've been hammering *nonstop*, and I can't get any sleep."

Absentmindedly, Deimos grabbed a strand of Abrielle's hair and played with it. Shivers ran down her spine and she suddenly had the urge to forget about the birthday party and spend the rest of the day hiding under the covers with him. Maybe they'd bring the cookies and some cream up with them...

Snapping back to the moment, she returned her focus to Tansy, "Wait, what news?"

There was a hint of panic in Tansy's tired eyes as she said, "Another gemtower has been fractured."

After the happily ever after...

brielle and Deimos found love in a bizarre set of circumstances. But while they are living out their happily ever after, trouble in Ellamere is far from over. For our neighbors, that means more magic and chaos to come. Follow Tansy's journey next! Thanks to the mayhem, the gemtower in Abrielle's backyard wasn't the only one affected. Tansy will soon discover that deer and rabbits aren't the only pests in her garden to contend with when a pestering new neighbor moves next door. Immerse yourself in her story with a light-hearted enemies-to frenemies-to-lovers.

Did you enjoy Abrielle's story? Don't forget to post a review! I love to hear from my readers!
Find more behind the scenes and bonus content here! https:/ /dl.bookfunnel.com/71wlyp9n7x

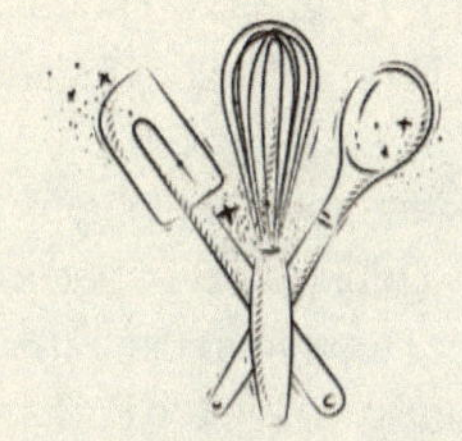

BRIE'S BAKERY

Recipes

ABRIELLE'S
S'mores Crumble

Ingredients

3/4 cup butter (softened)
1 cup brown sugar
1 cup old fashioned oats
3/4 cup flour
1 teaspoon baking powder
1 teaspoon kosher salt
1 teaspoon cinnamon
2 cups mini marshmallows (watch for fairies with sticky fingers!)
Coarsely chopped chocolate bars

Directions

1. If you're lacking a lord from the Otherworlds, then Preheat oven to 350 degrees. Spray oven-safe baking dish with cooking spray.
2. In a large mixing bowl, beat butter and brown sugar on medium speed until fluffy, about 3-4 minutes. Add oats, flour, baking powder, salt and cinnamon. Mix until well combined.
3. Press two-thirds of the crumble mixture into the prepared dish. Top with marshmallows and chopped chocolate. Sprinkle with remaining crumble mixture.
4. Bake until golden brown, 20-25 minutes. Let cool for 10 minutes before servings. Drizzle with more melted chocolate, if your heart desires it.

SIR PEAKBOTTOM'S
Frosted Hot Chocolate

Ingredients

4 ounces high quality semi-sweet chocolate
2 1/2 Tablespoons granulated sugar
1 Tablespoon unsweetened cocoa powder
pinch salt
1 1/2 cups milk
1 - 2 cups Ice cubes
Whipped Cream for topping, optional

Directions

1. Chop the chocolate into small pieces and melt on low (don't burn it like Deimos would!) stir vigilantly until melted.
2. Stir in sugar, coco powder, and salt. Slowly stir in ½ cup milk, until smooth like a gemtower.
3. Blend: Add mixture to blender with remaining 1 cup milk and 1 cup of ice. Blend well until smooth. Add more ice if you want it thicker.
4. Serve immediately, topped with whipped cream.

Acknowledgements

Writing this book filled me with so much contentment, and it never would have happened without my incredible readers who have supported and encouraged me throughout the last few years. I am forever grateful to you all.

To Grandma Pat and Grandpa Bob, the two of you have been an ever steady presence in my life. You've shown me so much love and encouragement and have played such a big role in shaping who I am today. That is the sort of love and dedication that inspired Abrielle's story. I love you both.

To Zach (honey). Who shows me every day what it is like to be loved. You are my best friend and I am so blessed to be on this journey with you by my side.

To Chelsi. This book literally wouldn't have happened without you. Getting a book ready during school summer vacation is NOT for the faint of heart. Thank you for taking my "mayhem makers" so I could make this release happen! But most of all, thank you for listening to my rants, reminding me to breathe, and for pulling me out of the "oh my God what am I even doing?" abyss.

To my own enchanted village; Chelsi (again because seriously, thank you), Justice, Michaela, Nicolle, and Stephanie. Thank you for your steadfast friendship, full moon celebrations (that include cover design brainstorming), and love for my stories. I love you all!

To my Chaos Corner (Danielle, Samantha, Jes, Emily H, Emily F, and Kate). Thank you for working through the kinks with me, keeping me on deadline, and for letting me celebrate (and groan) throughout this process.

xoxo

J.M. Wallace has spent much of her adult life moving around with her husband and their two children, making stories of their own. As a young girl, J.M. was fascinated with stories that she read and that she dreamed up herself. Even when she was horseback riding, she was never in her own yard; instead, she was in an enchanted forest or riding into battle alongside brave knights. Today, she puts those stories to paper, to share with the world.

Local to Eastern North Carolina, she does this in the little pockets of her day between giving her kids snacks, naps, baths, and putting them to bed.

Let's Connect via Social Media!
IG https://www.instagram.com/j.m.wallaceauthor/
FB Reader Group *Sword & Quill J.M. Wallace Reader Group*